SISTERS BEHAVING BADLY

MADDIE PLEASE

Boldwood

First published in Great Britain in 2021 by Boldwood Books Ltd.

Copyright © Maddie Please, 2021

Cover Design by Head Design

Cover Photography: Shutterstock

Every effort has been made to obtain the necessary permissions with reference to copyright material, both illustrative and quoted. We apologise for any omissions in this respect and will be pleased to make the appropriate acknowledgements in any future edition.

A CIP catalogue record for this book is available from the British Library.

Paperback ISBN 978-1-80162-124-3

Large Print ISBN 978-1-80162-125-0

Hardback ISBN 978-1-80162-123-6

Ebook ISBN 978-1-80162-126-7

Kindle ISBN 978-1-80162-127-4

Audio CD ISBN 978-1-80162-118-2

MP3 CD ISBN 978-1-80162-119-9

Digital audio download ISBN 978-1-80162-122-9

Boldwood Books Ltd
23 Bowerdean Street
London SW6 3TN
www.boldwoodbooks.com

For Teddy and Mabel, with much love xx

1

I thought I was ridiculously early that morning, but my elder sister was already there. Of course she was. Jenny had probably never been late for anything in her life and to be honest, I'd hardly ever been early.

I saw her before she clocked me. She was walking towards a row of seats in front of the plate-glass windows overlooking the sea. Still apprehensive about this meeting, I was semi-lurking behind the queue for the café. At first glance it looked as though she hadn't changed a bit since we last met. Still the same smooth, bobbed salt-and-pepper hair; the trim, precise figure; the same measured expression. Even the way she pulled her bag behind her was familiar and at that moment, slightly annoying. How could someone who was just walking and pulling a small suitcase irritate me? Perhaps after everything that had happened, all the time that had passed, my early start and several disturbed nights – thanks to my constantly partying neighbours in the flat above mine – I was just on edge.

I paused, hoping things between us would be better now, after all these years apart. The last time we'd met hadn't gone well at all:

a tepid carvery lunch followed by a blistering row. And then some door-slamming (Jenny) and flouncing (me).

I glanced over to where Jenny was now sitting, looking out of the window at the boats and the seagulls and for a moment was sad that she wasn't bothering to look for me. Why wasn't she looking for me? Perhaps she wasn't anticipating our trip with much pleasure either. What a strange frame of mind for us to be in, considering we were about to go off on a sort of holiday and would be living together for the first time in – how long was it? Forty years? Perhaps thirty-eight? Where had the time gone?

Well, I was younger than Jenny but that didn't mean I couldn't be more mature, and I was suddenly desperate to start the healing process, the explanations, the apologies. Perhaps it was up to me to break the ice. I took a deep breath, put a smile on my face and went over to join her. She was sitting very straight in her seat, her ankles neatly crossed, wearing a flowery dress and one of her many ghastly, hand-knitted cardigans. Nothing had changed there, then.

'Hi, Jenny,' I said, my throat giving an annoying croak that made it sound as though I was about to burst into tears. Actually, I did feel as if I might start crying. This was a moment I had thought about for a very long time.

She looked up. 'Hello, Kitty.'

That used to make us both laugh not so long ago. It had started every letter, every email. I can't think of the number of make-up bags, backpacks and T-shirts with that slogan Jenny had given me as presents in the past. But it had been nearly six years since we had met in person; a lot of water had gone under a lot of bridges. Still, you would think she might show a bit more reaction to the fact that we were meeting up at last. I felt very emotional, if I was honest.

I'd missed her so much. I hoped that she had missed me.

She half rose from her seat and we shared an awkward, rather mechanical hug. I sat down on the other side of the table that still bore the smears of when it had last been carelessly wiped, crumbs in the corners. I wasn't house-proud but I bet I could have done a better job than that.

The seat was slippery with polish and I thought about sliding down under the table to make my sister laugh, but at my age I might not have been able to haul myself back up again without a complete loss of dignity. So I didn't. Gone were the days when I could get up without sound effects.

Jenny hadn't appreciated my sense of humour in recent years, anyway. Perhaps that had been part of the problem. I sometimes think I have foot-in-mouth disease.

'How are you? Good drive down to Plymouth?' I said.

Now that the first awkwardness was over, I was excited, pleased to see her, hopeful that we could mend bridges.

She, on the other hand, sounded quite composed.

'Fine, thanks. Only about forty-five minutes from home. You?'

I nodded. 'Yes, so easy. Train straight through from Bristol to Plymouth and then I got a taxi from the station.'

'Great,' Jenny said. She pushed her glasses up her nose and looked out of the window again.

Oh God, it looked like this was going to be hard work, but I'd never been one to give up easily.

She did look older, which I suppose was to be expected. Her hair was greyer now, same as mine. Her face was a bit more lined. To a casual observer we would have looked exactly what we were: a pair of middle-aged, middle-sized sisters going off to France on the ferry together.

Her blue eyes behind the sensible, metal-rimmed spectacles were expressionless. I turned to see what she was looking at. Drake's Island, perhaps. Some dull concrete buildings on the dockside. A man in a high-vis jacket driving a forklift truck. None of it looked that interesting.

It didn't feel at all comfortable; the atmosphere was possibly worse than I'd expected. The ice needed a lot more breaking. Possibly with a pickaxe. Or some explosives.

'How's life? Okay?' I said.

'Fine, thanks. You?' Jenny replied, flicking me a glance.

'Yes, super, great, terrific,' I gushed.

There wasn't really anyone to mention that she would know. Chums from my latest zero-hour contract job at the estate agency. The noisy couple living in the flat above mine, who seemed to have taken up midnight clog dancing. My friends from the book club, who even now were ploughing gamely through some leaden book about death and disease in Guatemala.

Jenny sighed and flicked on her mobile. 'Oh, well, that's good. No more of your usual dramas, then.'

I clenched my teeth and didn't reply to this barb but watched while she sent a text message and wondered if I could think of someone to text too. I suppose I could have sent another cheery message to Diana or Scarlett at work. To see how they were coping without me, although the property market was a bit stagnant and they hadn't seemed to worry that I was taking so much time off. Or I could have sent a text to the neighbours, friends from the book group, but I'd already been in touch with all of them. I didn't think they needed a blow-by-blow account of my day. Maybe to my ex-husband, Steve, but his new child bride was expecting any day now. I couldn't think of anything that wouldn't have sounded sarcastic and why would I contact him anyway? Perhaps at that moment he was gowned up in the delivery room, patting Leanne's forehead with a damp cloth and feeding her ice cubes. Bastard.

Suddenly I was consumed with frustration and, as had so often happened in the past, I wanted to do something outrageous.

I wanted to throw my arms around Jenny and cry. Tell her how much I'd missed her. Suggest we all draw a line, forget what had happened between us. Remember the good bits. Apologise to each other. Make an effort. Laugh again. Reminisce about all the funny times we had shared. The excuses we had made for each other with our parents, our teachers. The scrapes we had got into and out of together.

But I did none of those things. I just sat there, fidgeted with my bag and wondered what we could talk about.

I decided on an easy topic, sure ground, the one she liked best.

'How's Paul? And how is Jason – I mean Ace?'

Years ago I'd taken her son Jason to see *Ace Ventura: Pet Detective* as a birthday treat and he'd been obsessed with the character, insisting on being called Ace from that day onwards and the nickname had stuck. It suited him, too; he was bright, cheerful and popular wherever he went. I liked him enormously. He was nothing like his father.

She gave a little smile and her face brightened.

'Fine thanks. Paul's busy with work. Accountants are always overwhelmed at this time of year. It's the end of the tax year and all his clients are desperate for his attention. We haven't seen Ace for a bit, although we text each other, of course. He spent Christmas in Scotland with some friends again, working at a homeless shelter before he went back to Nantes. Did you know he lives there now?'

'What a great thing to do. And Nantes! Yes, of course I remember. How exciting,' I said eagerly.

'He's teaching at the university,' Jenny added proudly. 'French and English history, his two passions.'

I widened my eyes. 'That's amazing. He's only thirteen.'

Old joke. For a long time it seemed that Ace was the perennially overprotected child of two helicopter parents. Chinooks, probably, or at least Sea Kings. I for one was secretly astonished when he actually left home.

She gave a polite smile, scrolled through her photos and passed her phone across the table to show me one of Ace mid-laugh, standing with a load of his friends, one arm around a woman with green hair. By the look of things, he was in a pub and a lot more than half cut. There were Christmas lights behind him, twinkling among the whisky bottles. Good to see he was enjoying life. He had also grown a really unattractive beard, which was a shame as he was a nice-looking chap. I couldn't understand this new passion for face fungus. But then I was probably out of the loop; I'd only just got to grips with 'designer stubble'. My husbands might have turned out to be losers but at least they all knew how to shave.

'How marvellous,' I said enthusiastically. 'He looks happy and you'll *both* be in France for a bit. And he's doing so well, I bet. He always was so clever.'

As I hadn't met up with her son for a long time either, this was a stab in the dark – I had no idea if he was doing well at all. Still, Ace had been to university, he had a teaching qualification and a PhD in some obscure facet of French history, and he could speak three languages the last time I'd asked. I expected he was now fluent in five more, knowing him.

'He is. I'm very – *we* are very proud of him,' Jenny said with a little smile.

'So, has he got a significant other, then?'

The smile faded and the shutters came down.

'Not that we know of. He's terrifically busy and he's never been a letter writer. Young people aren't these days, are they?'

Well, there were still emails and phones, surely? WhatsApp and FaceTime? And Ace was thirty-something, not a kid whose phone had run out of credit.

Ace, like me, had never got on particularly well with his father. Perhaps things had changed. Perhaps they hadn't. I didn't press the point. I wasn't going to mention Paul again.

'I wish I'd managed to travel more. I love planes and airports.

I've got an app on my phone that tells me what the planes are and where they're going. I love imagining being on one of them, sitting back in my seat with a glass of something. And ferries are marvellous too, aren't they?' I said after a while, nodding at the view spread out in front of us. Far out on the horizon it looked as though it was raining.

'Some of them are. I doubt this one will be,' Jenny replied rather dismissively. 'It's not exactly Cunard, is it?'

There was another awkward silence.

'Have you had breakfast? Do you fancy a coffee?' I was halfway out of my seat before I'd finished talking. 'I'll go if you do.'

'I'm fine thanks. I don't drink much coffee these days, only decaf, and Paul made me a packed lunch for the journey. But you go, I'll watch your bag.'

Was she keen to get me to go already? I hoped not. How long was it going to take before we could both relax with each other? Perhaps forgive each other?

I looked around. There was a line of people, parents mostly, with tired children hanging on their arms, requesting crisps and luminous drinks.

'It's okay, I'll wait,' I said, sitting back down again. 'There's still a bit of a queue.'

We sat in silence for a few minutes until I couldn't bear it any more.

'So this is exciting, isn't it? A trip to France to see our inheritance.'

'Yes, very. I was told Aunt Sheila's solicitors had sorted out all the necessary taxes and that sort of thing. I hope it's true.'

Jenny sounded as excited as though I'd suggested a day out at the dentist's.

I persevered, hoping to get the conversation flowing.

'I wonder what the house is like now. When I was there last,

Aunt Sheila was full of ideas of things she might do. She wrote telling me she was having new windows fitted, and the electrics done. You and Paul went there several times, didn't you? We almost joined you once, when I was living in Worcester.'

'With Oliver. Now, which husband was he? Oh, I remember, the bigamist?' Jenny said, arching one eyebrow.

'What a good memory you have,' I said frostily.

I hadn't known he was a bigamist; I think I deserved sympathy, under the circumstances, not scorn. It hadn't exactly been a picnic for me.

'That visit of ours was ages ago. The last time Paul and I went was when we just popped in on our way to Aquitaine. I honestly don't think much had changed since you went. Of course, we didn't *stay* with Aunt Sheila. It was still a bit rustic. Paul gets very edgy if there isn't air-conditioning. Or a buffet breakfast. The house still needed a lot doing to it, as I remember, so don't get your hopes up.'

'But I bet it's great now,' I said rather too enthusiastically. 'Aunt Sheila had a lot of plans, didn't she?'

'Yes, she did, but she was like her brother, like Dad, never one to do things in a rush. It had a great view of the countryside. And the sea in the distance. And she had planted a lot of trees,' Jenny said.

'I wish we could have gone to the funeral,' I said, 'but the lawyer said she didn't want any fuss. It seems a shame.'

Jenny pushed her specs up her nose again. 'I absolutely agree. It felt rather sad not to go, but on the other hand, I was quite relieved; Paul is very odd about funerals. A funeral in France, well, it would have been awful. He made enough of a fuss about his uncle in Yeovil and that was only fifty minutes away.'

'Well, I would have gone if I'd known,' I said. 'I wrote to her when she went into hospital. And even when she was really ill, she had lots of plans and ideas. She was such a positive person, so full of life, wasn't she? Sometimes I still can't believe she's gone.'

Jenny glanced at her watch. 'Look at the time. We should be leaving soon.'

She always was very good at changing the subject.

I resisted the impulse to shake my sister out of her reserve. I could remember the time when we had got on so well. If I looked back – okay, I was remembering years ago, so perhaps my memory was a bit rose-tinted – I remembered us laughing, squabbling, pinching each other's make-up, cheering each other up in bad times, celebrating the good. Late nights in our shared bedroom, laughing until we were nearly sick. Had she forgotten all that? I hadn't.

There had been boyfriends and our parents to deal with. School, exams to commiserate over. We had always been so close, allies, protective of each other. How had it come to this? If only it was possible to go back and do things differently. But, of course, it wasn't. Things had been said that could never be unsaid or forgotten. It was no good pretending otherwise. But there had to be something I could do to find a way for us to be friends again.

The engines far below us shuddered as the ferry shimmied away from the quayside, left Plymouth and headed out into Plymouth Sound. It was a mild spring morning, the sky blue above us and the sea reassuringly smooth. Jenny cleared her throat, took out her knitting and opened a book. Judging by the cover, it was something about miserable people caught up in a war. We used to swap books; we'd had a bookcase in our bedroom, filled with dog-eared paperbacks. I didn't much like the look of that one. What happened to her passion for Jilly Cooper? And Georgette Heyer? And why was she knitting a cardigan in such a dreary colour? A sort of sludge-green crossed with mud. In other words, dull.

'Still knitting, then?' I said.

Jenny gave a polite smile. 'It's for Paul.'

Yes, he would look quite the cool dude in that.

* * *

Across the aisle from us was a young woman who was taking surreptitious sips from a water bottle. Why were the younger generation so terrified of going anywhere without a water bottle clutched in one hand? Was it a sport thing? Was the girl pretending she was a marathon runner? Was she on her way to a Zumba class in Roscoff? Did she think the tap water was poisonous? Young people must spend their lives nipping to the loo. I wouldn't get anything done if I was drinking water all day. It would be asking for trouble.

And she had no coat and was wearing two different strappy tops at once, both of which were too small. I didn't understand that either. It was the end of March; she must have been cold. I suppose it was the fashion to go out half-dressed these days.

I thought about nudging Jenny under the table so she could share the joke, but at the last minute I didn't. Perhaps I should have brought a water bottle and filled it with gin. That sounded like a good idea. I looked at my watch hopefully. It was only nine thirty. Perhaps not.

A young man made his way down the aisle towards us. He was tall, stubbly and rather handsome, and looked as though he was the outdoors type. Rugged checked shirt, Aran sweater and sturdy-looking walking boots. He caught my gaze for the merest fraction of a nanosecond and then his eyes swivelled away to the girl and her bosom and her water bottle. You see, that's one of the rubbish things about being older: you're still there taking up space, needing stuff, wanting attention, but you gradually become invisible and unimportant. It's very annoying.

I wanted to reach out and grab his arm as he passed. *Excuse me, young man, I can assure you I was quite cute, back in 1843*, I wanted to say. *I had quite a lot of admirers. I haven't always been grey-haired with a slightly dodgy cholesterol count and a problem hip. I wore mini-skirts and I had a Biba flapper dress. I wore kaftans as a fashion statement, not to cover up my flab.* In my head, I was thirty-six at the most. In my head, I still had a figure that made builders whistle. Not that they were allowed to do that any more. Obviously.

* * *

Five and a half hours later, Jenny had got halfway through her book, which I think was called something like *The Worst Day in the History of the Universe.* Judging by her expression, there weren't many laughs. She'd also finished knitting one sleeve, which lay curled on the table between us like a huge, dead caterpillar, and eaten her packed lunch, which looked like a dull affair of colourless things and cardboard bread. I'd eaten an unsatisfactory panini, flavour unknown, from the ferry café, and had a walk around the boat and then a snooze.

And then we reached Roscoff.

It was much bigger than I remembered but with the same sort of uninteresting warehouses you'd expect to see at any ferry port. Far below us, the engine shuddered as the captain put the brakes on. Or whatever it was he was doing.

Jenny rolled up her knitting, put her bookmark in her book and closed it with a decisive thump.

'We'd better be going,' she said. 'We don't want to hold people up.'

'What people?'

She didn't answer.

Obediently, I picked up my case and followed her. We joined the queue of people heading slowly down the echoing, iron stairwells to the car decks below us. Jenny's car, a massive, fairly new, red Chelsea tractor thing, was near the front of the boat, presumably because she had been one of the first to arrive at the quayside that morning, and the ramp was already being lowered, allowing us our first glimpse of Roscoff and France. It was very exciting.

People many rows behind us who hadn't a hope of moving any time soon were already starting up their engines. Perhaps they were the people we didn't want to hold up. Some were panicking and shouting at their children, things like, 'Come on! No, Orlando, I've got Mr Teddy. For heaven's sake, Indigo! Hurry up, or Daddy will go without you.'

That was a waste of their nagging reserves; the ferry hadn't even stopped yet. And any child who had a basic knowledge of parenting fails – and they all seemed to – knew that *going without you* simply wouldn't happen. I didn't think children were allowed out of the front door without an armed guard where I lived.

But hey-ho, we had arrived safely and perhaps now was the opportunity to start some sisterly bonding. The miles of paperwork, angry-looking customs officials and terrifying (but strangely attractive) policemen with guns would soon all be behind us.

* * *

When we first planned this journey over the course of countless emails, Jenny had offered to drive – she told me she did all their holiday driving because Paul *didn't approve* of driving on the wrong side of the road, as though the French had done this out of a need to personally antagonise him – and I certainly wasn't going to argue about it. Jenny had passed her driving test first go. I had taken four attempts and I still wasn't very good at parallel parking.

When we were younger, Jenny used to drive us everywhere in her battered Mini: Glastonbury, the Isle of Wight, shopping trips and nights out. And she could change a tyre too, and had a far better sense of direction than anyone I knew. I owned a fairly basic car without the glories of air conditioning and sat-nav that Jenny's car had. And the MOT was about to expire.

To start off, the drive was really scary. Like being next to Lewis Hamilton at the beginning of a Formula One race when everyone roars away from the starting grid. I would have shut my eyes, but as Jenny hadn't owned the car long enough to know how to set the sat-nav and I was supposed to be navigating, it wouldn't have been a particularly helpful thing to do. She hunched over the steering wheel, her knuckles white. It was like a mouse driving a fire engine.

Gradually, the traffic thinned out and we plunged west, deep into the Brittany countryside, while other suicidal cars filled with tight-faced families also unfamiliar with driving on the wrong side of the road veered off towards Morlaix, leaving us on roads that were smaller and more winding as the journey progressed. Neither of us spoke much except when Jenny snapped out questions:

'Do you mean this roundabout?'

'Left? You mean left here or the next one?'

'For heaven's sake, you're the one with the map. Which way?'

Occasionally, I sneaked a look at my sister. After a while she had relaxed, and she seemed to be coping okay under the circumstances. I was filled with admiration for her. Even the unfamiliar road signs and roundabouts didn't seem to faze her. I would have been whimpering behind the wheel five minutes after we left the ferry port.

Jenny now had her prescription Polaroids perched accurately on her nose against the sun as we sped west through cute French villages where everyone seemed to be carrying baguettes. I wished – not for the first time – that I'd remembered my sunglasses.

Perhaps there would be a colourful little shop in a nearby village with a smiling owner with a beret who would be charmed by my ability to speak schoolgirl French, where I could buy some once we were settled. Every time I wore them, I would remember a happy shopping expedition with my sister.

Oh, these sunglasses? I bought these in France; my sister and I had such a lovely holiday...

Meanwhile, I was still busy trying to make sense of the road map that at no point appeared helpful or accurate and was covered in strange little icons I didn't understand.

'We will need to turn off soon,' Jenny said confidently. 'I remember this village. I don't think it's far now.'

'You're doing great,' I said, peering at the map again, hoping for some clue as to where we were.

Thank heavens one of us knew where we were going. By the time we had negotiated a couple of roundabouts and been through a few towns, I didn't have a clue, map or not.

2

About an hour later we reached our destination. In front of us, bathed in early evening sunset was the sign for the house. Jolies Arbres. Pretty Trees. Underneath that was a hand-painted, wooden board – *Galerie d'Art* – which had fallen over into the bushes. Behind the closed ironwork gates I remembered, we could see a weed-riddled track, leading between scrubby-looking – and not particularly pretty – trees towards the house. There was a tantalising glimpse of the stone walls and a roof with lichen-peppered tiles. It looked promising.

I got out of the car to push the gates open. The warmth of the day was past now and there was a chilly breeze. The air was fresher here, though, scented with something that was almost herbal. Whatever that was, I would have to find out. Anyway, it was gorgeous and much better than the smell I was used to at home in Bristol, which was dusty and urban with a top note of diesel and occasionally kebab.

I got back into the passenger seat.

'Put your seatbelt on,' Jenny said.

'It's not far,' I replied.

'You're making the car beep,' she said. 'It's annoying.'

I fastened my seatbelt.

Jenny drove through and up to the house. Yes, there were new windows, and a new front door. I remembered it now.

The porch was tiled and blocked with piles of leaves and small twigs. The windows were framed by wooden shutters, the colour of which had probably been blue, now faded to grey, the paint peeling after years under the French sun. There were ropes of a climbing plant up the front of the house – it looked like wisteria – and some empty terracotta pots on either side of the door. There was an unmistakeable air of neglect and slight disrepair. Well, the house had been empty for the best part of a year since Sheila had died. That's how long it had taken to sort out the paperwork, and our solicitor's understanding of French legalese had been stretched to the maximum.

I looked at Jenny, wanting her to be pleased, hoping she was happy. From her expression, I couldn't tell.

Never mind; we were here now, and Jenny had the front door keys in her hand. I was twitching with excitement and a pressing need for the loo, which at my age should never be ignored.

'Hurry up, hurry up. I can't wait to see inside. Do you think she put the shower in?'

'Yes, she did,' Jenny said, wrestling with the unfamiliar lock.

At last, there was a grinding squeak and the door opened.

* * *

I think I could speak for both of us. It wasn't quite what we had been expecting.

The hallway was darker than I remembered and smelled of dust. Piles of leaves had blown in under the door. To one side was the large sitting room with its low, beamed ceiling and three of the ugliest sofas I'd ever seen. To the other was the gloomy kitchen, still furnished with the same wooden cabinets and a huge stone sink like a horse trough, and then there was the rather poky dining room that Sheila had never used whenever I'd stayed with her. Further still was the bedroom I had slept in the last time with the same formidable iron bedstead and a massive oak wardrobe that could have led to Narnia. There was a second, similar bedroom behind the first and then two bathrooms.

Each one was reasonably clean but frankly hideous, fully tiled in brown and orange with dark brown paintwork and grimy, frosted windows. There was the biggest spider France had to offer, dead in one shower tray.

I heard footsteps tapping upstairs; evidently, Jenny was also exploring.

It might have been dark and a bit neglected now, but through the kitchen window was still the most magnificent view of the countryside, which flared away below us, yellow with gorse bushes, towards the sea in the distance. It really was wonderful. I could see a couple of yachts, their sails bellying in the breeze and what must have been a cruise ship, moving slowly across the horizon like a giant white pram.

I think I'd anticipated it would have changed more. Into something more exciting, I suppose. I remembered sitting with Sheila under a stone pergola, near the swimming pool. She had set the table for tea with an embroidered cloth and flowered china. My first husband, Frank, had topped up his cup from a hip flask when he thought I wasn't looking.

I'd hoped it would be sunlight-filled and jolly. Which was daft; at my age I should have been used to things not living up to expectations. And yet at the same time there was such a nice feel to the place, something comfortable and friendly. They say you can tell if

you want to buy a house within seconds, and it had nothing to do
with new carpets or accent wall colours.

'It hasn't changed that much, has it?'

'Not really,' Jenny said as she re-joined me in the sitting room
some minutes later. 'What were you expecting, Versailles?'

'No, of course not. It's got heaps of potential, though, hasn't it? I
like it. What's it like upstairs? Have there been any changes?' I asked
encouragingly.

'Not really, apart from the shower. It's all a bit dull, like this,'
Jenny said, flicking a hand over the back of the ugliest sofa. If one
could be singled out. 'I'll take the upstairs bedroom unless you have
any strenuous objections?'

There was the old Jenny: taking the lead again, actually making
a decision. I was delighted to see it.

'No, of course not. Whatever you want.'

We stood in silence for a moment, my excitement evaporating.
We were here, the journey was over; now we had to get to grips with
things.

'I'm going to find the pool. At least there is that to look forward
to,' I said. 'I've bought a new cossie specially. I went—'

'Well, I think we should bring the cases in first and get settled,'
Jenny said, turning briskly through the front door.

I followed her to where the car was sitting, covered in dust from
the gravel drive.

Jenny tutted at the sight of it.

'Paul would be livid if he could see that.'

'Good job he's not here, then,' I said.

Jenny laughed a bit uneasily.

Whatever the house was like, we both agreed its position was
fabulous. We stood together for a moment, admiring the sweeping
view down across the green landscape towards the shining sea in
the distance.

I sighed happily. 'Just gorgeous, isn't it? Sheila was happy here, wasn't she? It has a nice vibe.'

'Yes, she was. She said the light here was good for her artwork and the wine was cheap. Come and get your case out of the boot.'

How could the house be good for art when it was so dark? I wondered. I thought artists lived in north-facing attics with skylights and white walls. But didn't she work outdoors most of the time? Oh yes, I remembered her now, sitting in the garden with her easel in front of her, a paint-splattered overall covering her clothes. The memory made me smile.

Suddenly there was a loud, hooting cry behind us and, startled, we turned.

A stringy-looking man was coming up the driveway on a scruffy donkey.

He waved with excitement and hooted some more as he came closer and the donkey gave us a resigned look.

'*Bienvenue,*' he shouted. 'Welcome!'

He clambered off the poor animal and came forward, whipping his cloth cap off his head, nodding and welcoming us a bit more.

'*Bienvenue, mesdames. Charmantes dames. Bienvenue!*'

Jenny edged behind me.

'What does he want?' she hissed.

'He's just being friendly; he's welcoming us. He thinks we are charming.'

I stepped forward and took the newcomer's outstretched hand, which was tanned and calloused.

He shook each of our hands in turn, clutching his cap to his chest with emotion.

'*Bienvenue! Quelle belle journée.* What a lovely day. *Si heureux de vous voir!*'

'What?' Jenny muttered, surreptitiously wiping her hand down her leg.

'He's pleased to see us,' I said.

Jenny rose to the challenge. '*Bonjour.*'

The newcomer smiled, his teeth as yellow as his donkey's. He prodded himself enthusiastically in the chest.

'I am Bertrand. Friend. Sheila. Welcome, lovely ladies.'

'Thank you,' Jenny said.

Bertrand dug into a capacious trouser pocket and pulled out a bunch of keys, which he shook at us.

'I have keys. Keys to this house. Nice keys – *clés.*'

'God, Kitty, take them off him quick,' Jenny said, 'before he just lets himself and his donkey in.'

I did so, shoving them into my pocket.

'*Merci, m'sieur.*'

'*D'accord! Hourra!*' he cheered. 'Everything is good!'

The donkey joined in with an impressive bray and Bertrand smiled broadly, showing several more impressive teeth the donkey might have envied.

'*Âne,* donkey,' he said, patting the animal fondly on its neck and releasing a cloud of dust. '*Il s'appelle Hector.*'

'The donkey is called Hector,' I translated.

'I got that part. You should have closed the gate. Make it go away,' Jenny muttered.

'Stop being so anti-social,' I muttered back.

'I thought French men were supposed to be sexy and attractive,' she said, 'like Yves Montand or Sacha Distel.'

'Well, perhaps he was...'

'Thirty years ago,' she added rather too loudly.

'Stop it,' I said. 'He may be very helpful, and he might have been a good friend to Sheila.'

Jenny inched away around the car. 'That donkey is looking at me. And I think it's just made a disgusting smell.'

I giggled; Jenny had never really been an animal lover when we were growing up. I remembered a family trip to a zoo when she asked to be allowed to stay in the car park and was only lured out with the promise of ice cream.

'He knows you don't like him. They can smell fear, you know,' I said, teasing her.

'*Merci beaucoup*,' Jenny said and stalked back into the house, her shoulders twitching.

Bertrand and I exchanged a look; I was trying very hard not to laugh.

He held up a gnarled finger, his button eyes bright with excitement.

'Léo Bisset. *Je lui dirai que vous êtes arrivées.* I will tell him. I will tell Léo.'

'*Merci*,' I said, with no idea who Léo might be. Perhaps the local sex maniac or purveyor of unsightly donkeys.

'And, *demain* – tomorrow – *Mimi prendra les poulets. Bien sûr.*'

'What?' Something about chickens. I was quickly realising that schoolgirl French was one thing, actual French was quite another.

Jenny was back ten seconds later, her face panicked, her eyes desperate.

'Oh my God! Tell me it's not true! There's no mobile signal! Or Wi-Fi.'

Bertrand nodded and pulled a mobile phone in a surprisingly sparkly cover out of his pocket, waving it sadly in the air.

'Not today,' he said. He made a little motion, miming something with one index finger. '*Réinitialiser, il doit être démarré, mais dans le village.* Plenty of – um, um – *l'Internet*. In the village. *Dans le cybercafé*. Plenty!'

Hector brayed unattractively in agreement and shook his head, releasing another cloud of dust and another awful smell.

'Cybercafé,' Jenny said faintly, flapping her hand in front of her face. 'Who'd have thunk it?'

3

Jenny settled into the upstairs bedroom, which was large but cheer-less. I chose the bigger of the two downstairs bedrooms, next to the kitchen, so it was at least close to the kettle. The house was dull with disuse, but it had a lovely, friendly feel and was full of surprising things. An old linen press on the landing upstairs was filled with the sort of antique French bedlinens that would have sent Kirstie whatshername on the TV into ecstasy. There were cupboards in the kitchen filled with tinned food with unfamiliar labels and a walk-in pantry as big as my boxroom at home. On the shelves were Kilner jars full of pasta and rice and there was a vegetable rack containing a few fossilised and unidentifiable remnants and a large and surprisingly new fridge-freezer, which had been cleaned out, the doors left propped open. There was also a thrilling-looking and cavernous cupboard under the stairs filled to capacity with grimy bottles of wine. The locals must have been very honest; back home, that would have been ransacked in minutes.

I still wasn't allowed to go looking for the pool because the fridge-freezer was empty, so we switched it on, got back into the car and made a trip out to the nearest *supermarché* where we stocked up with milk, beautiful-looking fruit and vegetables, eggs and a fine selection of cheeses. There might not have been Wi-Fi, but this was looking really positive as far as I was concerned.

Jenny declared herself 'practically a vegetarian' and looked at the displays of meat with a shudder.

'I wonder why they have pictures of horses – oh. That's *awful*.'

'It's okay, we won't buy any. I wasn't planning to give you *hamburgers de cheval* anyway,' I said cheerfully. 'Perhaps they will have some nice soya ones for you in the freezer section.'

'Paul doesn't approve of soya; he says it uses up all the world's resources and most of it goes for animal feed. Perhaps we could just have some pasta?'

'With this luminous sauce?' I suggested, holding up a jar.

Jenny frowned. 'Surely you could make something. That's full of sugar and chemicals – ooh, look, proper baguettes!' She picked one up and held it to her nose, eyes closed. 'Oh, that's gorgeous.'

'And croissants!' I chucked a bag of about twenty into the trolley.

'That will help your cholesterol,' Jenny said.

'I don't much care.'

'Well, I won't pick you up off the floor when you have a coronary,' Jenny said.

'I don't suppose you will. Which reminds me – thinking about the floor, we need some cleaning things.'

'True.'

We added some cleaning products into the trolley and then I did what I always do: made some impulse purchases. A plastic tablecloth patterned with the silhouettes of ladies in lace caps and sabots, and a giant box of chocolate milkshake powder, which we both remembered from our childhood.

'Paul would go berserk if he could see that,' Jenny murmured, stroking the side of the packet.

'Well, he can't,' I said. 'Do you remember camping in the garden and we used to have that with hot milk? Mum would bring it out in a Thermos. And cheese-and-pickle sandwiches.'

'I haven't had a cheese-and-pickle sandwich for years!' she said wistfully.

'How about a cheese-and-pickle *baguette*? Even better!'

'Now you're talking! And we used to have a pile of *Jackie* magazines, and you used to read out the picture stories in a funny voice. And make up new words.'

'Emma, are you asking me to the dance, hen?' I asked in a gruff Glasgow docker's voice. *'I'd love to but I'm washing ma hair, and the day after is ma audition for the Royal Ballet School.'*

Jenny snorted with laughter and gave me a friendly shove.

Then I saw a stand filled with sunglasses that were rather glittery and odd and not what I had in mind. I picked out a pair that were more than a nod to some fifties starlet. Or Dame Edna Everage, depending on one's viewpoint. Oh well, they would do for the time being. Knowing me, I'd probably sit on them or lose them.

'What do you think?' I asked.

Jenny blinked. 'You look like Mum. That didn't come out right. I meant like Mum but better, you know?'

Well, that wasn't the response I had hoped for when I imagined buying new sunglasses with my sister, but it was a start.

* * *

We were both in a reasonably good mood by the time we got home. After a bit of casual questioning, Jenny had admitted she was looking forward to some *time to herself*, and not having to worry about *Paul's requirements*, which she said with a meaningful look.

Perhaps Paul, while approaching a late retirement, still had a spring in his step, so to speak.

I've always rather enjoyed the company of men, and sex as well, to be honest. Surprising, really, as my mother had always led us to believe that all men were foul fiends under their veneer of pretended domesticity. Jenny and I had once discussed whether or not our father was also a 'foul fiend'. He seemed pretty mild-mannered to us. The kindest, nicest man.

Mum had pursed her mouth disapprovingly when I divorced Frank and his alcoholism (*there's never been a divorce in this family, Kitty*), and almost laughed when she heard about bigamist Oliver (*I always had my doubts about him*). Thank heavens she hadn't lived long enough to know about Steve and his treacherous trousers.

I hadn't shared a bed with a man for several years and I felt quite wistful for a moment until I remembered the snoring and occasional unwelcome noises that went with it.

Still, there was one thing I was sure Jenny and I would both agree on.

'I'll get the wine.' I opened the makeshift *armoire à vin* under the stairs.

'Do you think we should?' Jenny said doubtfully.

'Sheila? Do you mind if we open a bottle of wine?' I called at the ceiling. I waited for a moment. 'There, she didn't say anything.'

'Mid-week drinking? Paul would... Well, maybe just a small glass, while we make dinner. I wonder what Paul is eating. He's terribly fussy about his food.'

She darted me a worried look, in case she had seemed disloyal, I suppose. This revelation came as no surprise to me; I remembered him dissecting a chicken dinner I once made for him as though he'd suspected me of hiding broken glass in it.

I pulled out a bottle and inspected the label.

'Château Monbrison,' I said. 'I've never heard of that, have you? Anyway, it will do.'

Jenny peered over my shoulder. '1988. It's a bit past its sell-by date, isn't it?'

'Well, if it's gone off we'll try another one,' I said, sloshing some red into two glasses, 'and red wine is very good for your heart, which will counteract the damage I intend to do with the croissants tomorrow morning.'

'Where did you hear that? Breakfast television?'

'An angel came to me in a dream,' I replied airily.

'You're still very silly. Even at your age,' she said, shaking her head.

'I am, and I intend to remain so. Cheers!'

We clinked glasses and exchanged a look.

'Don't tell Paul,' Jenny said.

'You worry far too much about your husband.' I was enjoying the warming glow from the first sip of wine. It was really nice.

'Well, perhaps you didn't worry enough about yours,' Jenny countered.

'Ooh! Touché,' I said. 'I'm not going to let you get to me. Now play nicely, Jenny.'

Perhaps she was right; perhaps I hadn't worried enough about the three men I had married. But what good would that have done in the long run? Had any one of them worried about me and my happiness?

'I'm just saying,' she said, a bit apologetic.

'Well, don't. I'm going to make a tomato sauce for the pasta. There's a huge basil bush by the kitchen door; I'll sling some of that in too. And we could have some garlic bread.'

Jenny tutted. 'Are you addicted to fats and carbohydrates? No wonder you've put on weight.'

'I haven't!'

She looked smug. 'I think you'll find you have. I bet those trousers have an elasticated waist, don't they?'

'Well, actually they don't, so yah boo sucks to you,' I said, feeling my good mood falter.

'Do you know, Paul is the same weight as the day we married?'

'How simply *marvellous* for you,' I said, banging the saucepans about. 'I expect he wears the same Crimplene *slacks* too.'

Jenny looked uncomprehending. I finished my wine and re-filled the glass.

* * *

In the end, we constructed a rather pleasant meal, linguine of uncertain age and a rich tomato and basil sauce, which I perked up with some of the red wine. The label seemed to suggest it was probably too good for cooking with, but there were dozens of other bottles so a small slosh wouldn't hurt. Jenny had watched me cook with an anguished look on her face.

'Don't you weigh anything? I mean, how much garlic? What did you do with the tomatoes?'

'Don't you cook at all?' I asked, amazed. 'You used to love it. Remember when we used to cook Christmas dinner together? And sneak the sherry while we were doing it?'

She laughed and her expression relaxed. 'I can still almost remember the Boxing Day hangovers we used to get too. Remember that bread sauce the year Auntie Jane came to stay? We had to practically pressure-wash the saucepan afterwards. To be honest, I haven't really cooked for years. Paul saw me licking a spoon once when I was making a casserole, and after that he took over. And he doesn't like the smell of food in the house, so he prefers ready meals so that he knows exactly how much fat and sugar he's eating. So it's more the art of the microwave than *Master-Chef* these days.'

Jenny wrestled for a bit with her linguine, and we tucked in. It was really rather good, though I say so myself. It made a change to be cooking for someone else, too. I loved messing about in the kitchen, but I'd been a bit toast-reliant over the last year. Sometimes it hardly seemed worth the bother just cooking for myself.

Jenny wiped the last of her garlic bread around her plate thoughtfully and placed her cutlery neatly together.

'That was rather good, actually. Miss Cattermole would be spinning in her grave if she could see the mess we've made. Do you remember her? Domestic science teacher. Tried to teach us how to cook at the grammar school. Sour old puss.'

'I do remember her; she told Mum I was unteachable and would end up an old maid because no man would want to marry a woman who couldn't make mayonnaise properly.'

Jenny snorted. 'Well, she got that wrong, didn't she? I can't make mayonnaise either and I've been married for thirty-five years.'

I stopped collecting up the plates and turned to look at her.

'God, have you? How awful. I can hear her now. Old Cattermole. *For heaven's sake, Katherine Patterson, why can't you be more like your sister?*'

'You're joking; the only thing I did properly was clean up afterwards – that's why she liked me. Most of my stuff was inedible. Custard you could cut with a bread knife. And what do you mean, "how awful"? I think I have a good marriage.'

'Do you?' I said doubtfully.

'I think so.' She didn't sound too sure all of a sudden. Perhaps it was the wine loosening her up a bit. 'And of course, I have Ace. That makes up for everything.'

'Ah, the trump card. The son and heir.'

'You never had children; you wouldn't understand,' Jenny said pompously.

This made me cross.

'It wasn't for lack of trying – and I did want them, it just never happened. Steve has a new child bride. She's half his age. And Leanne is about to undergo the miracle of birth any day now.'

Jenny guffawed. 'Miracle of birth? Don't make me laugh. Unless they have found a new way to do it, she's in for a thoroughly ghastly time.'

Still, I thought later as I unpacked my bags in my gloomy bedroom, I would have liked a child. A tall son to sling an arm around my shoulder and ruffle my hair when I did something daft. Or a daughter to make sense of life with, and to explain to why her many boyfriends weren't good enough for her.

My imaginary children were always well behaved and clever. They wouldn't have pinched gin from the drinks cupboard as I had. My daughter would not have rolled her school skirt up at the waistband as she walked with a smirk on her face to the train station. My son would not have got drunk on cheap cider behind the youth club and shoved his friends into other people's hedges.

I wondered which of my three ex-husbands would have made the best father. None of them, if I was honest. And would I have made a good mother? That was something I had wondered a lot over the years as the dream faded. Had I possessed the patience, the courage, to bring another human into the world and keep them safe? To guide them, steer them away from the sort of mistakes I had made.

4

The bed was possibly the most uncomfortable one I've ever slept on – or rather, tried to sleep on. The bedframe jangled like a wind-chime every time I turned over – and I turned over a lot – and the mattress was stuffed with Hector's hoof trimmings, as far as I could judge. Just after five o'clock I finally gave up the unequal struggle and went to make tea.

Outside, the dawn was breaking and the light over the sea was almost glowing. I unbolted the kitchen door and went out into the garden. The morning was cool and quiet, and the scrubby grass was flattened and damp with dew. I stood, breathing in the clean French air with my mug of tea, on a rustic patio made from old flagstones, the weeds thick between them, and felt unexpectedly happy. The basil bush by the kitchen door was looking rather lovely, covered in dew. I crushed a leaf between my fingers and inhaled the scent. Next to that was a straggling rosemary bush, the stems woody and dragging across the path.

Beyond the patio, the garden was a shambolic mess and nothing like the one I remembered. I'd always been a keen gardener and I used to be quite good at it too. That was one thing I missed about having to move into a flat after Steve and I divorced. Two flower boxes were no substitute for the half acre I used to look after.

I could make out several flower beds bordered by little stones, which showed that someone had once cared, but now they were filled with weeds. There was a substantial ironwork arch over which a rose, covered in rusty-looking rosehips, was trailing. I suddenly remembered Aunt Sheila mentioning this in one of her letters.

My friend Jean gave me such a lovely birthday present: a rose to train over the arch. I hope it takes.

There were trees, brambles, the promise of an old path leading deep into the shrubs and two broken bird feeders, covered with cobwebs and moss, but no sign of a pool anywhere. I knew there was one somewhere. I remembered it so vividly, filled with clear turquoise water. I'd imagined my sister and me lying on sunbeds next to each other with glasses of wine. I sometimes think I must be a cock-eyed optimist, which would explain some of the bad life decisions I'd made.

Why had I always been so relentlessly optimistic when all the evidence pointed to disappointment? The three men I had married, the various jobs I had taken, none of that had really made me happy. And here I was, in my sixties, various friends but not much family left, and still wondering what I was going to do when I grew up.

I found the pool, after a few minutes of wandering about through the trees and scratching my legs on the brambles that had obviously been left to their own devices for far too long. I stood on an upturned bucket I'd found and craned to see it, which was difficult, and I couldn't get very close to it because of the brambles.

From what I glimpsed, it was now a grave disappointment and also a grave for a couple of small birds. I wouldn't have dignified it with the name 'pool' any more; it was just a tiled hole, very shallow at one end and with some muddy water at the deep end. Hmm, I'd wasted £45.50 on my new swimming costume, not to mention the torment of the thirty minutes spent trying the blasted things on in Marks & Spencer.

My eye was caught by a stealthy movement in the underbrush, and I froze. What could it be? Were there wolves in France? No, of course there weren't. Perhaps it was just a fox or a rabbit.

I trudged back towards the house, wondering if Jenny was awake yet or whether she was still blissfully asleep, safe from the possibilities of *Paul's requirements.*

Did my sister have a satisfactory sex life? I wondered. Did I? Well, I didn't at the moment. I hadn't for a long time. Should I even consider it, or was that something that no longer troubled women of our age? If we did, we were regarded as slightly odd and younger people pulled disgusted faces. If we didn't, we confirmed we were past it and heading towards senility, complaining about everything. But I didn't consider myself odd to want male company. Perhaps I was just unrealistic? What did I have to offer them, and what could they give me? After the break-up with my last husband, I suppose I'd just assumed I would find happiness eventually, but at my age, how long could I keep my hopes up? Jenny seemed to know where she was going, but where and how would I find the next stage of my life?

Thinking about it, I could almost imagine myself in years to come, living alone with a fat dog that I was too infirm to walk, evenings spent watching soaps and asking where Dirty Den was and, if I was lucky, occasionally being taken out for a *nice drive* to a garden centre in someone's car.

At what point were women supposed to give up the hurly-burly of the chaise longue for the comfort of a Silentnight divan? Interesting thought. I wasn't nearly ready. I wondered if my sister was. And when and how had she changed from being my fun-loving sister who was always up for a party, an enthusiastic downer of cocktails, and first into the latest fashions and hairstyles, into someone so different?

* * *

When I got back, Jenny was up, showered and dressed and was washing the kitchen table with a bowl full of hot water and some disinfectant.

'Have you seen the state of this place?' she said. 'I didn't notice last night – the light bulbs are so dim. Everything is covered in dust. I wish I'd thought to bring some Mr Sheen. And the cobwebs in my bathroom are terrible.'

'D'you mean there are a lot of them, or they aren't particularly good ones?'

Jenny threw me an exasperated look and carried on scrubbing.

'I'll sort out breakfast, shall I?'

Jenny looked at her watch. 'It's only half past six.'

I shrugged. 'So?'

'We usually have breakfast at eight o'clock.'

'I usually have breakfast when I feel like it,' I said. 'Go on, live a little.'

I put half a dozen croissants into the oven and dried the table off with a beautiful, embroidered tea towel. Then I put out my new plastic tablecloth, which unfortunately smelled of cat's pee. Then I found butter, apricot jam, crockery and cutlery.

Jenny frowned at the table, fidgeting. She was obviously worried about something.

'What's the matter?'

'Nothing matches,' she said. 'All the plates and mugs are different colours.'

'Does that matter?'

'Well, no, I suppose not. But at home—'

I rolled my eyes. 'Let me guess: Paul likes everything to match. And I bet he prefers cups and saucers, not mugs. And when you buy cakes, he uses a set of cake forks.'

'Oh goodness, we never buy cakes,' Jenny said. 'I wish. Paul's got it into his head we might be pre-diabetic.'

I laughed. 'Goodness, I would have thought Paul would have gone for *proper* diabetes. A man of his ability. And are you – pre-diabetic?'

'No, but he's always making us go to the doctor to have tests. Sometimes I fall asleep in front of *Midsomer Murders*, and he goes mad if I have to get up in the night to go to the loo. He says they're both a sure sign of diabetes.'

'Doesn't everyone fall asleep in front of *Midsomer Murders*? I think I know the first half hour of every episode and none of the endings.'

She shook her head. 'Paul doesn't ever fall asleep in front of the television. Sometimes I have to pinch myself to stay awake.'

'That's awful,' I said sadly. 'I like a bit of a snooze on the sofa with a blanket. Especially if there's an old film on the television and I've got some chocolate.'

'Me too,' Jenny sighed. 'I'd love that.'

* * *

I ate three croissants and Jenny ate two, looking with some regret at the one we left. I made some proper coffee in a complicated machine that hissed and spluttered on the hotplate. While it did so, Jenny moved to stand in the hallway, obviously expecting the contraption to explode, and wittered on about caffeine and arteries. Still, it didn't stop her from grabbing a mugful and drinking it with evident pleasure.

'Oh God, that's good. I haven't had a cup of proper coffee for ages,' she said at last as she watched me top up her mug. 'I feel quite giddy. Paul insists on decaf.'

'What's the point in that?' I said cheerfully. 'And who knows where all the caffeine they take out goes? I bet he hasn't thought about that. Probably causes all sorts of ecological problems. Dolphins tragically trapped in caffeine sludge, rivers polluted with strands of caffeine, the landscape ruined with caffeine heaps. Anyway, it's good for you.'

'Is it?'

'Oh it is, I looked it up on the internet.'

I looked across the table at her and was pleased and slightly surprised to see humour in her eyes. That was more like it. We both burst out laughing; it felt really brilliant, too. It had been a long time since we had been this relaxed with each other, had the chance to enjoy each other's sense of humour.

'So what should we do today?'

'Well, this whole place needs deep cleaning before we can think about decorating. No one would buy it in this state—'

Oh yes, of course. We were going to sell Jolies Arbres when we'd sorted it out, that was the plan. I'd almost forgotten. We weren't here for a holiday; we were here to finish the renovations. Aunt Sheila had started to smarten the whole place up but hadn't got very far before she had died. But she had left a substantial amount of money in a special bank account to pay for everything that still needed doing and had insisted in her will that we do it together. When it was finished, then we would split the proceeds and Jenny and I would go our separate ways again.

But already I didn't want that; at that moment it felt as though my sister and I were finding each other, that we still had so many good memories, our shared childhood when it had been us against everyone. Jenny had been the one person I'd relied on, closest to me in the world, who understood me. She'd had my back and I'd had hers through everything. We had been inseparable once; I needed to find that connection and build on it so that we never needed to doubt each other again.

Jenny went to open the kitchen door, letting in the fresh spring morning air.

Almost immediately she gave a shrill scream.

'Oh my God! Oh God! Kitty, *do something!*'

I spun round to see what all the fuss was about.

A white hen was standing in the doorway, apparently not dissuaded by my sister's screams or hopping feet. It was fat and feathery with a bright scarlet comb that looked almost like a beret.

'It's a chicken,' I said, rather confused.

'Get it away! Shoo it!' Jenny said, cowering behind me.

'It's one chicken; you can't possibly be scared of a chicken, you chicken,' I added with a snort.

Jenny retreated, her hands over her face. 'It's not funny. I can't bear them. All feathery and pecky and *clucky*.'

Keen to put an end to all the drama, I closed the kitchen door.

Jenny heaved a sigh of relief.

'Perhaps it's a stray,' I said. 'Maybe we could give it some scraps; it could be ours. Like a pet. *Notre* hen *de la maison*.'

'Don't be ridiculous. And if there are wild animals out there, then I'm definitely going to leave that up to you; I'm no gardener.'

'Wild animals,' I scoffed. 'It's hardly a threat to life, is it? It's not like one wild chicken is going to stalk you and launch an unprovoked attack with a Gatling gun.'

'Are there such a thing as wild chickens? But the garden does look terrible, doesn't it? And Sheila used to be so particular about that.'

'Yes. By the way, I went to see the swimming pool,' I said. 'It's empty and there's a puddle of muddy water in the deep end.'

Jenny's face creased into worry. 'Oh dear. We are going to have to find some help, surely? We can't do it all ourselves, not at our age.'

I thought about it. I wasn't afraid of hard work, but we had to be realistic. Both of us in our sixties and only me with a rudimentary knowledge of O-level French.

'No, I know we can't. But Bertrand mentioned someone, didn't he? Léo someone – Bertrand was going to tell him we were here.'

'Sheila never mentioned him. Or perhaps she did and I'd forgotten. Who is he, anyway?'

'I don't know; I've only just got here too, remember? We'll just have to wait and see who turns up.'

Jenny looked horrified. 'Honestly, Kitty! We can't just have random people coming here, poking about and ripping us off. You know what will happen when people find out there are two feeble old women here on their own. We will be a magnet for every cowboy builder and con artist for miles.'

She put one hand to her throat as though she could already feel the garotte.

'I'm not a feeble old woman and nor are you!' I said, outraged.

'That's what we will look like to them. I can just imagine it: vans full of sinister-looking men queueing up at the gates, promising the earth and disappearing with fistfuls of our cash and before you know it, we will be broke, they will leave us with a place worse than it is now, and then we will have to go to the police and they will sneer at us in French. And we will be caught up in some futile court case and Paul will...'

Open-mouthed, I watched my sister ranting on in this vein for several minutes. When had she become so uptight? So suspicious of everyone and everything? I could remember both of us ripping the wallpaper off our shared bedroom on a whim one morning, much to our mother's horror. It had been the first day of the summer holidays and we had spent the rest of it decorating. Slapping paint up on walls, buying a couple of posters from Athena, stencilling the bookcase. We'd had such a lot of fun even if Mum had disapproved and closed the door with a shudder.

I realised there was a pause in the conversation.

'So, Jenny, when I ask you if the glass is half full or half empty, you'll be asking what glass?'

She paused to draw breath. 'What glass? You're not going to start drinking already, I hope.'

I grinned. 'Perhaps we should clear up the breakfast things first?'

5

'Have you seen this? Come and look!' I shouted.

Jenny came out of the kitchen, drying her hands on a tea towel.

'Where are you? What are you doing in there?' she said. 'Why are you poking about?'

Fed up with bumping into Jenny as we both tried to clean the kitchen, I had wandered off into the hallway to explore the parts of the house we hadn't examined yet. Apart from the wine cupboard, there was another door, fastened with a hasp and, where there should have been a padlock, there was a length of twisted garden wire. Behind it was a large room without a window, which smelled of paint and linseed oil. I switched on the light and an old light bulb glowed wearily from the middle of the ceiling.

Against one wall was a folded-up artist's easel, half covered with the paint-splattered overall I remembered. It was as though Sheila had just stepped out of the house and might be back any minute. I could almost imagine her bustling in through the kitchen door with an enamel bowl full of new potatoes or her arms full of flowers.

'*Put the kettle on, sweetheart. I'm gasping.*'

It made me sad that I would never see her again; I should have visited more often. I should have asked her more about Dad, what he was like as a small boy.

On the other side of the room, masses of canvases were stacked up, some in frames, most of them wrapped up in brown paper with the title and the date they were finished written on the side.

'I'm not poking about; I'm just looking. And I've found loads of paintings,' I said, flicking slowly and carefully through them. 'They're organised by date. The last batch are from about five years ago. There are lots of them. Look.'

There were some that weren't wrapped up: landscapes, a few still lifes and a couple of the sea.

'They must be Aunt Sheila's.' Jenny looked around nervously, as though Sheila might appear suddenly and demand to know what we were doing. 'I didn't know that room was even there. Are they any good?'

'I'm no judge, but I'd buy one if I saw one in a shop.'

'That's not saying much,' Jenny said, picking up a canvas of poppies in a cornfield. 'Your taste in pictures always veered towards the cheesy.'

'Alphonse Mucha is not cheesy,' I said. 'Just because Paul bought you a print of *Guernica* as a wedding present. Something which at the time I thought was incredibly inappropriate.'

'Well, actually, I liked it,' Jenny replied.

'Of course you did. There's nothing like a painting of a dying horse above the bed to get you in the mood for love,' I said.

Jenny snorted with laughter, which surprised me. I was fully prepared for her to be offended.

'It was a little bit unusual,' she agreed, 'but it went well with the taupe curtains. After a while I didn't even see it.'

'Anyway, some of these are really lovely. Look at these gorgeous colours. I wonder why they're all stashed in here?'

'Didn't she teach painting years ago? I seem to remember she did. Although now I think about it, she said she'd stopped. She didn't have the heart for it any more. Did she sell them?'

'The sign out by the gate suggests she did sell them. But we are a bit off the usual tourist route, aren't we?' I said.

I pulled out a small canvas of a tree reflected in a lake. It was really excellent. Sheila had a distinctive style of broad brushstrokes interspersed with fine detail. A border of wildflowers along the bottom of the picture added delicate colour. The more I looked at it, the more I liked it.

Jenny peered over my shoulder. 'Ace knows a lot about art; he might know if they are any good. What shall we do with them? I suppose we could always sell them. I wouldn't want to just dump them in a skip somewhere.'

'I'm going to hang this one of the tree in my bedroom,' I said. 'I think it's really good. And it's restful.'

'If you say so,' Jenny said, unsure.

'Well, it's better than screaming women and dismemberment in Spain,' I said.

She chuckled. 'You are daft.'

At that moment there was a knock on the door, followed by a loud jangling of the brass bell that hung beside it. Jenny and I exchanged a glance.

'Who on earth can that be?' she hissed.

'How would I know? Perhaps it's one of the axe-wielding, money-grabbing con men, come to check us out,' I said.

'Don't joke about it,' Jenny whimpered, her eyes wide with apprehension. 'What shall we do?'

I put the painting down. 'Well, we could answer the door? That might be a start.'

Jenny grabbed my arm. 'But it really might be a... an intruder.'

I shook her off. 'Calm down; are you always this suspicious of everyone? And it's hardly an intruder, seeing as they aren't even in the house. It could also be the Avon lady or the postman or someone from Amazon with a parcel.'

There was another brisk knock on the door.

'They're still there!' Jenny hissed.

'Well, yes. I think they might be trying to attract our attention. I've been reading up on it in my *Lonely Planet* guide. Banging on the front door is an ancient French custom.'

'I wish you'd stop being so flippant!'

I brushed the dust from the paintings off my hands and walked down the hallway.

'Should you pick up a weapon?' Jenny suggested. 'Before you open the door. Just in case? Have you got one?'

I looked around me. 'A weapon? What are you talking about? Still, I could take the can of kitchen cleaner and spray it in their face? Or you could pass me the Uzi submachine gun Sheila left propped up in the utility room? What do you think?'

Jenny picked up a newspaper that had been left on the hall table and rolled it up.

'Hit them in the eye with that,' she said, clutching my arm again.

'For heaven's sake, Jenny! You never used to be this neurotic,' I said, brushing her off.

I opened the front door just as the person outside raised a hand to knock again, which meant my first view of them was a large fist.

Behind me, Jenny screamed and grabbed a duster.

'What are you planning to do with that? Polish them to death?' I said.

I turned to look at the visitor, who was standing patiently on the metal doormat.

It was a tall, rather attractive man. Grey-haired, dark-eyed with a broad frame, he was wearing a padded gilet over a roll-neck sweater and jeans.

He smiled.

'*Bonjour, madame. Mesdames,*' he said with a nod towards Jenny behind me.

'*Bonjour,*' I replied.

He looked at a scrap of paper in his hand.

'You must be Mrs Price and Mrs Batty? Have I said this right?'

His accent was to die for – I mean, really lovely. That sort of broken, apologetic and yet masculine way that Frenchmen talk. I'd always thought that it was the most attractive accent in the world. If this chap was trying to sell something, I was susceptible. Unless it was fish. I'd bought fish once from a man at the door and it went off about five minutes after we concluded the deal. I wouldn't be doing that again.

'Yes,' Jenny said, her voice heavy with distrust. 'Jennifer Batty.'

He nodded. 'There is no need to be alarmed, *mesdames*; I am Léo Bisset. I am *un constructeur*, a builder – I was working on the renovations here before your aunt so sadly died. I commiserate with you for your loss. Sheila was a delightful lady. Our family were very fond of her.'

He reached into the pocket of his gilet and pulled out a business card. He handed it over to me.

'See, *madame* – Léo Bisset, builder. Here is my address and my contact details.'

Jenny peered over my shoulder suspiciously, her breath loud in my ear. I nudged her away with an elbow.

'Thank you, Mr Bisset...'

Jenny nudged me back, none too gently.

'Léo, please,' he said.

'I knew Sheila had plans for other renovations. But I don't know what.'

His expression brightened. His dark eyes twinkled at us rather attractively.

'Ah, but I do. All the permissions were in place some time ago. I assure you; it is all in order. Your aunt transferred a substantial amount of money to my firm already as a deposit. You should have been informed of this, but I can let you have copies of the documents. Perhaps you can let me have an email address?'

'Well, I think we would like to see exactly how much money my aunt paid you for work that hasn't been done. It all sounds very odd to me. And we don't have any internet,' Jenny said.

Léo's face cleared. 'But surely you do? This is one of the things I can sort out.'

'Really?' Jenny said rather quickly.

'We have been told we need to go to the internet café in the village,' I added, 'which isn't terribly convenient.'

'Of course. I can sort it out,' Léo said confidently. 'Sheila had excellent internet.'

'She did?'

'Oh yes. I expect the modem is switched off or needs' – he thought for a moment – '*redémarrer* internet.'

'I think that's French for "turn it off and turn it on again". That's what Bertrand was trying to tell us when we arrived.'

'But where is the internet thing? I haven't seen one,' Jenny said.

'I know where it is; I could come in and show you?' Léo said, raising his impressive eyebrows. 'You can hit me with the newspaper if you feel in danger.'

I smothered a snort of laughter and Jenny stalked back into the house with an audible *harrumph*.

I stepped back from the door and held it open for him. He was taller than I realised and had to stoop to get in under the lintel.

He had the internet fixed in under half an hour, making rapid phone calls on his mobile, making me talk to various people somewhere, taking my card details and explaining the situation. The house phone on the hall table announced success by giving a cheerful chirrup of approval.

'There,' he said. 'Now, is there anything else?'

By then Jenny already had her laptop out on the kitchen table and was firing off an email to Paul, presumably explaining our predicament.

'No, I don't think so,' I said, 'thank you.'

'My pleasure,' he said with a lovely wide smile.

We stood looking at each other for a second. And then I shifted uncomfortably.

'So, the building work?'

'Ah yes, I will send the documents as I suggested and also the details of the money Sheila paid to my firm. I would not want you to be distrustful. If you will just give me your email addresses. I promise I will not pass them on to anyone else.'

He handed over his notebook and a pen, and I wrote our emails down.

'Perhaps I could briefly explain what Sheila had in mind?' he said at last. 'She had been thinking about it for years. And then, well, there was the garden. She had some very precise ideas, but she lost strength, energy. She enjoyed the planning so much. But of course, then she was unwell.'

'Okay,' I said.

Jenny was now completely focused on her laptop, catching up with all the excitement she had missed back in Budleigh Salterton, which personally I wouldn't have thought would take long.

'The swimming pool,' I said. 'I'd like to know what is happening there?'

A flicker of something crossed his face. 'Of course, with the finer weather coming, I suppose you will want to use it. Perhaps we could go and see it?'

We walked out and round the back of the house over the weed-riddled patio and towards the thicket of shrubbery that hid the pool from view.

'I don't do this sort of work; I will speak to Pierre.' Léo made a note in his little notebook. 'He used to work on this garden, unless you are a good gardener and would not need him?'

'I like gardening, but I could probably do with some help with the really heavy stuff. And the patio needs re-laying. And I don't know anything about how I would get rid of all the green waste – are bonfires allowed?'

Despite the scale of the project ahead, I was beginning to feel very excited about the prospect. It was hard to imagine the garden being restored to something to be admired or even walked through at the moment, but there were the remnants of those flower beds, and some cobblestone paths hidden under the weeds and dead leaves. I remembered it being glorious, colour everywhere.

We picked our way through the undergrowth, until we reached the pool. Between us and it were ropes of brambles and nameless weeds.

Léo frowned and patted his pockets.

'I'll just go back to the van,' he said. 'I have a folder there. I will be able to show you what Sheila had in mind.'

He left and I turned to look at the poor pool in front of me.

Would it ever look as I remembered it? With tempting turquoise water, sparkling under the French sunshine. Me in my Marks & Spencer costume, swimming up and down with elegant strokes, while Jenny – probably still in her tweed skirt and hand-knitted cardigan – sat stiffly on one of the sunbeds under the stone pergola and disapproved. Perhaps she would have eased up a bit by then.

She'd always been a great swimmer. We had spent whole summer days at the pool in town, meeting up with friends and the local boys. We had surfed on holiday in Cornwall, sleeping in a tiny tent together, heating up beans on a camping stove. I'd been fifteen; Jenny was nearly nineteen. She'd been the first of our gang to get a bikini. Slim, long-legged and tanned, she'd caused a sensation on the beach. I'd been proud of her; I'd wanted to be just like her. I'd followed her, in and out of cafés and bars, loving her triumph, her chutzpah.

She'd batted away the boys with a look and a toss of her hair; she was unattainable and independent.

What had happened to that laughing girl? What had happened to both of us, for that matter? Was this it? Did we need to accept that nothing could or would change?

I didn't believe it; I wouldn't accept that we were damned by our mistakes, by our choices. There had to be more to life than this. For both of us.

I stepped carefully over the barrier of weeds, wanting to get a bit closer. How shallow was the shallow end? I couldn't remember. It looked about a foot deep. Were there still steps to get out of the deep end?

A bramble snagged at my trouser leg, and I pulled away from it, trying to dislodge it. I moved my other leg and tugged again. Then when I moved that leg, it too seemed stuck, in some primordial gloop of mud and leaf mould. I gave a good heave to get free and yet another bramble snaked up and latched on to my trousers. It was almost like some multi-tentacled creature trying to grab hold of me.

I spun slowly around, increasingly irritated and of course wanting to free myself before Léo came back and saw what an idiot looked like. Another bramble joined in with the efforts of its fellows to snare my legs.

I took a clumsy step forward; my foot twisted on a stone and I fell over.

I mean, that wasn't a great thing to do at my age. I didn't think I'd fallen over since school. Apart from that one occasion when Frank – fired up with his breakfast whisky – had stumbled into me and knocked me over an occasional table.

This time was different. Once brambles of that size get a hold of you, they are notoriously reluctant to let go. Of course, I twisted and struggled for a bit trying to get back to my feet, which only seemed to make things worse. At last, I gave a big heave and rolled over, hoping to get away. All I managed was to roll over the edge of the pool and fall into the (mercifully) shallow end. I landed with my hands braced on the floor of the pool in a big pile of wet leaves. And slime. My legs were still sticking up in the air. Slowly, my hands slipped away from me and I slid with a horrible inevitability, landing on my stomach with a thump and a squeal of outrage. I looked up to see the white chicken watching me from the edge of the pool, its head cocked to one side.

'Well, don't just stand there, do something,' I said.

The hen took another look and made a low, crooning sort of noise that could almost have been a hen laugh. Then it stepped daintily away.

I lay still for a moment, slightly winded, wondering if I had hurt myself. Perhaps I was concussed? I was certainly scratched and a bit bloody. I could feel something trickling down my face and wiped it away with a muddy hand.

'Ow,' I said reproachfully. 'Bloody ow.'

'What on earth are you doing?'

I looked up into the sun to see someone standing on the edge of the pool looking down at me.

It was Jenny in a sensible shirt dress and K Skip shoes, standing on the other side of the pool where the space around it was almost clear. Why hadn't I seen that?

'Are you having fun?' she said, trying to supress her giggles.

'Oh, terrific,' I said. 'Look, do you think you could give me a hand out of here?'

By that point I was lying on my side in the leaf mould. It was difficult to have a sensible conversation with someone standing two feet above me, laughing at me.

I got up onto all fours and then sat up rather painfully and pulled at some brambles, trying to detach them from my trouser legs and pricking my hands in the process.

Jenny reached down a hand and I grabbed it, but the mud meant I lost my grip and I fell back into the ooze.

She tried again but she was chuckling so much that, again, I slipped.

She started to roar with laughter and after a second, so did I. The pair of us were howling like a pair of hyenas, Jenny now kneeling on the edge of the pool and holding out an inadequate twig for me to grab.

'Catch hold,' she said, choking with laughter.

'I can't,' I spluttered back.

'*Madame!* Oh no! What has happened?'

Oh great. It was Léo back with a manila folder and a pencil, which he immediately dropped onto the ground before he jumped in beside me.

'Are you hurt? You are bleeding,' he said.

He pulled me to my feet and disentangled me from the vegetation that had followed me in. Jenny stood up, gasping for breath, one hand pressed to her chest.

'No, I think I'm okay,' I said, flexing my knees to check.

It was a miracle I hadn't killed myself. Of course, what had saved me from injury was the cushion of sludge and leaves, much of which had transferred itself to me.

'You'd better put those trousers in the wash straight away or you'll never get the mud out. What were you doing?' Jenny asked.

'I think it's called falling into an empty swimming pool,' I said.

'Only you could manage that,' she said, grinning. 'I wish I had my camera.'

Léo hopped out onto the side and reached both hands down towards me.

'Please be careful, *madame*,' he said. I had the feeling he was trying not to laugh too. 'I do not like pools; they always seem to cause trouble. I hope you are not injured?'

Well, nice to see someone cared. I shot a dark look at my sister.

'You could have hurt yourself,' Jenny said, 'especially if you'd landed in the deep end.'

'Gosh, could I? I hadn't thought of that,' I said, spitting out some grit.

'I'll go and get a dry towel and then I'll put the kettle on,' she said, trying hard not to laugh. 'I'll make some tea.'

'I think I'd rather have a drink,' I shouted after her.

Her shoulders were shaking; I think she was giggling again.

I plodded up the garden after her, following Léo. I insisted he went in front of me; I didn't really want him walking behind me, observing my wet and muddy rear end. I must have looked an absolute sight.

'Are you sure you are not injured?' Léo said as we reached the house. 'No broken bones?'

'I'm fine,' I said, 'just a bit shaken up.'

'Sit, *madame*; I will get you a brandy. For the shock.'

Oh, yes please. That was the best idea I'd heard for a while.

Léo pulled up an old ironwork chair that had been propped against the wall, brushed the cobwebs off it and made me sit down. That was fun, sitting down in wet, muddy trousers.

He was back a moment later with a pretty hefty slug of brandy in a glass.

He watched me as I sipped it.

Then he crouched down in front of me and held up one finger.

'How many fingers?' he said.

'One,' I replied and took another sip.

He waved his finger slowly from side to side, watching me.

I think perhaps I was supposed to be watching his finger, not his beautiful brown eyes, but he really was tremendously good-looking. Even though he too had a muddy splodge on one cheek. It just seemed to add to his rustic appeal.

'I'm fine, honestly,' I said.

We watched each other, rather warily on my part.

He must have thought I was a complete fool. I wondered what that was in French. I didn't think it had cropped up during my O-level French all those years ago.

Voilà la dame; elle est une nitwit *complète.*

It could have been so different too. It should have been.

In an ideal world, I would have been in a flowing summery dress and possibly a shady hat. Out in the garden with a wooden trug over one arm, deadheading the roses or something. Maybe spraying the greenfly, and Léo would have come around the side of the house and his face would have lit up at the sight of me and we would have talked intelligently about the proposed building work and he would have found me amusing and attractive.

Instead, I was sitting on a wobbly old chair, my bottom covered in mud, my hair plastered to my head, dirty water dripping off my trousers onto the ground like some sad old git, knocking back a large brandy. Meanwhile, the most attractive man I had met in years was trying to see if I had concussion and talking about seeing the doctor.

6

Léo left soon after that.

Jenny came out of the kitchen with a mug of tea and burst out into giggles again.

'But what on earth were you trying to do? That's what I don't understand,' she said.

I finished my brandy. 'I tripped, got caught up in some brambles. It was an accident. Okay?'

'Well, it's one way to pick up men.' She nodded.

I looked at my trousers. 'Oh yes, he won't forget me in a hurry. Anyway, I'm not the only one to have accidents. Remember that time when you were working in the Cosy Café and spilt a tray of chocolate milkshakes over yourself?'

'I was fifteen. I'd have thought you would have stopped doing daft things at your age.'

I took the tea she held out to me. 'Well, in my experience, age doesn't stop you doing daft things; you just do them slower. And it's more undignified.'

'Come inside; you need to get out of your wet clothes before you catch a chill.'

I did as I was told, standing in the doorway while Jenny went to wipe a few water splashes off the floor.

'So what did that man say about the building work?'

'His name is Léo Bisset and he didn't get the chance to say anything. He helped me out of the pool, sat me down and said he would come back.'

'You do realise that we have to get this place smartened up as soon as possible so we can sell it for some sort of a profit?' Jenny said, as she came to stand opposite me. She held up three fingers. 'How many?'

'Twenty-two,' I said.

'Very funny. Perhaps you should see a doctor.'

'I'm fine,' I said, 'absolutely fine now, but I need a shower. Then we should take a good look around this place and perhaps make a list of things that need doing. I mean, it looks like the window frames were done fairly recently although the shutters need repainting. The light switches are all new and so are the sockets so I'm guessing the electrics have been sorted out.'

'There's a very nice new shower upstairs in my bathroom,' Jenny said.

'So why am I using the nasty-looking brown and orange one down here?'

Jenny shrugged. 'Because the one upstairs is mine?'

I decided not to make a thing of it, took a deep breath and went to have a shower in my bathroom. Peeling off wet, mud-sodden clothes was very unpleasant. I remembered something similar a few years ago when I had fallen into the garden pond. And there had been tadpoles. I wasn't very keen on them.

Steve had laughed at me when that had happened, but it hadn't felt the same. He'd been unkind and he *had* taken a picture, which he had shared on his Facebook page even though I'd begged him not to, but Jenny and I had been able to share the joke this time.

When I came back, Jenny was sitting at the kitchen table with her tea.

'We'll make a list,' I repeated.

Jenny rummaged in her handbag and came out with a pencil and a shopping pad.

'Go on then,' she said, looking at me.

'No, *we* need to make a list, not me.'

'Paul always does this sort of thing,' she said doubtfully. 'He's good at lists.'

'Well, he's not making this one because he's not here. We need to ask what exactly has been done and what Léo is planning to do. We need to ask about the plumbing and the damp in that corner where the plaster is falling off. We need to ask about the downstairs bathrooms, the lean-to garage thing. Is that staying or going? What about that room with the paintings? What about the decorating? Do we do that?'

'Paul always does the decorating,' Jenny said firmly, looking up from her notepad. 'He says I do it wrong and he will only use magnolia paint.'

'How splendid for you, but as I keep telling you, he's not here. And we can choose any colour we want to. A blue kitchen, a yellow bathroom, a pink hallway. And don't tell me what Paul would do because it's unimportant. This is our house. These are our choices.'

'Oh,' Jenny said, looking worried.

'So go on, what are your thoughts?' I said encouragingly.

Jenny looked intently down at her notepad but didn't write anything.

'I don't know,' she said at last.

'That's not very helpful.'

'Don't go on at me,' Jenny said unhappily.

I reached across the table and put a hand over hers. 'I'm not going on at you; I'm saying we should do this together. Like we used to, remember? We used to share a bedroom – you split it in half with some masking tape on the carpet. You decorated your side with Tom Jones posters, and I had Paul McCartney. You had a hideous orange and yellow bedspread and I had blue and green one. With a white fringe.'

Her face brightened. 'Oh God, I remember that bedspread. My friends all thought it was marvellous.'

'I'm not sure it was. It was *of its time*. What I'm saying is you used to choose things and like things. You can decide colours and you can make mistakes and then change them.'

This sounded like really good advice to me on many levels, not just when it came to interior decoration. Heaven knew I'd made some rubbish choices over the years, and so had Jenny. Perhaps this process would help her to see that life didn't always have to run on someone else's lines. She was entitled to her own opinion.

Jenny stared down at her notepad again.

'Yes, I see that. Okay. Those sofas,' she said at last, rather thoughtfully. 'What do you think of them? They are pretty awful, aren't they?'

I waved a hand. 'They are beyond ugly. Write it down: new furniture.'

'You're looking forward to this, aren't you?' Jenny said.

'I am,' I admitted. 'Look, I used to have a lovely house and a beautiful garden when I was married to Steve and I lost it all. I moved into a ghastly flat where some of the neighbours are were-wolves. And the garden is a concrete yard full of recycling bins. This is a chance to – I don't know, express ourselves. Have a bit of fun.'

'Well, yes, I see that too, but how long is it going to take? I can't leave Paul to his own devices for too long.'

'No idea, but the sooner we start the sooner we finish. Person-ally, I don't mind how long it takes.'

I thought about this for a while. It was true; I was feeling more enthusiastic, more alive than I had felt for ages. There was nothing drawing me back to Bristol with any urgency. Yes, I had friends, a social life and a reasonably interesting job, but this, being here, was far more exciting.

'And you heard what Léo said: a lot of money has already been handed over to pay for the building work. And remember what Sheila said in her will – we could do what we liked. And who knows, it might be a chance for us to reconnect.'

'She hated that, when we fell out,' Jenny said, looking away.

'How did she know?' I asked. 'I never told her.'

'I told her; we used to write to each other too, and I'd send her updates at Christmas.' Jenny looked a bit uncomfortable. 'I told her about us because I was upset; I still am, actually. If I think about it.'

'Are you? Were you?'

I sat rubbing my bruised arm and thought about it. I'd said some pretty awful stuff that day in the Old Duck and Trumpet, and so had she.

'I didn't mean those things I said. Honestly, I was just hurt by what *you* said.'

I was about to say *you started it* but then I realised how childish that sounded. I didn't want to waste time doling out blame in order to make myself feel better. I was just as much at fault, if I was honest.

'Paul says I shouldn't open up all that again.'

She sounded a little doubtful, as though she *did* want to talk about it. I certainly did; I'd spent countless nights awake, thinking about it and worrying about her. Wondering how on earth we could build bridges. But at the same time, it was much easier to build a bridge if there were people helping. And it felt as though Sheila might have been trying to help, even though she wasn't here any more. Maybe she had seen this as an opportunity for me and for Jenny? I hadn't seen that before; what a wise old bird she was.

'Paul's not here. And we are, and don't you want us to be friends again? I know I do.'

I felt a bit emotional; I could feel the sting of tears for a moment.

If my falling into the pool and making myself look a complete twit had brought us to this moment, then the embarrassment had been well worth it.

* * *

We spent the rest of the day cleaning. Which was strangely satisfying. Jenny was obviously an expert in the task, and whizzed around upstairs, her footsteps echoing down through the floorboards. I concentrated on the sitting room, moving all the furniture and hoovering the threadbare rugs. Really, the room needed to be emptied and redecorated before we brought in some new furniture. Where did French people buy paint? And white spirit? I'm sure they had DIY warehouses like ours – *bricolage*. I'd ask Léo if and when he returned.

I was a little distracted from my dusting by the contents of Sheila's bookcases, which filled the deep alcoves either side of the wood burner. There were books on many different subjects: art, famous painters, biographies, romance novels, classics, history, Fabergé and France. Aunt Sheila had always had eclectic taste. It would have been tempting to sit back on one of the sofas with a glass of wine and have a nice read, but the busy noises from my sister upstairs put me off. She would have been bound to catch me.

In the corner was a wooden cabinet hiding the smallest television I'd seen for years. The sort Jenny and I had watched as a child. In fact, it might have been identical. I could almost hear the *Blue Peter* theme tune. I fiddled with the switches, wondering if it still worked.

The screen gradually cleared to reveal – in black and white – five women arguing around a table. I watched it for a few minutes, trying to understand what they were saying. Something about *mariage* and *les hommes* that necessitated a lot of eye-rolling and hand-waving.

I stood looking at them, absolutely fascinated, and then tried unsuccessfully to imitate their exaggerated gestures and Gallic shrugging. Was it genetic? Did all French women do that instinctively? And if so, why?

That was an interesting thought. British women didn't stand in the street gesticulating wildly, shrugging their shoulders and pouting like Brigitte Bardot over their shopping, did they?

'What on earth are you doing?' Jenny said behind me. 'Are you having a stroke?'

I jumped. 'No, I'm just—'

'What are you watching?'

We stood looking at the television, side by side, both of us bemused.

Jenny tilted her head to one side. 'What has that woman done to her face?'

'Lip fillers?' I suggested.

'Why do women do that to themselves? She looks as though she has been punched in the mouth.'

On the television, a man started singing. Really badly.

'Oh, for heaven's sake,' Jenny said, striding into the room and switching off the television.

'Look, I've been scrubbing away like a mad thing upstairs and you're just watching television,' she grumbled, bustling around, straightening the (rather nasty) curtains.

'I just got distracted for a minute. Literally a minute,' I said. 'I was just seeing if the television worked.'

'Well, now you know it does,' she said. 'I'll get back to work.'

The sound of her voice tailed off as she went out of the room and stomped back upstairs.

Busted.

I looked at my watch. It was four thirty in the afternoon. Was it too early to open a bottle of wine?

I wiped the shelves and the spines of the dusty books and then switched the ancient vacuum cleaner on again and crashed around for a bit as noisily as possible to show Jenny that I was doing some manual labour. Just as I was about to switch it off, there was a loud burping noise from somewhere deep within the machine and the ominous smell of burning. Then, with an impressive bang, the back flew off the hoover and all the dust and debris I had collected up, plus presumably some of Sheila's, flew out into the room.

I stood feeling rather limp and hopeless, watching as tumble-weeds of fluff and dust floated gently onto their preferred location of the floor and bookcases again.

Oh, for heaven's sake.

Better add *new vacuum cleaner* to the list.

I gave a resigned sigh, dropped the hoover hose onto the floor, opened the windows and shut the door behind me, leaving the dust to settle.

Hoping to appease my offended sister and trying to ignore the mess I had just left in the sitting room, I went out into the kitchen and washed out the dirty dusters. Then I couldn't resist it: I had a sneaky glass of Sancerre, a rather uninspiring label but nice enough, while hiding in the pantry with the door closed.

I sipped it, looking at the Kilner jars of pasta and the unusual labels on the tins. It was rather interesting, actually. The French ones were of two types: colourful with pictures of huge fruit and vegetables and smiling farmers, or faintly nostalgic and elaborate with curly writing.

My life over the last few years had become very predictable. It had taken two hours to clean my flat from top to bottom; I'd timed myself once, which in itself was rather tragic. During the week I always caught the same bus with the same people at eight thirty; I shopped at the same supermarket and bought the same food; I went to the same wine bar with the same friends; I tweaked at my window boxes; I thought the same thoughts. I'd been cross and irritated by Jenny's life but perhaps, if I was honest, my life was equally as dull as hers was? Wow, that was quite a realisation. Perhaps I should stop being quite so complacent.

Being here could be a really positive change for both of us. New challenges, new possibilities and something I'd never thought would happen again: time on my own with Jenny. I raised my glass towards the cobwebs on the ceiling.

'Cheers, Sheila,' I said and finished my wine. 'I rather think I owe you one.'

I began thinking about what to cook for our evening meal seeing as the 'shared cooking' we had agreed on didn't seem to be materialising. It was, after all, Jenny's turn. But on the other hand, I was rather pleased to be cooking for someone else; it made a nice change. Too often I hadn't bothered cooking for myself, and I might have been critical of Paul and his microwave meals, but heaven knew I'd eaten enough of them in my time. There were few things less likely to encourage the appetite than stabbing a fork into the film cover of a ready meal. Well, no more of that; I was going to make the effort for both of us.

There was some chicken in the fridge and a whole basket full of fresh vegetables. Of course, coq au vin. There was plenty of *vin* after all. I set to work, and naturally enough, Jenny came in at the exact moment I was yanking a cork out of a fine old bottle of red. A 2012 Médoc this time.

'Drinking already?' she said, nudging me out of the way to get to the sink.

'Of course not; I'm cooking,' I said, ignoring the sneaky tipple I'd had ten minutes ago in the pantry.

'I'm glad to hear it. You should know what it's like living with an alcoholic,' she said.

I tried to think of something terse and witty to say but of course I couldn't.

So I blew a raspberry at her instead, which didn't really do the trick.

'Well, don't hold back – pour me one too, then,' she said.

'You've changed your tune!'

Laughing, Jenny went out into the back garden to empty her bucket of dirty water down the drain and I took a swig straight out of the wine bottle and wondered when Léo Bisset would return.

7

Léo came back at mid-morning the following day, just as I had finished sweeping up the debris from the sitting room, using a scrubby old broom and a dustpan with a broken handle. Perhaps Aunt Sheila hadn't noticed the less-than-effective cleaning methods available to her, or perhaps she wasn't as houseproud as my sister.

This meant that when I opened the front door, I was red in the face, sweating and rather grubby. Added to that I was wearing a filthy old T-shirt and some jogging bottoms that were less than flattering.

'Ah!' I said brightly.

'Good morning, *madame*,' he said with the usual broad smile.

I took a quick look at myself in the hall mirror next to the door. I had a couple of cushion feathers in my hair and a large smear of dirt down one cheek.

'*Bonjour*, Monsieur Bisset,' I replied cheerfully, trying to brush away the feathers with a casual hand. '*Comment ça va?*'

'*Ça va bien, madame*, but please would you call me Léo?'

'You can call me Kitty,' I said.

Well, you can call me any time, actually, I thought.

'Kitty,' he said. It sounded like 'Keetee' and was rather nice. He held out the familiar manila folder. 'I have brought the plans I drew up with your aunt. Perhaps you and your sister would like to look over them when you have time and tell me what you think?'

'Do come in,' I said, stepping back.

He held up one hand. 'Oh no, I can see you are busy.'

'Not at all busy,' I said, wiping the grime around my face, 'and I have a lot of questions to ask you already. Come through to the kitchen and I'll make coffee.'

Not waiting for him to say no, I hurried off, hoping that as he was wiping his boots on the doormat and closing the door behind him, he wouldn't have time to notice my back-end-of-the-pantomime-horse bottoms.

Jenny was in the kitchen, scrubbing something in the stone trough sink. She looked up.

'I've just seen that chicken again, down the end of the garden. Perhaps we should get someone in to deal with it.'

'Who? The chicken police?'

'Don't be daft. Who was that at the door – oh.'

'It's Léo,' I said unnecessarily. 'He's brought us the plans for the building work.'

Léo held out the cardboard folder and Jenny took it, holding it with her fingertips as though it was forensic evidence from the FBI.

'How kind,' she said, 'um – do sit down.'

'I'm sure you want the work to start again as soon as possible,' Léo said. 'We managed to do most of the vital work in the years before Sheila died. The roof, the window frames, the electrics and most of the plumbing. You will see there is still some work that needs doing on some of the plasterwork in that corner now that the damp course has been resolved.'

'Yes,' I said, nudging at some flaking stuff on the wall next to me.

A chunk of rotting plaster detached itself and landed on the floor with a thump. I looked up guiltily.

'I promise you, *mesdames*, the problems can be sorted and we will resolve such things,' Léo said reassuringly.

That was nice – to feel that he could be relied on, that he would do what was needed. I hadn't known many men like that recently; they all seemed to be averse to changing tap washers or the batteries in anything. And heaven forbid they should be expected to multi-task, have a conversation while the football was on or interrupt their meal for anything.

'It's going to cause a mess, isn't it?' Jenny said.

Léo pursed his mouth in the way all French men since Maurice Chevalier seem to do, and nodded.

'It will. I will get Claud and Benoît to be here first thing tomorrow, and they will make a start. I would suggest that you clear away all the things from the worktops; there will be a fair amount of dust.'

'Who are Claud and Benoît?' Jenny asked suspiciously.

Well, I expect one of them is a drug dealer and the other one is a mafia hitman...

'My sons. They work with me; they are excellent craftsmen, very – um – industrious. You will see,' Léo said, 'and I will ask Bertrand to come along for a few days to help.'

'Does he have a donkey called Hector?'

'Ah yes, he does. You have you met them both?' Léo asked, his face brightening.

'Yes, they were here when we arrived,' Jenny said.

'Ah well, that's good. Bertrand has been keeping an eye on this place while it was empty; he lives only a short distance from here. In fact, he is almost your neighbour, so he is never late.'

Jenny raised one finger. 'He won't bring the donkey with him, will he?'

Léo laughed. 'Not if you prefer he didn't. He has a car. Of sorts.'

'Thank heavens for that,' Jenny murmured. 'The smell...'

Honestly, Jenny, it's just a donkey.

Léo accepted a cup of coffee and shuffled some more papers around.

'You see, there was also the need for work in the garden. The pool for one thing and the – 'ow do you say – overgrowth.'

He actually did say it like that. It was rather sexy, to be honest. I said it in my head. *'Ow do you say. 'Ow do you say.* I think I was doing the French pouting thing too because I suddenly realised Jenny was giving me a hard look.

'Sorry,' I said.

'This is important, Kitty, do pay attention. Léo is asking about the garden. Do we need help? Because Sheila used someone in the village.'

'Pierre,' Léo said helpfully. 'Pierre Desgrandes. I mentioned him yesterday. He's very good. Young and very strong.'

A young, strong Frenchman to help me in the garden – whoopee! What part of that didn't I like?

'Marvellous,' I said, 'definitely yes. Please ask him to come along as soon as possible.'

'I will do,' he said. He pulled his mobile out of his pocket and pressed a few buttons. 'Pierre? *Ça va? Oui oui, bien.*'

Jenny watched him with suspicion, while I ploughed mindlessly through a couple of biscuits and admired Léo's profile. There was a lot of rapid-fire French conversation and Léo looking at his watch and nodding.

'There,' he said, 'he will be here, possibly after lunch.'

'So he's not very busy with work?' Jenny said.

The implication being that if he wasn't gainfully employed somewhere else, he must be rubbish. Honestly, why did she always have to be so negative? Still, I had to admit, in the days when I had a garden and tried to employ someone reliable to help, it had been a

hopeless task, like searching for decent broadband. Or a comfortable bra.

Léo wagged his head from side to side and pushed out his
lower lip.

'Oh yes, he is very busy, but Pierre admired your aunt a great
deal. And he promised her he would do this as *une priorité*. A prior-
ity. You could always ask him about filling in the pool. It would
reduce the maintenance. Now, after we have sorted the plasterwork
in here and the downstairs bathroom, the next thing will be the
new dining room, the decoration and the outside of the house. The
shutters, and there are a few stones that need repointing – is that
the right word?'

'Yes, absolutely,' I said, trying to concentrate on his words and
not focus on him. I mean, he was very attractive and gave off an irre-
sistible air of being capable. He had big, strong hands too, rough-
ened from years of manual toil, I expected. Much more impressive
than someone who thought they needed to go to A&E when they
had a splinter.

'*Et bien.*' He shuffled his papers together and hesitated before
handing them to Jenny. 'There is the plan. I translated it into
English for you. If you have any questions, then please ask me. We
will be back to start early tomorrow morning, if that is convenient?'

'Absolutely,' Jenny said.

He finished his coffee and left, his big workman's boots treading
carefully over the recently washed floor.

'Well, he's rather nice,' I mused. 'I always say there's nothing
more attractive than a man with a tool in his hand.'

'Don't you dare,' Jenny said warningly.

'Dare what?' I asked innocently. 'I don't know what you mean.'

'You know perfectly well.' She snorted a little. 'This is time for
us, to get this done *together*. I don't want you wandering off with the
first man who catches your eye. We were supposed to be going to

Spain together when you met Frank. Oliver put a stop to just about everything and there was that car dealer who sold you two cars welded together and you let him because he looked like Brad Pitt.'

I thought this was a bit one-sided, because Paul had been far more controlling, but I didn't say anything.

She put all the dirty mugs into the dishwasher, found an empty cardboard box, and started taking everything off the worktops and packing it away. At the same time, she was wiping the draining boards and taps. Now this was multi-tasking at its finest. Why could women do that without thinking and men couldn't? I remembered Jenny when she was expecting Ace, packing her bag for the hospital, cleaning the kitchen floor and putting on mascara, all at the same time.

'You heard him – they will be back tomorrow morning, first thing. Actually, what do you think that means? Nine o'clock? Ten? I'll be surprised if they get here before lunch, and then they will mess about and expect coffee and cigarette breaks, and then they take long lunch hours, don't they?'

'Do you think they'll need a siesta for a couple of hours in the afternoon? Followed by an early departure? Yes, I expect it will take months before this is finished,' I said. 'Talk about stereotyping!'

Jenny started lugging boxes about, banging into the kitchen chairs and complaining.

'Perhaps you'd like to start helping. Honestly, all that cleaning we've done since we got here will have been a waste of time.'

'We need a new vacuum cleaner,' I said, 'and with builders in the house we will definitely need one soon.'

Jenny ran one hand through her hair. It fell back into its usual, smooth bob.

'It's going to be chaos,' she said, 'absolute chaos. I hadn't realised.'

I suddenly felt sorry for her. The last time I'd visited her house there had been coasters under every cup, doilies under every vase and no shoes allowed indoors. And I'd been wearing odd socks: one blue and the other patterned with ducks. She must have been hating all this. I went and put an arm around her stiff shoulders.

'It will be a challenge, Jenny, but it won't last forever. It might be exciting,' I said.

'Oh yes, with dirt and dust everywhere, builders clomping through the house, noise mess and muddle, and you forgot to ask about the wild chicken—'

Her voice was rising to a wavering shriek by this point, when someone knocked forcefully on the kitchen window, making her yelp.

We turned to look and were confronted by a young man, waving at us.

I went to the kitchen door and opened it.

'*Bonjour, mesdames,*' he said, sweeping a woolly cap off his curls and treating us to a look at his dimples. *I say!* 'I am Pierre. I am the gardener. Léo Bisset has asked me to call round to say *allô*. I would have brought my brother Sylveste *aussi*, but he is in the village, *il mélange le béton* – mix the concrete. He will be here *demain* – tomorrow – if the weather is good.'

Behind me I heard Jenny's low moan, and she sank onto one of the kitchen chairs, her head pillowed on her arms.

'Excellent,' I said with a bright smile, moving around so he couldn't see her. 'Thank you for calling around so promptly.'

He smiled. 'Ah, yes, well, Madame Sheila was *une amie* – a friend. I promised I would be here, and here I am.'

Excellent. I thought it was kinder to take him away from Jenny so that she could carry on cleaning and perhaps calm down a little.

'Well, no time like the present,' I said, holding out an arm towards the garden. 'Shall we take a walk around the grounds, and we can decide what to do.'

8

'Jenny, it will be fine,' I said. 'What did you expect? We knew there was work to be done, didn't we? There's bound to be a bit of a mess at first. But then it will all be lovely again. You don't need to panic; they haven't even started yet. And when they do, leave them to me; I'll sort them out.'

'You'll be saying something about omelettes and eggs next,' Jenny said gloomily, sloshing some of the Sancerre into her glass.

This was most unlike her as it was only six fifteen and, predictably, Paul didn't usually allow midweek drinking. If they did have a drink, she said it had to be an actual event like a birthday or Brexit, and even then, not before seven o'clock. She was obviously coming round to my way of thinking, which was an improvement as far as I was concerned. And the wine was rather good; we hadn't had a dud bottle yet.

We were sitting outside in the garden, under the pergola. There was a plant growing and twining around it; I think it was a clematis. There were birds twittering in the hedges and it was all very pleasant and relaxing. We had cleared the worktops and a few of the kitchen cupboards, packed everything away into boxes, and put

them in the cramped dining room. This had produced the unfortunate effect of a 1970s student squat with the saucepans and casserole dishes crowding onto the table and two huge vases filled with
kitchen utensils on the windowsill.

Behind my sister I could see the feral chicken, standing quite
brazenly on the little wall by the pool watching us. I decided not to
mention it. Jenny had brought her knitting bag out with her, but it
lay unopened on the floor beside her.

'Should we empty *all* the cupboards, do you think? Or move the
fridge?' she said at last.

'No, I'm sure we don't need to do that. Look, once they are here
and they've got started, we should go out somewhere. Léo and his
sons will be knocking the damaged plaster off, and Pierre has
plenty to get on with in the garden.'

'But what about giving them tea and coffee? Surely we should
be here for that. And what if they go – you know – *rummaging
around*?'

'If it makes you feel better, we can put all your knickers into the
car and take them out with us for a little drive,' I said.

'Oh good God, I hadn't thought of that!' Jenny said, her eyes
round with horror. 'They wouldn't, would they? Yes, I shall definitely do that.'

'Not that there is much to be excited about as far as my knicker
drawer is concerned,' I added. 'They would have to be pretty odd to
find anything stimulating there. Although back in the day I did
have some rather good stuff. Although I never got on with—'

Jenny flapped a hand at me. 'Change the subject. What's for
dinner?'

'I don't know. Got anything in mind?' I fired back.

She looked a bit wild-eyed. 'Well, what have we got in the
fridge?'

'Loads of stuff. All those vegetables and salads. Some burgers—'

'Not the horse ones?'

'No, beef. And we have lots of pasta. You choose.'

Jenny finished off her wine and immediately topped up her glass. For someone who claimed not to drink very often, she was getting into the swing of things quite well.

'I have no idea,' she said at last. 'You're the one who cooks. Not me.'

'But it's your turn,' I said. 'We said we were going to share the cooking.'

'I know we did! But I did say I haven't cooked anything for years. Paul always—'

'Paul isn't here, I keep telling you. What would you *like* to eat?'

She looked a bit misty-eyed. 'My favourite meal...'

'Yes?'

'My absolute favourite meal – and I haven't had it for years because Paul says it's labour-intensive and not very healthy – is...'

'Yes? Yes? The suspense is killing me.'

By this time, I was imagining something like chateaubriand or lobster thermidor and wondering if lobsters were even in season. Was it something to do with having an R in the month, or was that oysters?

'Lasagne,' Jenny said at last, looking faintly embarrassed.

I did a bit of a double take. 'Really?'

She nodded. 'The last time I had it we were in Oxford; it was my birthday, and we went to a wine bar for lunch as a treat. And it was nothing special, but I think it was the last really hot, really tasty thing I ate. You know what Paul is like; he hides the saltshaker and is always keeping an eye on preservatives and carbs and good fats, whatever they are. And I know he's right, and he's doing everything to keep us healthy. That and the regular long walks. I should be thanking him, not complaining.'

I thought for a moment what it would be like to take regular long walks with Paul and gave a little shudder. My daily existence might be rather boring but at least I didn't have to put up with that. I think on balance I would rather have been lonely.

Was I lonely? I'd never allowed myself to go too far down that path; I'd been too busy assuring everyone I was enjoying my independence, but with me that only lasted for a bit. And then, I had to be honest, I made one bad decision after another, chose the wrong men for the wrong reasons. It was easy to be wise after the event.

I slapped my hand down on the rickety ironwork table.

'Preservatives? I think people our age need all the preservatives we can get. I'm going to make lasagne for you tonight. It might not be as memorable as the last one you had but I'll do my best.'

Jenny looked across at me and I was startled to see tears in her eyes. Good God. What sort of state had Paul reduced my sister to that she was ready to cry about lasagne? I felt a surge of protective fury and deep sadness.

I put my arms around her and gave her a hug. She did a bit of sniffing and nose-blowing and managed a smile.

'Thanks,' she said, 'and I'll help.'

Yes, despite everything there was still someone really nice underneath those cardigans, I knew there was. Someone who was fun to be with, who had been in love with David Cassidy. Someone who had taken on the school bullies on my behalf with a swinging satchel, someone who had taught me how to use eyeliner, someone who had been systematically crushed over those thirty-five years of marriage.

How *could* I have just left her to get on with it? I should have done something, anything to help her. To stick up for her as she had done for me.

'No time like the present,' I said. 'Come on, let's make a start.'

* * *

We spent such an enjoyable evening together. The lasagne was no more than okay if I was honest, but Jenny hoovered it up with enthusiasm as though Marco Pierre White had paid us a visit. We knocked back another bottle of Aunt Sheila's wine too – a red one this time, with a very attractive house on the label, Château something, 2014.

We talked about Ace and his progress through university, how he had once smoked something herbal in the garden and how Paul hadn't spoken to him for days and threatened to go to the police. We discussed clothes and where we liked to shop. We paid each other compliments. Jenny still had better legs than I did, but I had great hair. That sort of thing.

It was fantastic to be able to feel connected with her again; it brought home to me how much I had missed her, how much we had missed each other. And for the first time in years, I felt useful and needed. Because she needed me, I could see that. More than that, we needed each other; that's what I had forgotten. Having someone at the other end of a phone that I could talk to at any hour, about any subject, knowing she would listen to me, and I would listen to her. Maybe – horrible thought – if I had been there for her more instead of criticising her life when mine was such a mess, things might have been different. For both of us.

We went to bed quite late for us. We both agreed that the older we got, the earlier it got late. But we were content. It was the best evening I'd had for a long time.

The last thing I heard before I went to sleep was Jenny's voice resonating through the floorboards as she had her usual bedtime call with Paul. I hoped she hadn't mentioned the lasagne or the quantity of wine we had shifted during the short time we had been here. I wondered about recycling.

* * *

I woke the following morning very suddenly with a jerk that almost catapulted me out of bed. There was a noise from somewhere. An aggressive sort of rumbling noise that was rattling the windows. And then a shout and a loud laugh.

I got up and went to the sitting room to peer out at the driveway.

There was some sort of mechanical digger being unloaded on huge caterpillar tracks from a flat-bed truck. As I watched, it trundled away and round the side of the house. Then as the truck manoeuvred its way back down the drive, three more vans appeared.

Two of them had *Léo Bisset* on the side and the other one was larger and had a ladder strapped to the top, a small trailer covered with tarpaulin and *Travaux de Jardin* inscribed on the bonnet.

After a moment I sprang into action, horrified. When Léo had said they would be here early, I hadn't really believed him. My bedroom was on the ground floor and I liked to sleep with the shutters open. I didn't want the first view the workmen got of me to be in my Primark pyjamas.

I went into the bathroom, dragged on yesterday's clothes and then looked at my watch. What time was it, anyway? It wasn't properly light yet. Seven thirty? Really? I hadn't seen that coming.

I went to the foot of the stairs and hollered for Jenny. It was still quiet up there, not even the sound of BBC World Service that Paul apparently liked to wake up to so he could listen to the shipping forecast and reassure himself the world hadn't gone to hell in a handcart during the night.

I spent the next ten minutes dodging from the sitting room window to the bottom of the stairs, where I yelled for my sister.

'Jenny! Jenny! Wake up!'

There were five of them out there, all dressed in padded jackets over hoodies like some sort of uniform. Two had woollen beanie hats and two had baseball caps. The fifth one was Léo. There was a lot of Gallic shrugging going on. I wished I could hear what they were saying.

'Jenny! Wake up, the workmen are here!' I shouted.

It seemed there was a bit of a conference going on, a couple of them smoking, one of them sipping at a takeaway coffee. The one I now recognised as Pierre was opening the back doors of his van and then taking the tarpaulin off the trailer to reveal all sorts of garden paraphernalia.

I took a deep breath and shouted as hard as I could up the stairs.

'Jenny! Paul's here. He wants to know about the lasagne last night!'

There was a thump from above as though Jenny had fallen out of bed, and a muffled shout.

I opened the front door.

'*Bonjour!*' I called.

They all turned to look at me and then called out a chorus of '*Bonjour, madame*' back. Well, so far so good.

What now? I'd always been rather sycophantic with workmen, trying to get them to think favourably of me. As though Nescafé Gold Blend and a packet of Hobnobs would get them on my side. I still wasn't sure it worked and had a sneaking suspicion it made me look like a soft touch instead. But anyway, why break the habits of a lifetime?

'*Du café? Du thé?*' What was the French word for biscuits? Ah yes. '*Les biscuits?*'

They politely declined my offer of refreshment, which was just as well, as Jenny suddenly appeared behind me. I didn't think she would have approved of me delaying them from starting work.

'What's happening?' she hissed over my shoulder. 'Did you say something about Paul?'

'I was joking.'

'I've got such a headache,' she said.

'Yes, you do look a bit grey about the gills,' I said.

Jenny was wearing a strange mishmash of clothes, obviously grabbed in haste. A green cardigan over a yellow polo shirt and a floral elasticated skirt. This was finished with a red beret pulled down low over her ears for some reason.

'Interesting outfit,' I said mildly.

'I was panicking,' she said, following me into the kitchen, 'and I'm having a bad hair day. Is there any coffee?'

'I'm just making it. Look, sit at the table and I will bring you some and I'll find some drugs too.'

'How are you so bright and breezy?' she grumbled.

'My liver has been on a more advanced training course than yours,' I said.

I handed her a mug of coffee and she blew across the top and sipped it cautiously.

'Who are the two younger ones with Léo? The youngest looks very familiar. He's got the sort of face that would be on the Interpol most-wanted list.'

'I thought that; perhaps he looks like a celebrity you know.'

'I don't pay any attention to celebrities.' She sniffed dismissively.

'No, I don't suppose you do.'

She took another look. 'But he does look familiar.'

There was a roar of heavy machinery from the garden, just outside the kitchen window. I went to look.

'God almighty! What's that?'

'It's Pierre, the gardener,' I said. 'He's digging up the patio.'

'Why on earth is he doing that? Oh God, my head.'

'Because we asked him to,' I shouted over the noise.

'Couldn't he do something *quieter*?' she shouted back.

'Go into the sitting room with your coffee, and I'll ask if he can turn the volume down on his digger and then I'll bring you some breakfast.'

'I don't think I want anything,' she said. 'Perhaps just some orange juice?'

Jenny scurried off and I opened the kitchen door.

Léo and two young men I took to be his sons were standing there looking at their plans. His face brightened as he saw me.

'Ah, Kitty! I should introduce you properly. These are my boys, Benoît and Claud. They will be working on the plaster in the kitchen while I make a start on the downstairs bathrooms.'

Benoît was tall and muscular with a beard and a piercing gaze, while Claud was quite a chirpy-looking soul who really did remind me of someone. Maybe an actor or some sports star? Anyway, they were a nice-looking pair. Definitely a resemblance to their father.

We did a bit of handshaking and *bonjour*-ing and I repeated my offer of coffee, which again they politely declined. They were keen to get started. This meant that they took big canvas bags into the kitchen and in a matter of minutes were down on their hands and knees examining the patches of plaster that needed sorting. Or rather – as I discovered a short time later when they had spread out canvas dustsheets – bashing it off the wall with big lump hammers and chisels. I think the foundations of the house were shaking although I had managed to kick one chunk off without any trouble. I didn't tell them that. I just stood looking until the dust drove me out and I went to see what Jenny was doing.

I eventually tracked her down in her bedroom, where she was in the middle of a phone call.

'Terrible. You'd hate it. They've only been here five minutes and the noise is incredible. What? No, I didn't realise you'd still be asleep. Sorry. No, I didn't think.'

She looked up at me and rolled her eyes, mouthing *Paul* at me.

I rolled my eyes back, not sure if I should stand there eavesdropping or go away. I decided to stay.

'No, I don't know. There should be a card somewhere from the council. Well, it was on the hall table.'

She mouthed *recycling* at me, and I tutted sympathetically.

'No, I don't know. Look, I'm not even in the same country, Paul, how am I expected to know? No, I'm not using a tone with you, I just don't know. Who was that? Really? It doesn't sound like the radio.'

I went to look out of the window to see where Léo was. He was standing by one of his vans, taking a phone call, and then he started pacing about, accompanied by a lot of hand gestures. I wondered what he was up to. He really was very handsome.

I stopped. No, I wasn't going to think like that and certainly not about him. I'd learned my lesson the hard way and suffered a lot of knocks in the process. I needed to be rather more selective with my choices. Just because Léo was tall, tanned and attractive with the hint of a muscular frame underneath his padded gilet and had a certain sparkle in his smile and dark eyes that crinkled attractively when he laughed, it didn't mean he was any more trustworthy than the others. And I wanted to feel I could trust a man, not be suspicious of him, his lateness, his mobile phone calls. I had to also take responsibility for the uncomfortable fact that the common factor in my three failed marriages was me.

Did he have a wife? I wondered. I bet she didn't have to nag him to change a light bulb or read the electricity meter, because she wasn't tall enough to see it. I bet he did all sorts of handy things in the house, putting up shelves and changing tap washers without being praised or rewarded.

Behind me, Jenny was still on the phone.

'No, I don't know where the sink plunger is. Perhaps where you left it last time you used it? No, I'm not getting uppity at all. I'm fine by the way, thank you for asking.'

I looked over at her, surprised by her tone. She met my gaze, and I gave her a fist pump of encouragement. She straightened up and stuck her chin out.

'Paul, I have to go. The builders are here. No, I'm sure they aren't cowboys. Sheila used them in the past and presumably trusted them – yes, even though they are foreign, they seem very pleasant. The main builder has his two sons with him. And there's a gardener too, and his brother. Well, that's a very xenophobic comment if you don't mind me saying so.'

I mouthed at her *I'll go, shall I?* but she flapped a hand at me to stay. She was – unbelievably – standing up to her husband. There was a definite mottled flush to her neck and her eyes were a bit wild. I was astonished and, if I was honest, rather pleased that she was showing some spirit.

Well I never.

I went back to the window, but Léo wasn't there any more. Perhaps he was in the house, about to knock seven bells out of something.

'Look, Paul, Kitty says—'

I waited, breath bated. I'd been mentioned. This wasn't a good sign; Paul disliked me as much as I despised him.

'Well, possibly,' Jenny said, 'but that's not the point.'

What? What wasn't the point?

'Look, I can tell you are annoyed because I woke you up, but I thought you wanted me to keep you updated?'

There was a pause while Paul twittered. Jenny stood up and flashed me a look.

'No, absolutely not. I do not want you to come over here and sort anything out.'

I made an agonised expression, which Jenny returned. I think we were both horrified at the prospect of introducing Paul into this mix. Then she turned away.

'Yes, I'm sure they need you at the office. What are you having for dinner? Well, there is plenty of bread in the freezer and the milkman will deliver more eggs if you leave a note out for him. There are some frozen meals – yes, I realise that. There are always shops.'

There was another long pause while Paul's voice wittered on. Jenny put her hand over her phone and held it away from her face. She rolled her eyes at me.

'Honestly I hadn't realised how useless he is,' she whispered. 'I'm rather enjoying this.'

'Go for it,' I whispered back.

I felt a silly little leap of pride, hearing my sister talking like this at last. It could be that being together again, away from him, had helped her. Maybe I had helped too in some small way. Maybe she was feeling braver. Perhaps things were changing, for both of us.

'Right, I'm going, Paul. I have a lot to do. Well, have a nice day – Sainsbury's, I expect. Yes, they should be open. Right, bye.'

She ended the call and turned to look at me, her eyes haggard.

'I'm beginning to think you were right,' she said. And burst into tears.

I gave her a hug. I could see how much courage that had taken on her part, to stand up for herself at last. I was proud of her.

9

'We're going out,' I said firmly. 'It's not even nine o'clock yet. We need to get away from all this noise and mess. And I'll take you out for lunch. Okay?'

'That would be lovely. But will the workmen be able to get on without us here?' Jenny said, mopping up the last of her tears and taking deep breaths.

I put my arm around her and gave her another hug.

'Why – were you thinking of picking up a sledgehammer and helping?'

She giggled rather shakily. 'No.'

We'd gone back downstairs and were in the sitting room with the door closed, drinking a reviving cup of tea while the noise from the digger outside and the din from the kitchen melded into one long background racket.

'They'll probably get on better if we aren't here,' I said firmly, 'and we need a break.'

'If you think so,' she said.

'I do. I'm going to have a quick word with Pierre. You go and wash your face and fetch a coat. I won't be a minute.'

Outside, the patio already resembled a disaster zone. There were stone slabs all over the place. Pierre, his curls covered by a yellow hard hat, was lifting them with the bucket of the digger and stacking them into a heap on one side of the garden. His brother, Sylveste, was starting to remove a network of roots that had burrowed underneath over the years and was creating an ugly pile, which occasionally he looked at with some satisfaction. There was a pipe running away from the house in the middle.

'*Tuyau de drainage.*' Sylveste pointed and shouted over the noise. 'Drainage.'

'Really?' I yelled back, as though this was the most fascinating thing I had seen in years.

'*Il va au cloaque,*' he added happily, rubbing his hands together.

'Excellent,' I said, not really wanting to know where it went.

Léo came around the corner with an empty wheelbarrow at that point. He'd taken off his padded gilet and rolled his sleeves up. He had the most beautiful arms. Brown and muscular and no tattoos that I could see. I wasn't a great fan. It was surprising the way the younger generation had taken to tattoos; it used to be just salty old sea dogs who had them.

Should I get one? I wondered. And if I did, what would it be? A Chinese proverb, perhaps, but no, I had heard of someone getting one that was eventually translated as *chicken chow mein*.

What about a bluebird of happiness? Surely my happiness should come from inside me, not be inked onto my arm. And had I been happy or was I just keeping my head above water? Could I look at myself, at my age, with my health and my sanity intact and some money in the bank and not want more from life? What would it take for me to be truly happy? It wasn't a man; it wasn't a bigger house in a quieter street. It wasn't a better job.

What was making me happy, really happy, was being back with my sister, talking together, sitting opposite her at the kitchen table for our meals and getting to know each other again. I wondered if she felt the same way about me? I had been so used to her looking at me with annoyance or exasperation that it was fantastic to see kindness in her eyes again. I almost felt like crying, too.

'Kitty,' Léo said with pleasure when he saw me, and I think Sylveste chuckled. Pierre, not wanting to miss anything or pass up the opportunity for a fag break, turned the digger off and jumped down.

'I'm taking my sister out for the day,' I said. 'We need a new vacuum cleaner.'

We discussed the best place to buy such a thing for a few minutes, which meant Sylveste and Pierre came over to add their two euros' worth.

'And then we are going to take a trip somewhere, for a change of scene.'

The three of them started suggesting where we might go. After a few minutes Benoît and Claud realised everyone had downed tools and joined us. A discussion started, which became more and more confusing and heated. I mean, it was bad enough asking for directions to one place but when five men were discussing how to get to several places *and* in French, then you knew you were on to a loser.

Eventually, Léo went to find a book of road maps from his van and brought it back, opening it up on the garden table. Some of the route was obscured with coffee-cup rings and smears of plaster, but eventually we decided to visit Quimper and picked out a suitable route that would avoid the worst of the Brest traffic system.

'It will take about an hour,' Sylveste said confidently. 'You will be there in time for lunch. I dug out – um, um – *basin de jardin* – a garden pool there.'

'Was that the woman with the dogs?' Pierre said. 'And the strange husband?'

Sylveste nodded seriously. 'We had to go back and put a guard rail in a week later; *il a continué à tomber dedans* – he kept falling in and the dogs would jump on him. *Wouf wouf. Incroyable.*'

'You have to be careful with pools, and falling in,' Léo said.

He had a straight face, but I think he was laughing at me all the same.

I swallowed a giggle, bit my lip and said nothing.

* * *

We left about ten minutes later before Jenny could talk herself out of it. Léo even programmed the sat-nav for her to make sure we wouldn't get lost.

'So, I hope you don't mind me asking, but Paul's *not* coming over here, is he?' I said after a while.

We had wriggled our way out of the little lanes, through the village where everyone was still walking around with baguettes, and got onto a road leading south towards Brest.

'No,' Jenny said with feeling, 'he's not.'

Thank God for that, I thought.

Perhaps it wouldn't be the thing to comment at this point – to launch into another snarling, spitting diatribe about what a complete and utter twat Paul was. How he was anally retentive in a way that should come with an award from some organisation specialising in such things. I'd voiced my opinions before, and it had cost me a lot. I wasn't going to risk it again. Jenny needed, had needed, my support and now she was going to get it.

We drove on in silence for a few miles, but it was somehow okay this time; it wasn't uncomfortable. The sun was shining, the scenery was lush and green and the roads good. There wasn't much traffic either and Jenny was doing well, driving confidently and even over-taking sometimes, which was slightly scary because of course I was on the 'wrong' side of the car, and hanging out in the middle of the road instead of being snug against the kerb.

'So you're okay,' I said at last.

'Of course.' Jenny didn't look at me, which wasn't surprising, I suppose, as she was negotiating a roundabout.

'And Paul?' I said temptingly. 'He's coping without you.'

There was a long silence.

'I don't know,' she sighed at last, 'I think I should ring him back and apologise. It can't be easy for him and I was rude.'

'Apologise? Why would you do that?' I said, outraged. 'Presumably you left him with enough food in the house and everything clean and tidy. All he has to do is go to work and have his lunch in the subsidised canteen and look after himself.'

'I know you think I'm daft,' Jenny said, 'but Paul is used to me being there.'

'Well, now you aren't. I would think it would make him appreciate you more,' I said.

Jenny gave a short laugh. 'You really don't understand men, do you? Even after all your various adventures.'

'Anyone could marry an alcoholic, a bigamist and a philanderer one after the other,' I said, hoping to inject some humour into the situation, but saying it out loud like that made me feel rather embarrassed.

How had I sailed through my life with such little self-knowledge? How had I got to this age and still not got my act together?

I might not understand Jenny's marriage but then I hadn't understood mine either.

'Don't be daft,' she said. 'After all, they had something to do with it too—'

Mercifully, the sat-nav interrupted us at that point. '*Follow the E60 to Quimper.*'

We swung around a curving slip road and joined a motorway

that developed the annoying habit of turning into the N165 and back again without warning.

The road stretched in front of us, lined with thick trees on either side. There was hardly any traffic to speak of, not like the motorways in England where all the lanes seemed permanently full.

I watched the occasional truck on the other side of the motorway. Should I say anything more?

There had never been a time when we were growing up when Jenny and I hadn't squabbled with each other, but it had never been a threat to our sisterly friendship. Neither of us had held a grudge – well, not for long. We'd always made up; we had been able to laugh and seal the deal with a little gift of something silly. Several Hello Kitty items had been mine as a result, and after one particular screaming match I'd put a Walnut Whip on her pillow without even biting the walnut off the top first.

I opened my guidebook.

'Quimper has fine medieval streets opposite the cathedral, which is dedicated to Saint Corentin,' I read out. 'It has ribbed vaulting and flying buttresses. Quimper is famous for faience pottery, which has been made there for over three hundred years. Perhaps we should buy some?'

'We could,' Jenny agreed. 'That's a good idea.'

'It might be a nice souvenir. Do you remember when Ace was little and he used to collect snow globes from everywhere he went?'

'He did,' Jenny said rather wistfully. 'He had some awful ones, too. Did you ever see that terrible one from Blackpool? With the tower and a donkey in the snow?'

'I should have; I bought it for him,' I said.

She laughed. 'Did you really? He had dozens. He used to scour junk shops for them, too; we had them from all over the world. There was one absolutely horrific one from Egypt – pyramids and the sphinx in the snow with a three-legged elephant, for some reason. Ace said perhaps they'd ran out of camels and this was a collector's piece. It was his absolute favourite.'

'Let's find one for him in Quimper,' I said. 'There's bound to be one.'

'How could we get it to him?'

'You could hop on a train to Nantes. Go and see him.'

She frowned. 'He's probably very busy; he won't have time for snow globes.'

'No, but he would have time for his mum,' I said. 'It's a brilliant idea.'

'Oh, I don't know—'

'I'll find out the train times. You could stay for a couple of days while the worst of the building work is going on. Or you could drive; you're a great driver. You're coping incredibly well with this. I certainly couldn't do it.'

Jenny looked pleased. 'I like driving, actually. It's the one thing Paul leaves to me. I mean, it doesn't stop him criticising, but he never takes over.'

Arse, I thought.

'But I couldn't do that because then you'd be left without a car,' she said after a bit of a think.

Aha, so at least she was considering it. Unusually for me I just gave a casual shrug.

'I'd cope,' I said. 'The weather is okay; I could get started on the garden now I have Pierre and Sylveste. There's plenty there to keep me busy.'

'I suppose.' She was quiet for a few minutes, obviously wrestling with something. 'Do you think Claud looks like Ace? But without the beard?' This last bit came out in a rush.

Light dawned; she was absolutely right!

'Yes! Of course! Now you say it, it's obvious! *That's* who he reminds me of.'

'I noticed the resemblance as soon as I saw him this morning. It made me really sad, actually. To realise how long it is since I've seen Ace.'

I patted her arm. 'Of course you need to see Ace. Of course you've missed him. I've missed him; we always got on so well.'

Jenny laughed. 'Oh, you! The crazy godmother everyone needs. I used to get quite jealous when he would talk to you about school, and he would never talk to us about it. You knew he was applying to Edinburgh before we did.'

'He swore me to secrecy,' I said.

We were distracted then as we had left the motorway a while back and were driving through the outskirts of Quimper. There were houses and building sites and supermarkets. We stopped at one and bought a new vacuum cleaner and some supplies. Then we pressed on towards the bright lights.

'*Take the last exit from the roundabout signposted D39,*' said the sat-nav, and then a few seconds later, rather smugly, '*You have arrived at your destination.*'

'Well, that's all well and good,' I said. 'How do we know where to park?'

'We could park here,' Jenny replied, smoothly pulling into a space next to a canal. 'You panic too much. I mean, have you ever just gone home from somewhere because you didn't know where to park?'

'Well, yes, actually,' I said. 'Many times.'

'Really? I didn't know that; I didn't know you were so timid.'

I snorted. 'At least I'm not scared of chickens!'

* * *

We set off into the sunshine. There were several narrow streets leading off into the city and we just picked one.

Quimper was absolutely delightful. One little cobbled lane led to another. There were chic fashion shops and the most unbelievable patisseries. We stood outside one, transfixed by the window display. Tarts with glossy fillings, croissants and pastries like pillows, chocolate confections decorated with fragments of gold leaf, quiches that would impress any man who saw them.

A couple of little girls stood next to us, dressed in dear little linen pinafores and cute straw hats. I listened, entranced, as they chatted away in French to their mother. She, of course, was chic in a striped Breton top and loose, white linen trousers – the sort of outfit that would look like an unmade bed on me. I wondered about her and her daughters for a moment and felt a stab of envy.

She looked like a nice woman, the sort of woman I would have liked to be. Confident, casual, elegant in a throwaway sort of way that French women have. I expected her husband adored her and worked in business earning shedloads of money. I bet he didn't sneer at her when she ate doughnuts out of the bag or sit her down on the sofa one day and guiltily admit he was actually still married to someone else.

'Well, come on,' Jenny called. 'You don't want to get lost *again*, do you?'

She was standing a few yards away, smiling at me. I grinned back.

I knew we were both remembering the same thing: the time when I had been lost for half an hour at Bristol Zoo, wandering around hopelessly while the animals jabbered and jeered at me through their cages. I could still recall the relief when Jenny had found me sitting on a bench and taken hold of my hand, offering me a square of her chocolate and her handkerchief to mop up my tears. She had been everything I could have wanted in a sister. Kind, funny and trustworthy. Still, I'd hated zoos ever since.

'We deserve coffee,' she said, 'and a decadent pastry. To hell with the calories and the cholesterol and the fat. Let's choose somewhere.'

A few minutes later, after much discussion, we sat in a café with huge bowls of café au lait and a cake each: *macaron pomme caramel* for Jenny and *millefeuille au fruits rouges* for me. They were like works of art. Fabulous.

We sat opposite each other with a lovely view out of the window of the cathedral, which reared up into the blue sky. It wasn't something I allowed myself to do very often but I thought about those two little girls again and wondered how my life would have been if I'd had children.

I was only too ready to criticise Paul's parenting skills, but how would I have coped? Would I have been a good mother, or would I have been self-absorbed and disinterested as our mother had been? I might have been over-protective like Jenny. Would I have been overtaken by the need to be my children's best friend? Would they have loved me, for all my faults, or would they appear on some chat show in later life, complaining about me and blaming me for their failures?

'You're lucky to have Ace,' I said at last.

Jenny looked at me. Her eyes were very kind. It was as though she knew what I was thinking.

'Yes, I know,' she said. 'You'd have been a great mum.'

'Well, too late now,' I said, with a courage I didn't feel.

'Never give up,' Jenny said.

'That would be a miracle, for many reasons.'

We looked at each other and both burst out laughing.

10

We went for a walk around the cathedral, which was of course glorious with its barrel vault ceilings and flying buttresses, the interior dim and scented with wax candles and history. Then we discussed going into museums but decided we would rather go shopping, looking for faience pottery and possibly a snow globe.

We found both in no time, mainly because Jenny said we could have lunch afterwards as a reward. She was in unusually good spirits that day, looking around her with pleasure at the timbered houses and cobbled streets. It was almost like having the old Jenny back. It was so great; it reminded me of the many times we had been together when we were growing up: shopping, gossiping, swapping confidences and clothes. That new little glow of happiness I'd noticed inside me was growing.

Remembering her liking for matching things, we each bought identical pottery café bowls with our names on them and an almost tasteful snow globe of the cathedral. Then we ventured into a shop selling the sort of homeware – embroidered towels, lace-edged sheets, pale, distressed furniture – that made you want to throw away everything you owned and start again.

I bought a platter decorated with flowers and Jenny bought a sweet little milk jug, which she predicted Paul would never use because it was 'too small'. She said he was unable to understand the concept of buying something just as a decorative novelty. Personally, I thought it was just the right size to hold a drop of arsenic for his breakfast muesli, but I didn't say that.

Then we had lunch, having decided on a gorgeous-looking bistro near the covered market with seats and tables outside under a canopy. There were a few people there already, sitting around with tiny cups of espresso. I almost expected the drift of a Gauloises cigarette but of course no one was allowed to do that any more. Instead, we sat, enveloped in the scents of garlic and wine and herbs that emanated from every good French restaurant. It was wonderful.

'I'm having *moules marinière*,' Jenny said, surprising me. 'I love them and Paul won't let me have them. He says they are disgusting bottom-feeders, which of course they aren't.'

'They come with *frites*,' I warned.

'He won't let me have those either,' she said, and she hunched her shoulders like the mischievous girl she had once been.

'I won't tell if you don't. I'm having the *planche de charcuterie et fromages.*'

'You mad, crazy thing! What's in that?'

'I don't really know or care,' I said. 'Meat and cheeses.'

She laughed. 'How typical. You live close to the edge, don't you?'

We sat in the sunshine, sipping water and eating the French bread that was deposited on our table the moment after we had sat down.

'I wonder how things are back at the house?' Jenny said later, dabbing her bread into some of her garlic and wine sauce.

'Noisy and very dusty, I'd guess.'

'Yes, I expect so. Well, we can play with the new vacuum cleaner when we get back.'

'What fun,' I said. 'You can't buy entertainment like that.'

She snorted. 'Remember that time when you hoovered up Mum's earrings? We had to go through the bag to find them.'

'She was so cross.'

'She was always cross about something,' Jenny said.

'Usually me,' I said.

'Do you know, it absolutely broke her heart when you divorced Frank,' Jenny said after a few minutes, pinching the mussels out of their shells.

'Well, it was no picnic for me either. It's not like I did it to upset her. How was I to know his favourite hobby was booze? He hid it well; I think they call that being a functioning alcoholic these days. Mum only ever saw him when he was in the cheerful life-and-soul-of-the-party phase. She never saw him slumped on the stairs shouting abuse at three in the morning. He used to get in a furious temper with politicians and occasionally the milkman.'

Jenny shook her head. 'It must have been very difficult.'

'It was, and I know you think I should have worked harder at things, but it wasn't for want of trying.'

'Well, perhaps we didn't realise what you were dealing with,' she said at last. She patted my hand. 'I'm sorry.'

Well, that was nice; I hadn't been expecting that at all. I felt quite emotional for a moment. Physical contact between us had been non-existent over the last years. Until we came here. This felt like a bit of a breakthrough to me.

* * *

After lunch we wandered on, passing all sorts of chic boutiques and gift shops. Perhaps I had my rose-tinted spectacles on that day, but everywhere was clean and attractive and people were smiling and looked happy.

Then we passed the windows of a bijou-looking gallery. The sort that usually had one thing in in the window with a spotlight and no price tag.

There was a display of two ceramic bowls decorated with splatters of red paint that looked as though they might have been used for some sacrificial ritual, and the other window contained one painting. I almost walked on.

Then I stopped, went back and stared. It looked sort of familiar. I peered at it. No price tag, of course.

Jenny was still looking at the sacrificial bowls with a frown on her face.

'Come and look at this,' I said.

'What?'

I waved her over and we both stood staring in at the painting.

'What about it?' she said at last. 'It's a donkey standing under a tree. With some *flowers.*'

'Don't you think that looks likes one of Sheila's paintings?' I asked.

Jenny took another look. 'It's the same style, I suppose. Is it signed?'

We peered a bit more.

'Let's go in and ask,' I said.

'Oh no, we shouldn't,' Jenny said. 'I mean, it's not as though we are going to buy it, are we?'

'Maybe not, but it would be interesting to know how much they are selling it for,' I replied with a meaningful look.

Her eyebrows shot up under her fringe. 'Oh. Yes, I see.'

We dithered about for a few seconds and then I went in, Jenny at my heels.

Inside there was some music playing very softly, a cross between pan pipes and whale noises, and everything – floor, ceiling and walls – was painted a tasteful pale grey.

A bell dinged somewhere, and a thin, floppy-haired man in a grey suit and blue brocade waistcoat came through a door at the back of the room.

'*Mesdames?*' he said, with a little neck bow.

I dug deep in my French O-level memory.

'*Bonjour, voilà un* painting *dans la fenêtre,*' I said.

'Ah, you are English,' Floppy said, sweeping his hair back from his forehead.

'*Nous sommes,*' I agreed.

'We'd like to know more about it,' Jenny said, suddenly bold.

She looked at me and I nodded.

'*Bien sûr,*' he said, leading us over to gaze at the back of it.

'Who is it by?' I asked.

'And how much is it?' Jenny added.

'This is by a Brittany artist, Sheila Salter—'

'I knew it,' I said. 'I was right!'

'*Malheureusement*, Madame Salter is no longer with us, but her work is now much collected, much admired. You are familiar with her work?'

'She was our aunt,' Jenny said rather proudly.

'Ah, how interesting.' He flicked his hair back again. 'Do you collect her art?'

'Not exactly. Can you tell us some more about the painting? How old it is?'

Floppy examined the little paper label on the back.

'2012,' he said. 'It's called *Le Prince de Troie – The Trojan Prince.*'

'That's a weird name for a donkey,' I said. 'I wonder why she called it that?'

'How much is it?' Jenny said again.

Floppy went over to a white desk and leafed through a book.

'*Un moment. The Trojan Prince* – hmm, hmm, let me see. I think I need to check elsewhere; it has not been with us for very long.'

Jenny went to look at the sacrificial bowls in the window, her lower lip stuck out uncomprehendingly.

I wandered over to look at some other paintings on the grey walls. One was a big canvas of a neighing horse trapped in a bomb crater entitled *Mélodie de Vie*; another depicted a stone Breton longhouse perched on a cliff, while white waves battered below, called *Folie Tranquille*. I found a sculpture shaped like a bucket, made out of paperclips and sticky tape, grandly called *Tout est Prêt*. I think this meant 'everything is ready', which seemed like misrepresentation of the highest order to me. But what would I know?

'Ah, yes.' It was Floppy back again. '*Le Prince de Troie* is priced at *douze mille euros*.'

'What does that mean?' Jenny said. 'A million euros?'

I counted on my fingers. '*Douze* is twelve and *mille* is thousand.'

'Good grief. That's ridiculous,' she said, giving Floppy a hard look.

Floppy looked slightly annoyed and made a *pfft* noise. 'But no, this is a very good price. It is an investment piece.'

'Do you think you will sell it?'

Floppy flared his nostrils at her. 'Of course. This piece has been with us for three days and we have already several enquiries from America and England.'

'Really? You're having me on,' Jenny insisted.

'I'm having no one on – or off,' Floppy said stiffly, jamming his thumbs in his waistcoat pockets. 'In the last few months these pictures are suddenly becoming very popular. They have a certain *charme nostalgique*. Tell me, do you have any of your aunt's paintings? Because if you do, I would be interested in selling them for you.'

'Well, we do have quite a few,' Jenny said.

His eyes glistened.

'My card,' he said. He fished out a business card from one of his waistcoat pockets and handed it over with another little neck bow.

Capitaine Jean Picard, Marchand d'Art.

'Oh, look! Do you have a cousin who is on the Starship *Enterprise*?'

'Well, thank you,' Jenny said, grabbing my arm and steering me towards the door. 'Thank you so much for your time.'

Jenny bundled me out into the street, and we watched as Capitaine Picard put the painting back in the window, favouring us with a look. He then came out and wiped a smudge off the glass as though we had been pressing our philistine noses on it.

'Starship *Enterprise*. You are a twit,' Jenny chuckled. 'But twelve thousand euros for a painting of a donkey? I've never heard anything so preposterous. It's not worth that. Who is going to pay that?'

'I expect he knows his business; someone will. Like they say on *Antiques Roadshow*, a picture is worth what someone is willing to pay for it.'

We walked on in silence for a few yards and then Jenny stopped very suddenly.

'That painting is priced at twelve thousand euros.'

'Yes.'

'And we have loads of her paintings in a room protected by a piece of old garden wire.'

'Yes,' I said.

I realised we were now blocking the narrow pavement.

'They weren't mentioned in the will. Are they even ours?'

'I suppose so,' I said, pulling her arm to get her moving again. 'She said *house plus contents*, and they are contents. Someone must have gone round to value the place for the inheritance tax.'

'Good grief.'

We walked on towards the place where we had parked the car. I think both of us were trying to do the mental arithmetic. Jenny got there first.

'But... but that might be getting on to half a million euros.'

We both stopped this time and looked at each other, horrified.

In my mind's eye I could see the paintings, wrapped up in brown paper, stacked any old how in a dark and grubby room, and, as Jenny had said, protected only by a rusty twist of garden wire.

I felt a bit faint. I had a bit of money in the bank and some savings, but that sort of money was on another level.

'I think I need a sit-down and a glass of wine,' I said.

'Well, I think we should get home,' Jenny said.

'Good idea. But calm down. Let's be honest; they've been there for ages and no one has touched them. Like the wine in the cupboard. And I'm sure the builders aren't going to go rummaging around.'

'Let's get home quickly,' Jenny repeated, giving me a look across the car roof. 'I forgot my knickers.'

'You might want to re-think that sentence,' I said.

11

I think we were both a bit stunned by our discovery, and we didn't talk much on the homeward journey. I kept sneaking little looks at Jenny's profile. She looked rather grim.

'It'll be fine,' I said. 'Nothing is going to happen to the paintings.'

'Okay, but what do we do?' she said. 'I mean, when we get home and assuming everything is fine. We can't just leave them there, can we?'

'We could put them in a storage locker, or a bank?'

'I need to think. Should I ask Paul?'

'Absolutely not!' I said firmly. If Paul got wind of this he would be on the next ferry over. 'We need to move them anyway, because that room is due for renovation or demolition or something. It was on the plans.'

'It was, wasn't it? Right, perhaps we should look for a storage unit. If you think that would be secure enough?'

'People put all sorts of stuff in them. Furniture, clothes, guns, drugs, bodies.'

Jenny huffed at me. 'Oh, stop it. You're winding me up.'

'It's true. I read about it in the paper.'

'Oh, it must be true then.'

At last we reached the little lane leading to Jolies Arbres and Jenny turned in to the drive with a sigh of relief. I think she was expecting to see a couple of masked burglars making off with bags marked 'swag', but what we did see was a huge skip, the builders' vans, the gardener's van and a familiar donkey tethered to a concrete post.

'What the...' Jenny exclaimed.

'Ah, now I see the joke,' I said. '*The Trojan Prince*. Get it?'

'No,' Jenny said rather grumpily. She parked the car and switched off the engine. 'What I see is *that donkey*. And it's done an enormous pile of doings in the garden. Well, I'm not clearing that up! I expressly said I didn't want Hector here again. Léo said he had a car.'

'Perhaps Hector failed his driving test?'

'Oh, very funny. Can't you take anything seriously?'

'Well, not this. There are a lot of things to get cross about, but a donkey isn't one of them. Perhaps Bertrand forgot, or perhaps the car has broken down,' I said. 'It's just a donkey. In fact, it's *that* donkey. The one Sheila painted. Hector. And you know who Hector was.'

'No, who?'

'In ancient history, Hector was the prince of Troy. That's what Sheila called the painting of Hector. That's brilliant.'

Jenny got out of the car and slammed her door closed in a marked manner. 'I shall have words with him. Or with Léo. I said expressly no donkey. Especially one that makes that smell.'

'Oh, lighten up. He's not doing any harm and donkey doings, as you call them, are probably excellent for the roses.'

Jenny had bustled off with a couple of bags of shopping, to let herself into the house while I went to fetch the new vacuum cleaner from the boot.

As I got to the front door, I heard Jenny give an anguished wail.

Oh God, now what?

I lugged the vacuum cleaner into the hallway. The door to the storage room where all those potential art treasures were stored was blocked with several bags of wall plaster, countless boxes of nails and screws and some other stuff that I couldn't recognise. In the kitchen I was met with a pile of wreckage; Benoît, who was covered in dust; and a large pile of new timber stacked up against one wall.

Léo emerged from the passageway that led to the downstairs bathrooms.

'Ah, there you are,' he said pleasantly. He was dragging a large bag of rubble. Broken tiles, chunks of plaster and bits of old pipe. 'I'll just get rid of this.'

He lugged it out of the kitchen door, presumably to take it to the skip, and a few minutes later he returned.

'Have you had a good day, *mesdames*?'

Jenny came downstairs. I guessed she had been up in her bedroom checking for signs of knicker-drawer invasion.

'Well, yes, we did,' I said uncertainly, looking around at the devastation. 'We have a new vacuum cleaner.'

Léo held up his hands. 'Please don't use a new vacuum cleaner on this mess. It will burn out the motor. I have an industrial one, which I promise will deal with this before we go home.'

Jenny straightened up as if preparing to launch into a speech. 'Léo, why is that—'

At that moment, a familiar hooting greeting echoed through the kitchen door and Bertrand hove into view, looking just as disreputable as ever.

'*Jolies mesdames! Bienvenue à vous deux! Bienvenue!*' he cried cheerfully.

Jenny backed away slightly.

'*Bonjour*, everyone,' she said coldly. 'What on earth is going on?'

'We are busy busy busy,' Bertrand said cheerfully. '*Abeilles occupées.* Busy bees!'

'I did warn you there would be a mess,' Léo said, 'but don't worry, we will be clearing up soon. You will hardly know we have been here.'

I thought that was very unlikely.

More than ready for a chat, Bertrand leant on the handles of his wheelbarrow and behind him, moving slowly into view, were five chickens.

Jenny gave a strangled scream. 'It's a pack! A herd!'

Bertrand looked around him, bewildered.

'*Ce ne sont que des poules, madame. Poulets coquins,*' he added fondly. 'Only naughty chickens. *Cotcotcot.*'

Suddenly, the chickens scattered and a rather handsome tabby cat came out from the hedge and began to wind itself around Bertrand's wellington boots. It looked up at him adoringly and gave a squeaky miaow.

Bertrand gave a little cry of surprise and bent and ruffled the cat's ears.

'Gigi! *Que fais-tu ici? Méchant chat!* Bad cat! *Colette va s'inquiéter.* Colette will be looking for you!'

Claud came into the kitchen at that point and Jenny shot him a searching look. I stared at him for a bit too; he did look very like Ace. Very nice cheekbones and a noble nose.

'I'm going up to my room,' she said with a furious glare at Bertrand. 'All this dust and livestock is giving me one of my headaches. And my back is aching with the stress. I'm going to take a paracetamol. I might even take two.'

She went out of the kitchen and even went so far as to slam the door firmly behind her. Then it opened again, and she stuck her head into the room.

'I'm very annoyed indeed. Kitty, say something about the donkey; the smell is unbelievable. What on earth do they feed it? And the hens. And now a *cat*. Good God, we're not Whipsnade Zoo. Although I'm beginning to wonder.'

Her voice was shrill with a mixture of temper and hysteria. It reminded me of many instances during our childhood when I had annoyed her. Borrowed crayons, broken toys or misplaced lip gloss. I'm ashamed to say I had to bite the inside of my cheek to stop myself from smiling.

We could just about hear the sounds of her footsteps thumping up the stairs in a marked manner. Léo didn't know this but *taking a paracetamol* was as close to drug abuse as Jenny ever got. Claud gave a shrug and lugged another bag of rubble outside. The cat slunk away.

I turned to Léo.

'She's a bit upset,' I said. Understatement.

Léo looked sympathetic. 'I do understand. This is always the worst part. When there is demolition, and it seems as though it will never be right again. It is always a shock if the customer is not used to it. But trust me, the worst will soon be over. Tomorrow we will perhaps start to repair the damaged plaster in here. It was a smaller problem than I first thought. Come and see the bathrooms. You will need to choose new tiles soon.'

I followed him, picking my way carefully over the rubble. The floor was gritty under my shoes. Benoît and Claud were starting to sweep up the dirt and debris, releasing clouds of dust into the air, which floated out of the open door.

The two downstairs bathrooms had been practically gutted. The walls were bare, except for odd lengths of new pipe and cable sticking out. The hideous brown and orange tiles had been removed and so had the baths and sinks and toilets. The dividing partition between the two rooms was nearly down; just part of a small brick wall was left.

'Good, yes?' Léo said. He was as enthusiastic as a boy. 'This will be a very good space. Plenty of room, and excellent for you.'

'Will it?' I said weakly. I couldn't see it myself. No wonder Jenny couldn't either. 'I'm sure you are right.'

'I couldn't stick to the plan without demolishing them both, do you see? You still have the upstairs bathroom to use for the time being.'

Oh yes, Jenny would love that. My face must have reflected my doubt.

Léo laughed. '*Chère madame*, trust me. It will be outstanding.'

I looked at him, liking the way his face was filled with such excitement. He must have done this sort of thing hundreds if not thousands of times. Taken a battered building or room, seen the problems and the solutions and built it up into something better. It was all very clever and admirable.

Perhaps it was a philosophy to apply to life, too. Knock down the old stuff and replace it with something better. I liked that idea.

'If you are happy with it, then okay,' I said.

'Please can you reassure Madame Jenny?' he said.

'*Madame' is about right*, I thought, *storming off like that in a strop.*

'I will,' I said, 'and about that – do you know where the hens are from? And Jenny wasn't very happy to see Hector again. She did say she didn't want him here. I know it sounds silly but she's not very keen on animals.'

'I see,' Léo said, rather puzzled and obviously not seeing at all. 'It's just Bertrand is unable to drive at the moment and he needs Hector to carry his tools. I should have said something. The chickens must have wandered over from his place.'

'I think the cat might be a stray. Although Bertrand seem to know whose it was. He mentioned Colette.'

'Ah, Colette is Bertrand's daughter. She works in the village, at the museum. She took Bertrand's car to drive to Rouen at the weekend, to look after a friend who has a new baby. She had a difficult birth and is not doing well. That's why Bertrand had to bring Hector.'

'Of course, I do understand – how kind of her. Then forget about it, please. I mean, I don't mind Hector being here. I'll tell Jenny there is a good reason. Personally, he doesn't bother me at all. I mean, he's a sort of lawnmower, isn't he? Hector, not Bertrand.'

Léo nodded. 'I will ask Bertrand to keep Hector out of sight. Perhaps it was *insensible* – insensitive – to put him somewhere so visible. Bertrand is a good sort, trustworthy.'

Léo called Bertrand over and they had a rapid conversation that involved a lot of shrugging and '*bien sûr, bien sûr*'.

'Ah, Bertrand understands; he will speak to Mimi again.'

Who the hell was Mimi? I didn't have the energy to ask. I wasn't sure I didn't need a paracetamol too. That or a strong drink.

'Well, would you like some tea?'

Always tea with English people, wasn't it? Tea and biscuits, the universal panacea to arguments, birth, death, panic, despair. He was bound to politely decline, though. What must he think of us?

'That would be nice,' he said with a smile that made me feel a bit fizzy inside. 'Let me get the men packed up first. I would like to ask you some things.'

He walked off, back to some cleaning and tidying. Carrying out the last of the day's debris. I heard things crash into the skip with a clang and Hector gave a braying accompaniment, rather tactlessly under the circumstances, I thought. Especially as he was parked under Jenny's bedroom windows.

What things did Léo want to ask me? I wondered.

Things about myself, about Jenny and her tantrum? Where would I like to have dinner with him? How did I keep my youthful good looks? No, probably not the last two. I was probably getting a bit overexcited.

Claud and Benoît, who had been pretending to tidy up while actually listening with interest to our conversation, started working at top speed, neither of them looking at me. Both of them exchanged sneaky looks with each other and at one point Benoît grinned. They must have thought we were two typically neurotic, middle-aged women, when, personally, I'd always prided myself on being reasonable and tolerant. I could feel myself blushing.

Filled with excited anticipation – which was really rather tragic, but sometimes one has to take pleasure in the oddest things – I took the new vacuum cleaner into the sitting room. Everything still seemed to be covered in dust, even though the door had been closed and the workmen had pinned a dustsheet across it. Jenny would like to have one room where everything was ordered when she came back downstairs. That might cheer her up. I hauled it out of its box and plugged it in.

My word, it was powerful. We did a sort of frantic tango together as it dragged all the cushions off the sofa and possibly some of the remaining pile out of the rugs. With a gulp of glee, it pounced on a tissue it found under the coffee table, then inhaled a biscuit wrapper and tried furiously to eat one of Jenny's scarves that she had unwisely left on the coffee table. I clung on to the hose and wrestled with it, feeling it was escorting me around the room rather than the other way round. Through the closed door I could vaguely hear the echoing roar of the workmen's vacuum, like some sort of primordial mating ritual. Anyway, it didn't take long before all the dust was gone. I disentangled the end of one of the curtains that the hoover had ambitiously tried to eat and switched if off. I was hot, sweating and panting.

I opened the door and went to see how the workmen were getting on. I was pleasantly surprised by what I found. In as far as a building site could be spotless, it was. Even the worktops, the stove and the table had been cleaned and wiped.

'Ah, there you are.'

It was Léo, who was standing just outside the kitchen door, hands in his pockets, looking out at the patio, which had not been cleaned up with anything like the same care. I went to look. There were two towers of stone slabs, a huge pile of tree roots and rocks and several big dumpy bags of sand to one side. The hole had been filled in so I no longer had a tantalising view of the sewer pipe, and the grass had been trampled and churned up by the caterpillar tracks of the digger. There were three hens pecking happily at bugs and worms in the dirt. The white one with the beret – I'd begun to think of her as Blanche – was standing with a very confident expression. If hens could be said to have expressions.

'This too will be fine, *madame*,' Léo said as he saw my face.

'Oh, I know. It will be fine. I mean, grass recovers quickly, doesn't it? It's hard to stop it half the time. These hens – who is Mimi?'

'Bertrand's wife. They live in a place that backs on to the other end of your garden, which is why the hens have been coming through the hedge. I have told Bertrand to warn her they are out and wandering and causing distress.'

'Well, not distress—'

'Don't be alarmed. They are not trained to attack.'

I laughed at the thought. 'I'm sure they aren't. Now, I promised you tea, didn't I? Have the others gone?'

Around the side of the house I saw Pierre's van moving slowly down the lane, and behind it the unmistakable figures of Bertrand and Hector slowly swaying home together. I could even hear

Bertram's encouraging call of '*Hoo hoo, Hector, bien, bien,*' as they went.

'I think we are safe,' Léo said, and he twinkled his eyes at me.

I grasped my opportunity. 'Would you like a glass of wine instead?'

'That would be very pleasant,' Léo said. 'Will Madame Jenny join us?'

'I think we might leave Madame Jenny where she is for the moment,' I said carefully. 'You know. She might be asleep.'

I went to get a new bottle of wine from the store and washed two glasses, which, although they had been in a closed cupboard, had been liberally coated with dust.

Léo was sitting at the garden table with his long legs stretched out in front of him.

'You have plans for the garden?' he said. 'It used to be beautiful. My father planted that rose, the one growing around the arch. I think it was a birthday present to Sheila.'

'Oh, that's lovely – what a great thing to know. Yes, I will be glad to get started. I'd like to get the flower beds cleared first and the overgrowth around the pool cleared away.'

'Of course,' he said.

He was watching closely as I uncorked the bottle and poured out two hefty measures. I handed one over.

He took the bottle and looked at the label. 'Kitty, what is this?'

I was puzzled. 'Red wine. Isn't it very nice? Would you prefer white?'

He shook his head. 'Kitty, this is a Château Chantelune Margaux, 2009,' he said.

'Is it?' I asked. Was that good or bad?

'This is very expensive. You shouldn't be giving it to your builder,' Léo said, his brow creased.

'Don't you like it?'

'Of course I like it. Perhaps you don't understand what I am saying. This is possibly a seventy-euro bottle of wine.'

I took a sip, and spluttered a bit. 'Oh! I think it's rather good. You can have a cup of tea if you'd prefer?'

We exchanged a look and he burst out laughing. 'Ah, Kitty, you are priceless!'

12

I took that as a compliment and tried to smile in a way that would suggest I knew what I was doing. Actually, I was remembering the other bottles Jenny and I had knocked back since we had been here, the faded, dusty labels, the dates on the necks of the bottle, the wax seals I had sliced off so carelessly. Heaven knew how much those had been worth. Recently, if I spent more than a fiver on a bottle of wine, I'd thought I was pushing the boat out.

I gave it some thought. If there were five glasses of wine in each bottle, that meant I was now swigging back fourteen quid's worth. Seventy euros for one bottle? I would have hoped for a whole case at that price. And free delivery and a gift of a novelty corkscrew.

Anyway, we sat out there drinking wine and quietly chatting while the hens crept nearer and pecked away at the earth in front of us. They were quite cute, really, and they made little crooning noises, which was rather endearing. It made it sound as though they were happy.

Léo told me he lived in a house he had restored in a wooded valley. His sons shared a house in the village and his ex-wife had moved to Spain with her new partner. It sounded all very amicable, neat and tidy. And in a strange way it was rather encouraging to hear that he was single.

Should that thought even have crossed my mind? Did I always have to look at men with that sort of interest? I did have a poor track record when it came to my choices.

I told him about Steve and his new wife but held off telling him about Frank the alcoholic and Oliver the bigamist. That wasn't quite so ship-shape and, to be honest, I was rather embarrassed by my marital history. It had caused me nothing but grief over the years and also a spectacular falling-out with my sister. She would be very annoyed if she knew where my thoughts were going. I should calm down. I was employing him, that was all.

'Your sister – Jenny – I think she is not a happy woman,' he said as he swirled the fourteen quid's worth of wine in his glass. 'She seems *anxieuse* – anxious about all this.'

'Yes, she isn't used to mess and muddle,' I said. 'Her husband can be very...'

What could I say? That Paul had seemed quite a nice sort when he and Jenny had first married, a bit reserved perhaps, clever but slightly dull, but he had morphed into an uncontrolled package of intolerance and twattishness over the years? That he would switch off the television if there was swearing, the possibility of nudity or any Labour politician. That he had become unthinkingly racist, xenophobic and immune to reasoned argument if he didn't agree with something.

But then my husbands had been far from ideal. Who was I to judge?

'... difficult,' I said at last.

Léo nodded. 'And you? You laugh a great deal; I hear you. You make jokes, you find things funny. I like that. And yet your eyes are sad. Why is that, I wonder?'

I had no idea what to say to this.

'Oh, you know,' I said, brushing off the comment, 'sometimes life is ridiculous. You have to laugh.'

'Perhaps,' he agreed, 'and yet I still wonder.'

Time for me to change the subject.

'Tell me what will happen next with the house. When will the bathroom be finished?' I said. 'I don't think Jenny is going to like sharing her bathroom with me for long.'

He looked surprised. 'But she is your sister. Oh well. We will be finished demolishing things tomorrow, and then Benoît can begin with plumbing and the electrics. I will build the shower cubicle, put the tiles on – which reminds me, you must choose some.'

'Where do I go to do that?'

'I can bring you some samples if you tell me what you like.'

I flicked on my mobile and turned to my Pinterest page. This was a mish-mash of all the things that I had seen over the years that I liked, that took my mind off the dull actuality of my life. One day I would wear this dress. One day I would have this garden furniture. That sort of thing.

And yet I'd always known that I probably wouldn't have any of those things. Maybe that was the magic of social media, the feeling that you could reinvent your life for the benefit of strangers without actually doing anything? Photoshop, for example. The camera could lie, after all. Perhaps that was why people seemed so dissatisfied, looking at the reality when the fantasy was so preferable.

Among my pictures was a tile mural of the sea I had seen in some Italian palazzo and was probably hand-painted by Michelangelo. The chances of something similar in a far-flung corner of Brittany was slim.

'Ah yes,' Léo said as he enlarged the picture, 'I see.'

'Too much?' I said. 'And far too expensive?'

'I'm sure I could find something that would give the same effect.

I will do some research. These things are popular these days. Leave it with me.'

I watched as his fingers patted the screen of my mobile. They were strong, grimy with ingrained dirt, and the nails were bitten. He wasn't *that* carefree, then.

He bent over the screen, frowning slightly.

I wondered how he spent his time when he wasn't working. He might be divorced but did he have *une amie*? A lady friend, a partner who helped him with the business. She would be capable and attractive and younger than him. She would be disciplined and not possess a wardrobe full of impulse sale purchases she had never worn. She would probably go running and wild swimming. Or kayaking. For the fun of it. I could think of no other hobbies to inflict on her that would make her less like me. I preferred gardening, reading and eating. Plus a fair amount of sitting around scrolling through Pinterest and imagining a more interesting life for myself with a capsule wardrobe and a customised camper van.

There was no reason why I couldn't have a capsule wardrobe and a camper van. If I could take on managing the renovation of an old French farmhouse while reconnecting with my sister, I could probably do anything. Now that was an exciting thought. At least I was media savvy. I might be sixty-two, but I had a Harry Styles CD and could name most of the Kardashians. At least I was down with the kids. Whatever that meant.

'So you knew Sheila quite well?' I asked.

'She was a lovely lady, kind, pleasant and gentle. My father was very fond of her. Oh, *rien de scandaleux* – after all, he was a widower, she was alone. They had a nice friendship until he died five years ago.'

Friendship? What did that mean? Had they been more than just friends? Was there some sort of connection between us other than builder and client? I mean... hang on, Sheila had mentioned her friend Jean quite a lot in her letters. I'd always assumed it was a woman.

'What was your father's name?'

'Jean – well, Jean-Louis, actually. He used to live in the village, the house where he lived for many years. Quite often he would walk up the lane to visit her, help in the garden. They were good company for each other.'

'That's lovely.'

So Sheila, even at eighty-something, had had an admirer. But why not? Good for her.

'I lived near him until he died and then I moved to where I now live. My house is quite traditional. It was an old stone cottage, which was *abandonnée* – derelict. I bought it for a song years ago and almost forgot about it, but then circumstances changed and I wanted something peaceful, different. So I lived in a caravan for over a year, nearly two while I restored it. It was my hobby, but then it became my passion. You would think I was mad, working out there in the woods, in the snow, in the rain, in the dark. But then I was able to move in and make it my home, somewhere where there were no memories, no sadness.'

'After your divorce?'

'Yes, and other things.'

Hmm, what could that be? I wondered.

He shook his head. 'I am talking too much. I am telling you far too much; I don't know why. Let's talk about you. What sort of house do you like?' he said. 'How do you live?'

I sighed. That was a good question. How did I live?

I had a rather ordinary two-bedroom apartment with a view of other two-bedroom apartments. My neighbours were mostly noisy, occasionally kind, often busy disembowelling cars in the shared car park below my kitchen. I had window boxes. I had Fez next door, who enjoyed taking out the wheelie bins and lining them up with precision on recycling day. Joan in the flat below, who was a retired teacher who never spoke to anyone if she could avoid it. Melissa and Harvey upstairs, who liked to argue, and next to them, Derek.

Derek had invited me out once for 'a day in the country'. I ended up watching him umpire a cricket match, parked in a canvas chair in front of the pavilion for five hours. I passed the time by trying to think of some domestic emergency that would mean I had to leave, but he had driven us there so I was a bit stuck. Afterwards he made a clumsy comment about 'bowling a maiden over'. We spent the next six months avoiding each other.

Good grief, my life had become pathetic; I had allowed all my enthusiasm and energy to dwindle, my parameters to shrink. I had to do something about that. Perhaps that was why I was enjoying this experience so much, because both Jenny and I had been forced out of our respective comfort zones.

'It's a flat,' I said at last. 'I used to live in a nice house with a big garden. I miss it. I'm looking forward to working on this one.'

'Pierre is young but capable,' he said. 'Sylveste not so much, but he's strong. They make a good team.'

'How old are they, these workers?'

'Benoît is thirty-three, Claud thirty. I think Pierre and his brother are much the same. Why do you ask?'

God almighty, I really was old enough to be their mother.

'Just curious,' I said airily.

I wasn't curious; I was sad. There was yet another reminder of what my life might have been like if I had made different choices.

There was no point agonising about it but what would it have been like to be the mother of one or two of them? How did it feel to be pregnant, to give birth to a new person, to watch them grow from a baby, a toddler, a boy and eventually into the sort of man who could dismantle a patio with a digger?

There was a pause in the conversation while Léo finished up his wine and I twirled the stem of my glass between my fingers.

'Come and see my house, one day,' Léo said suddenly. 'I'm proud of it; I think you might like it.'

'Oh, I don't—'

'Just think about it. Don't say no. Just so you can look around and perhaps get some ideas. The garden is nothing special. Quite wild. As I said, it is in the woods; there are trees with a hammock and there is a stream. It's very pleasant.'

'I'll think about it,' I said, knowing that indeed I would. I would probably lie awake that night thinking about it.

He looked at his watch and then slapped his hands down on his knees, making the sort of moves men make when they are about to leave. The hens clucked and scattered in alarm. Then he looked at me, his eyes very kind.

'I ask because I would like it,' he said, 'because I am a nice person and so are you.'

He reached across the table and gently wiped his thumb under my eye.

'You have a smudge of dirt on your face. The dust gets everywhere when we are knocking down walls.'

I looked at him, hardly able to breathe.

'You don't play cricket, do you?' I asked, a bit hoarse.

'No, I don't.'

Then he smiled. And so did I.

'So, what's happening here?' Jenny said behind us.

I sprang up like a startled cat hearing a balloon burst. Jenny clapped her hands and the chickens fled back into the shrubbery in a flurry of feathery undergarments.

'Nothing,' I said, my voice rather shrill. 'Léo and I were just talking about the building work.'

'Hmm. I see those hens have come back and they have brought

some friends. This isn't on. Have you asked him about the storage units around here?'

'No. You could always ask him yourself, you know.'

Then she huffed, rolled her eyes and turned to Léo.

'We need to put some things into storage. Can you tell me where you would recommend? Somewhere secure.'

'Of course, I know a few places,' he said.

They had a tedious conversation about storage for a few minutes, Jenny taking notes on her little shopping pad with a pencil with an irritating tassel on the end. I watched it dangling and twitching until I felt like biting it off and spitting it onto the ground.

Blast. Léo and I had been having such a nice chat, and I'd begun to think there might be a connection between us that had nothing to do with the renovations.

Eventually Léo offered to ring around and find somewhere nearby, which was a relief as I didn't think my French would have coped with it.

We stood side by side in an uneasy silence and watched Léo's van disappear down the drive.

'I've been thinking,' Jenny said, sitting down in the chair Léo had vacated.

'Oh yes?' I was still slightly cross with her for interrupting us.

'I've been thinking about Ace. I do want to go and see him.'

My annoyance evaporated instantly. What a brilliant idea.

'Great, that's excellent news,' I said.

'I really want to go and see him. I think the way that younger boy – Claud – reminded me of him made me feel very nostalgic.'

'Of course! That's only natural!'

'I sent him an email while I was upstairs asking if it would be convenient.'

'That's marvellous!' I said, clapping my hands.

Jenny shook her head. 'Calm down, for heaven's sake. Do you have to get so hyper over everything at your age?'

'I'm not hyper, I'm just pleased,' I said, composing my face so I looked sensible.

'That look fools no one,' Jenny said knowingly. 'I've seen it too often over the years.'

'Really, genuinely, I am pleased,' I said. 'I bet he misses you too.'

That was a mistake. I should have quit while I was ahead.

'Oh, I don't suppose he does,' Jenny said, looking worried. 'It's probably a stupid idea. He'll be too busy. He'll have his work and his friends. He won't want his mother hanging around embarrassing him.'

'I'm sure you're wrong,' I said.

'How would you know?' Jenny fired back. 'You don't know what you're talking about; you've never had children.'

I took a deep breath and we looked at each other for a moment.

She flushed. 'I'm so sorry, Kit. I didn't mean—'

'No you're right, Jenny. I never had children but if you think it's because I didn't want them then you're sadly mistaken. I would have loved to have children; you know I even thought about IVF at one point but – well, I didn't. So count your blessings because if I *did* have a son I hadn't seen for months and he was only three hours away, nothing *on earth* would stop me from seeing him. Even if I was embarrassing and in the way.'

Jenny had the grace to look uncomfortable.

'I didn't mean what I said,' she said, 'but it's complicated. He had a terrible row with Paul when they last saw each other. And it wasn't a few months ago... it was two years ago.'

'What? You haven't seen your son for *two years*?'

Jenny swallowed hard. 'No. Paul said that Ace needed to apologise first. But Paul said some terrible things: how Ace would never amount to anything, how he was just immersed in an academic life and needed to get out into the real world. That sort of thing. Ace said some awful things back: that Paul was a bully, that he was self-centred and cruel.'

'Well, he is,' I said. 'He's been all of those things; surely you can see that?'

'I was hoping with time Paul would relent but he never did. And if I mentioned Ace, Paul would pull a face and give me the silent treatment. He didn't speak to me for a month once.'

I shook my head in disbelief. 'And you put up with this?'

'What choice did I have?' She started to cry, silently. 'He's my husband.'

I passed her a tissue. 'And Ace is your son. And you are here now and you have plenty of choices. It's never too late to change things. What Paul did, what he's been doing for years, is a sort of abuse.'

'Oh, Kitty—'

'Look, let's not waste any more time thinking and talking about it. Go and pack yourself a bag; take the car; don't forget the snow globe. I'll be fine here on my own. Go and see Ace and stay as long as you like. A week, two weeks. You won't be missing anything here except a lot of noise and mess. Léo is going to be needing some decisions about tiles and sinks and boring stuff. I can deal with all that. As long as you don't complain about what I choose.'

'I wouldn't mind getting away from...' she said, blowing her nose and wiping away a tear. 'I don't much care at the moment. It's all right for you.'

'What do you mean, it's all right for me?'

'Well, you can cope with these things. You always bounce back.'

Was that how she saw me, as someone who brushed off disasters and sprang forward unaffected? Well, it was very far from the truth. Perhaps I just hid it better. Maybe that was my way of coping.

'Er, I'm going to stop you there before you say something else to annoy me. Set off tomorrow morning, first thing. I'll hold the fort here. I'll deal with everything.'

'Okay.' Jenny stood up and then put one hand on my shoulder. 'Thank you, Kitty. I'm sorry for what I said. You know, I always thought I was the successful one, having one long marriage when you had three chronic failures. It was funny; you always seemed to like men and you didn't mind admitting it. Sometimes I'm not sure if I even like – well, never mind. You were so optimistic; you went into every marriage as though you wanted them to work.'

'Well, of course I did. Doesn't everyone? Didn't you? Some men are rubbish, but I still believe most of them aren't. They don't understand us any more than we understand them. But one thing I do know is a boy needs his mum. He's more important than Paul and his ridiculous behaviour. He's an absolute *dinosaur*.'

Jenny blinked a bit, as though she was trying to hold back the tears.

I watched as the hens sneaked back into the garden towards us, irresistibly lured by the prospect of grubs in the earth.

'And talking of dinosaurs, did you know hens are not just *descended* from dinosaurs, but actually *related* to them.'

'Don't talk nonsense,' Jenny said, blowing her nose and doing a bit of throat clearing.

'It's true. I read it in the papers. Imagine if those hens were four times the size. They would be like those things in *Jurassic Park*. Veliocraptors.'

'I think you mean velociraptors,' Jenny said with a shaky laugh.

'Imagine a flock of them all over your garden, with their feathers and claws and beaks. Then you would have something to worry about.'

'You are a fool.' Jenny laughed, giving me a friendly shove. 'What goes on in your head?'

I grinned. 'Well, at least it cheered you up a bit.'

'Thanks. I know you're right about Paul. I can't believe… I'm sorry for what I said.'

'I know. Forget about it. Look, I'm going to see what we can have with our evening meal. We could have salad? Or how about burgers with a side dish of rubble and grit?'

I walked away into the kitchen and she followed me.

She stood looking around rather bleakly for a few minutes and reassured herself that the paintings were blocked off behind a considerable weight of building materials. Then I chivvied her upstairs to pack a bag and although I wasn't sure what I was going to make for our evening meal, I chopped up some onions because that was where a lot of my meals started, and I thought about things.

This trip was making me look at the future in a very different way. It had made me realise I could do just about anything now. Perhaps it was having the same effect on Jenny, making her look at her life too, and seeing it for what it was.

And perhaps getting away from *Paul's requirements*, as she had so delicately put it, hadn't been about sex at all. More about his horrible, controlling behaviour.

I held up the knife I was using and looked at the blade thoughtfully. Then I wondered about stabbing Paul with it. I bared my teeth and lunged slightly forwards, wondering what it would feel like. What would Paul's expression be like? Outrage? Disbelief?

But I've watched *Line of Duty*, *Vera*, *The Bill* and countless other police dramas over the years. They'd know it was me. They'd be at my door in minutes with a battering ram and a search warrant.

13

Jenny left at first light the next morning. That previous evening she received a reply to her email from Ace and, bless him, he sounded really enthusiastic about her visit. I tried very hard not to say *I told you so* too many times.

I made sure she had the snow globe, safely wrapped up in a towel, and I was almost as excited as she was as I waved her off. Then she stopped and reversed up the driveway to remind me about the hens and ask yet again if I was going to be all right on my own and I reassured her yet again that I would be fine.

'Now go! Drive safely. Enjoy yourself! And give him a hug from his mad auntie Kitty! And give him my love!'

She hesitated for a moment.

'I've forgotten my knitting,' she said at last.

'Good,' I said, and she grinned.

'I wasn't enjoying it anyway.'

'Shall I get Pierre to bury it under the new patio?'

She smothered a laugh and didn't answer, just waved and set off up the drive.

I watched, waving until she had disappeared through the gates and then I stood and looked around. It was still early, the sky a delicious pale lavender with the slimmest of crescent moons low over the sea. The air was still, and it was absolutely quiet. A faint scent of thyme and rosemary hung in the air.

Above me were the vapour trails of two planes, heading in from the Atlantic. I scrolled through my phone to find the flight app. One was from Cancún to Liège and the other was JFK to Paris. How marvellous. I loved knowing things like that, wondering about the people on board. Why were they travelling? What would they do when they arrived?

I could be on one of those planes soon, going anywhere in the world, a brave explorer boldly going to seek out new worlds. Ah, wasn't that *Star Trek*? Perhaps I wouldn't go that far.

I thought about Ace. I remembered him as a tiny baby, as a toddler, then in his first stiff school uniform. We had always liked each other. I had been a pushover; he had made me laugh. He'd sent me emails occasionally and pictures of himself with various friends. Up mountains. Surfing. Camping in the Lake District. I had sent him silly presents for his birthday and money for Christmas. He had even come to stay with me a few times when Jenny and Paul had gone away for a weekend. I'd returned him to them, filled with junk food and high on sugar and always received a stern look from Paul and a cautious rebuke from my sister.

Ace and I had both sworn each other to secrecy about the visits to fast food places, the rubbish we had eaten on the sofa in front of all those episodes of *NCIS*. '*Gear up, we've got a dead marine*' became our catchphrase. I'd missed him. I hope he'd missed me.

Soon the workmen would be arriving, bringing with them chaos and noise. I wondered where I could make a start on the garden without getting in Pierre's way.

I made a cup of tea and went back outside to inspect what was left after Pierre's digger had made its mark. There were the begin-

nings of a patio, and beyond that an area of loose earth. The minia-
ture velociraptors were finding it intensely interesting. Further still,
a barrier of shrubs and trees, shielding the pool and the stone
pergola from the wind from the sea. There were odd little walls and
a thick, tangled hedge where winter jasmine was flowering. It didn't
look very promising. And yet the more I looked, the more I could
see possibilities.

I imagined sitting under the pergola, the sunlight filtering
through the trees. Maybe when the work was all finished, we would
have a garden party to say thank you to all the workers. There
would be chairs and a table with some of Sheila's exquisite table
linen, china plates of cake and sandwiches. Maybe even some
bunting. A lazy afternoon of chatter and merriment. Jenny, Léo,
perhaps friends from home. Although, I realised with a bit of a
shock, *this* place could be my home. I hadn't expected that at all. I
mean, there was a difference between liking a place and feeling as
though you belonged there.

The party would be like one of those spreads in a lifestyle maga-
zine, with children running about in Mini Boden and the adults
laughing together over the table and jugs of Pimm's, perhaps. The
men in panama hats, the women in floral tea dresses.

There were flowers beginning to bloom in the untidy soil. The
pebble edges of the flower beds I had noticed were green with moss
and overgrown with weeds. I went to fetch an empty cardboard box
and bent down to pull a few up. I should have known better. It was
really therapeutic and too enjoyable to stop.

Before I realised what I was doing, my tea was cold, the box was
full of green waste, the sun had risen and two hens were standing
watching me. I worked on, fetching some cutlery and a pair of
kitchen scissors to help with the bigger roots. The soil was dark and
rich. Obviously, Sheila really had been a keen gardener because it
didn't look like the soil I had seen in the surrounding fields. It felt

pleasant to be continuing her work and I enjoyed thinking about her, the way she had been so happy, so welcoming.

I thought about Léo's father, planting the rose bush for her birthday. I could almost imagine them, together in this garden, friends and perhaps lovers? I wondered about their relationship, wishing I had known, that I had asked her about it when there was still time. Perhaps they had been friends; maybe they had been more than that to each other, and why not? I liked the thought of Sheila having a significant other, partner, lover, whatever they were called these days. After all, we were always the same age inside, no matter what the outside resembled. Good for Sheila.

Under the trees I found a bed of lily of the valley, growing like a weed. Some cyclamens, all shades of pink and white. Spring bulbs trying to push through the grass. Across the front of the house, the climbing thing that had almost looked dead had started to sprout leaves. I examined it more closely. Now I could tell it was a wisteria, which was very exciting as it was one of my favourites.

By now I had filled my third box of green waste. I hadn't stopped to find gardening gloves, or even proper garden tools, so I was on my knees, grubbing in the dirt with a kitchen knife when the builders turned up.

They hailed me with cheerful shouts, and it was then I realised I was still in my pyjamas. I clutched my dressing gown tightly around me and tried to brush the mud off my knees. The chickens made their usual lumbering dash for the hedge.

'Good morning!' Léo called across the scrubby lawn. 'You're making an early start.'

'Um, er, um,' I said rather wildly. I must have looked an absolute sight. I hadn't even brushed my hair.

I trotted across towards the kitchen door, head down. I was aware Benoît and Claud were standing just behind him.

'Pierre will be here soon,' Léo said. 'I'm sure he has some proper garden tools you could use.'

I looked down at the old, bone-handled dinner knife in my hand and feigned surprise.

'Goodness. I was just...'

Just what? I couldn't think of a suitable explanation, so I made a run for it, back into the kitchen and upstairs to Jenny's bathroom for a shower. Out of the bedroom window, I heard one of them laughing. Great. How to make myself look a complete twit before breakfast.

* * *

I decided the best thing to do was pretend nothing had happened; I was English, and we were well known for eccentricity. I made breakfast and a big mug of tea and took them into the sitting room and closed the door. Ten minutes later, the rumbling of the digger announced Pierre had started work, and the banging and crashing from the downstairs bathroom indicated that Léo was hard at it too.

To be honest, at that moment I would have liked to be able to clear off in the car somewhere, but of course I couldn't. I hadn't ever been one for aimless, brisk walks around the lanes. I could never see the point unless there was a pub at the end of it.

A prime example of this was Boxing Day walks with the family.

Having worked myself to a standstill on Christmas Day, someone – usually Jenny – would always pipe up, '*Let's all put our new scarves and gloves on and go for a ramble. Blow away the cobwebs.*' I mean, why? I would rather be the one left at home in the warm, with my cobwebs, a new bottle of Baileys and a book.

I took a deep breath and went back out into the garden.

Pierre was shifting piles of sand onto the new patio and his brother was raking it flat. They both acknowledged me with a brisk wave.

'Can I have a quick word?' I shouted up at Pierre.

He turned the digger off and it rumbled into silence.

'*Madame?*' he said politely.

'I'd like to borrow some tools, a spade, trowel?' I had no idea what these were in French so I just made vague digging motions and pointed to the flower bed.

'*Les outils de jardin,*' Bertrand called, midway between the house and the skip with yet another load of rubble. '*Elle aimerait en emprunter.*'

Pierre gave one of his brisk nods and clambered down from the cab.

I followed him to his van, and he waved an expansive hand.

'Please, 'elp yourself,' he said. 'I am starting *un feu* – a fire.'

He pointed towards a pile of roots and broken wood and made blowing noises, accompanied by whirling motions with his arms. Then he stopped.

'And, *madame*, you wish to remove the pool? Is this right?'

'No, absolutely not!' I said. 'I never said I did. I want someone to get it cleaned and filled up again.'

'Ah, right. *Mon erreur.* I must have misunderstood. I will make some phone calls. I know a few people.'

Thanking him, I picked a few things out and set to work on the other side of the pool, where they couldn't see me. I worked steadily all morning, digging and pulling up the stuff I didn't recognise. I suppose the best advice would have been to wait and see what was growing, but I was pretty sure the French didn't appreciate thistles and nettles any more than the British did.

It had been a while since I'd done any serious gardening, probably three years if I thought about it. I was older and certainly not as fit as I had been when I had taken on my last garden, but I was really enjoying it. Maybe I wouldn't be able to work at the pace I used to, but there was a lot of satisfaction from clearing away a flower bed and seeing the soil, clean and ready for new planting.

After a while I took a break, sitting on a low wall with a drink of water, and remembered how much I had put into my garden the last time. A beautiful lawn that was scarified every two years and mown into stripes. A metal trellis covered in Generous Gardener roses, the fishpond beyond that with its water lilies and darting fish. There had even been a fountain in the middle, something preten- tious with pouting cherubs that Steve's mother had given us when she had her pond filled in just after we married. She'd done that because she had been afraid her much-anticipated grandchildren would fall into it. Obviously, she hadn't minded if *our* prospective children drowned in our own pond. Well, that was a waste of time. She should have kept it.

I looked up at the trees that were coming into full foliage and wondered how Jenny was getting on. It had been nearly three hours since she'd left; with any luck, she would almost be there for her long-awaited reunion with Ace. There were birds twittering away above me in the branches and every so often one of them would dart down to snatch a worm unearthed by my digging.

I was remembering a time when I was younger and had more energy. As it was, my back was aching, my dodgy hip twanging away like a banjo. Had Steve ever helped me with this sort of thing? I supposed he had but I couldn't remember it. The garden had been 'mine'; he had encouraged the impression with our friends that I was too particular, too territorial, that I didn't want his input. None of that had been true. I supposed while I was pruning and dead- heading and mowing, it had given him plenty of spare time for emails and messages to women with less horticultural interests who preferred their fingernails painted rather than rimmed with dirt.

'How are you getting on?'

It was Léo, standing there in his big working boots, the sleeves of his shirt rolled up. I feasted my eyes on his forearms for a moment.

'Oh, not bad. There's a lot to do, but I'm enjoying it,' I said, looking around at the area I had cleared. It didn't look that much compared with what I still had to achieve but it was a start.

'You are like your aunt. She was always out here. And Madame Jenny? She is out for the day and has left all the work to you?' He gave a mock stern expression.

I laughed. 'She's gone for a week or two, to see her son, at the University of Nantes.'

'Ah, how pleasant for her,' he said. 'So you have no car, Kitty?'

'No, but it's fine. I don't mind,' I said.

'You will be glad to hear that I have finished knocking down the wall. Come and see.'

Glad of the excuse to stop working for a while, I followed him into the house.

Léo stood looking at the shell of the room that was left, the horrible tiles, the toilets and iron baths all gone. He sketched out some shapes with his hands.

'Here will be the shower, the sink, *les toilettes*. There will be storage, the new cupboard. You need to choose flooring. I have brought some books and some samples. Perhaps you would take a look. And do you want a curtain? A blind? *Verre opaque?*'

'No, I'd like wooden shutters. White ones.'

'Good, that is fine. And taps? And window catches? And door handles?'

'Something easy to clean,' I said. 'After all, as Jenny said, it's not Versailles, is it?'

Léo made a few notes in a journal and tucked his pencil behind his ear.

I'd always found that rather a turn-on; it was a sign of a man who was in the middle of doing practical things. I'd dated a carpenter for six months because of that. He was tight-fisted, snored like a walrus with sinus troubles and left me to hoover up all the wood shavings that fell out of his clothing. But every time he tucked that pencil behind his ear, I was enchanted.

If I was honest, I couldn't imagine the bathroom in its finished state at all. It looked quite small, in fact; not what I had been expecting.

Léo seemed to sense my feeling.

'It never looks good at this stage, Kitty, but you will be pleased, I assure you. Ah, before I forget.' He pulled a couple of leaflets out of his pocket. 'These are two places where you can store things. One is the other side of the village, quite convenient, and this one is a few miles away, but cheaper.'

I took them. 'Thank you, I'll take a look.'

'And Madame Jenny will be away for a while?'

Hang on. Why was my sister Madame Jenny and I was just Kitty? I wondered. Did he recognise her as the sensible one who did the driving and wasn't afraid to show her displeasure, while I was the other one, who fell into things and did the gardening in her pyjamas? I would work on cultivating a no-nonsense demeanour.

'I'm not exactly sure. A week perhaps or maybe two. I told her to take as long as she wanted. She hasn't seen her son for about two years.'

Léo shook his head. 'That's a long time. I wouldn't like that. I had trouble getting my boys to move out; it was too easy, too comfortable. But I still see them, nearly every day. And you have children of your own?'

'No, I don't,' I said. 'Is it good, working with your sons? Don't you get on each other's nerves sometimes?'

'Oh, yes.' He pulled a thoughtful expression. 'Of course. But they are very protective of me, now it is just the three of us. Sometimes they try to find me – never mind. Usually we get on well.'

'That's good to hear. And Pierre will find someone to sort out the pool?' I asked.

The pencil was retrieved, and another note was scribbled in his journal.

'Right.' He snapped the journal shut. 'I will get back to work.'

'Me too,' I said.

He walked off, and I watched him go. He really was a fine man. He seemed genuine enough. Thoughtful, hard-working. He didn't look like an alcoholic or a bigamist. Not that I was an expert, obviously. I wondered what his sons were trying to find him. What did Léo need?

* * *

About ten minutes later I saw someone coming up the drive: a furious-looking woman muffled up in a huge, padded coat, furry boots and a woolly hat. She was pushing a pram.

When she saw me, she diverted in my direction.

'*Bonjour*,' I called out cheerfully.

She gave me a narrow-eyed look. '*Bonjour. Mes poules.*'

I thought she'd said 'maypoles' for a moment, and I must have looked a bit dense. Maypoles?

'*Mes poules*,' she repeated, and she flapped her elbows.

'Oh, your chickens! You must be Mimi. Bertrand's wife. *La épouse de Bertrand.*'

'*Oui. Dieu aide moi.* My chickens, yes,' Mimi said, rolling her eyes.

She looked about my age, but her face was weather-beaten and lined. The face of a woman who didn't smile very often.

'They were here earlier on,' I said, looking around.

Could you attract hens? Could you call them to your side, like spaniels?

Mimi sniffed and wiped her nose on the back of her hand. She then started to make chicken-calling noises, which sounded like *chuck, chuck, chuck, coo coo*.

As if by magic, ten hens – *ten* – scurried out from the undergrowth, their legs very high with enthusiasm, and clustered around her boots, pecking hopefully at the fur tops.

Mimi bent over and crooned back at them. I think she was calling them naughty chickens. She pulled out some fossilised crusts of bread from the pocket of her coat and threw them onto the ground, provoking a spirited fight.

'I take them back,' she said at last. She sent me a glowering look from under her woolly hat. 'You hate my chickens.'

'No, absolutely not, I don't hate them,' I said, feeling like David Attenborough's evil sister. 'I was just worried about them.'

'*Ne sois pas ridicule,*' Mimi muttered.

I think she meant I was being ridiculous, and maybe I was. I couldn't exactly tell her that it wasn't me making the fuss, it was my sister, who probably hated all animals equally. Why had our parents insisted on taking us to zoos and wildlife parks?

'Would you like a cup of tea?' I asked, feeling that some sort of hospitality was required of me. '*Une tasse de thé?*'

Another dark look.

'No, well, okay, that's fine.'

Mimi bent and scooped up the hens and deposited them into the pram, where they sat clucking and crooning at each other until the last one was in place and then she turned and pushed them back up the garden, down the drive and out of sight. She only paused to shout something at Bertrand, who shouted back.

I breathed a sigh of relief.

* * *

The days continued uneventfully and I was very happy. I was finding a new routine which was busy and productive.

The Bisset men made a lot of noise and dust in the house, Pierre and Sylveste finished re-laying the patio and I carried on working through the flower beds, weeding and clearing. It was satisfying to look back at what I had done, to see some sort of order coming to the neglected garden. I was achieving something on my own, something I could be proud of. The weather was bright and sunny, and the workers even started to have their mid-morning break on the garden chairs instead of in their vans.

The kitchen was still a place to be avoided, because of the dust. At lunchtime, I usually went into the sitting room and finished up some leftovers from the night before, with cheese, which we seemed to have a lot of. Biscuits seemed to feature heavily in my diet too. Then, always conscious of my five a day, a compensatory apple.

At lunchtime, Léo would usually go out somewhere in his van, picking up various pieces of wood or building materials while his sons sat on folding chairs in the garden and ate chocolate bars and salad out of plastic boxes, their fingers busy on their phones. Bertrand liked to sit on his own, next to Hector, sharing their lunch. Afterwards, Bertrand would tip his hat over his eyes and snooze while Hector, minus the hat, happily passed wind at regular intervals and did the same. It was all very pleasant and satisfying. That life, that work, suited my need to feel I was doing something constructive; I wasn't wasting the days, stuck in a rut of repetitive behaviour.

About an hour later, the sound of Pierre's digger would roar through the silence, showing they were back at work, and I would return to the garden, wanting to finish off clearing the flower beds so at least Jenny could see on her return what I had accomplished. I wanted her to be pleased, with both the garden and with me. I think I was doing it for her as much as for myself. My industry was, in a funny sort of way, a gift to her and to Sheila, too; I liked the thought of that.

It was warmer those days, the sun higher in the sky. I stood up, wishing yet again that I had a kneeler, and stretched my arms out. Pierre and Sylveste were starting to clear the dense undergrowth away from the pool area; Bertrand was trundling another full barrow around to empty it into the skip.

Just as I was resuming my weeding, there was a yelp from Sylveste and quite a bit of shouting.

'What's the matter?' I shouted.

'*Imbécile! Merde!*' Sylveste shouted, hopping around, flapping his arms.

It seemed Pierre had dropped an unexpected rock on his brother's leg. I encouraged him to sit down and unlaced his boot while Pierre told him how stupid he was to get in the way.

'No real damage,' I said after a few minutes, 'just a nasty scrape to his shin. I'll get some disinfectant and a plaster.'

I knew we had both; Jenny had brought a bulky first aid kit that Médecins Sans Frontières might have used.

Typical man, there was an inordinate amount of fuss and flinching from Sylveste as I cleaned his wound and dried it. Then he sat cringing and watching me as I bandaged his leg, occasionally throwing reproachful looks at Pierre, who by then had gone back to work after calling his brother *un bébé pitoyable.*

Still, it was nice to do something for him, and kneeling at his feet, fastening the rather smart bandage with a safety pin, I felt almost maternal.

'Do you need a painkiller?' I said as I stood up rather painfully. I did; my back was definitely feeling sore after all these days of digging.

Sylveste gave a shrug.

'*Un* paracetamol?' I offered.

'*Non, merci*,' he said.

'*Arrête de faire des histoires*,' Pierre shouted from the seat of his digger, which I think meant Sylveste was making an unnecessary fuss.

Still, somehow I could see Pierre felt a bit guilty from the concerned looks he kept giving us, and when Sylveste limped rather dramatically over to continue work, I heard him mutter, '*Fais attention, imbécile*,' which was as close as Pierre was going to get to an apology. Sibling affection was the same the world over, it seemed.

Bertrand, having enjoyed all the drama, had stood watching, smoking a roll-up and making sympathetic noises from the side-lines – '*mon Dieu*', '*zut*' and '*merde*' among them. Then he went off to give Hector's ears an affectionate tug and swig some water before he resumed his barrowing. Obviously, he was used to Hector's intestinal explosions.

Thankfully, Léo returned a few minutes later.

'*Ça va?*' he said, intercepting the black looks between the two gardeners.

'Slight accident,' I said, re-packing the first aid box. 'A nasty scrape to Sylveste's leg; he's fine. I've cleaned him up and bandaged his war wound.'

'Thank you for helping,' he said, 'and look what I have found. On display.'

He held out his phone towards me, to show me a picture he had taken, presumably in a tile warehouse. It showed a tile mural very close to what I had wanted.

'And it's *en vente* – on sale,' he added, 'although they don't have it in the local branch. But I will keep searching.'

'Excellent, that would be ideal; let's go for it,' I said.

I stared at the picture for a few seconds, trying to imagine it on the wall in the shower room. Perhaps it would be there forever, a memento of our time here and of my choice, this moment, long after we had gone. I felt quite sentimental, and ridiculously pleased that he had gone to the trouble of finding it.

'And this,' he added, scrolling through his phone.

We spent the next half an hour looking at pictures of taps and window catches. Door handles and sinks. It was nowhere near as interesting.

'I just want something easy to clean,' I said at last. 'I mean, it's not as though we are going to be living here forever, is it?'

At that point we looked at each other and his expression changed. He frowned slightly, his mouth a tight line.

'No, I suppose not,' he said at last. He shoved his phone back into his pocket. 'I was forgetting. Now I must get on.'

I did a bit more weeding and then, as my hip was beginning to really ache with all the unexpected activity of the past week, I cleaned off the garden tools and put them back in Pierre's van. I should get some of my own. Difficult to do without transport, though. Surely Sheila had some somewhere? Perhaps I should look a bit more carefully.

Late that afternoon it began to rain anyway, so I had a shower to wash off the dirt, and then I stayed inside, wondering how Jenny was getting on, how her reunion with Ace was going. I sent her a text asking if everything was okay. An hour and a half later I got a one-word reply.

Brilliant!!

Oh well, I mean, don't tell me anything, will you?

By then the workers were packing up for the day, storing their tools in the van, washing out buckets. Bertrand had draped a towel over Hector's ears to keep them dry. Hector had eaten his body weight in grass, leaving behind the usual evil aroma and a surprising amount of 'doings' as evidence; I'd have to clear that away before Jenny saw it.

'So,' Léo said, as he slammed the doors of his truck closed, 'we have achieved a great deal this week; I hope you are pleased?'

We went indoors to inspect the day's handiwork. The repairs to the ravaged kitchen wall were done, there was a new skim of pink plaster in the bathroom, too, and the bouquet of electrical wires and pipework sticking out of the bathroom walls and ceiling were starting to connect up to other wires and pipes. There was a new sink and loo propped against the wall, still with blue-and-white protective tape around them. As usual there was the smell of dust and the acidic tang of new plaster.

'Lovely,' I said, unconvinced.

Léo laughed. 'It will be fine, you'll see.'

'I'm sure you're right.'

'So are you lonely here without Madame Jenny?' he asked.

'I'm fine,' I said, 'absolutely fine.'

This was mostly true; I *was* fine, but it would have been nice to have her there too, to see how well everything was progressing.

'It must be hard to cook anything here at the moment. You could join me for dinner?' he said almost carelessly.

'Oh,' I said, a bit taken aback.

We looked at each other for a moment.

'Nothing difficult; I am not exactly cordon bleu. Just a steak, perhaps?' he asked, fussing about with his jacket.

'That would be very kind,' I answered, giving myself some thinking time.

'No, no, not kind. I would enjoy some company for a change, and you might too. You could see the house I built. See if you like what I have done.'

'I'm sure I would,' I said.

Could I go over to his house on my own? For no real reason? I mean, I could cook myself a steak here – if I had one. Which I didn't. Jenny had resisted them when we'd gone to the supermarket in case the staff had somehow muddled up the beef with something equine.

'And I could show you where the storage units are; I pass them on the way here.'

'That would be helpful,' I said.

His face brightened. 'Then' – he made a sweeping motion towards his truck – 'let's go.'

I was a bit startled. 'You mean now?'

He wagged his head from side to side. 'Well, yes.'

I took a deep breath. I wasn't exactly prepared for this. Not the prospect of leaving the house, getting into a handsome, relative stranger's truck, going who knew where. I couldn't possibly do that. He might seem a reasonable man here, at work, but he might turn into something very different when he wasn't. Perhaps this was a bad idea. I would make an excuse, remember something I had to do. I could put him off for a few days.

'Okay then,' I said, 'I'll get my bag.'

That was me all over. Sometimes I wonder if I'd learned anything at all.

14

Léo's house was down a steep driveway and mostly hidden by trees. I could see why he had chosen to live there; it was a beautiful spot. On one side of the hallway there was a living room, which was large and furnished with comfortable sofas. I made a mental note to ask where he had bought them; Sheila's looked even more raddled in comparison.

On the other side was a splendid kitchen with a dining area. Everywhere was functional and practical but a bit lacking in heart, to my way of thinking. I suppose it was a man's house, devoid of softness, cushions, decoration, pictures. In my opinion, the huge slice of oak that had been polished and used as a mantlepiece over the fireplace cried out for some candles. The beams should have fairy lights strung around them; the small table placed near to an armchair needed a lamp.

I had always found it interesting to see how men on their own organised their lives. The things they bought, the way they organised their fridge, the colours they chose. The lights in their rooms were either on or off. It was the same with the radio; there was no middle ground of table lamps and background music. They seldom filled the ice trays; they bought boring bed linen, usually reduced in the sale, just because it didn't have flowers on it. Not that I was planning to investigate that particular theory.

It was very different from the way women did things; not better, just different. Men equated tidying up with putting things into piles. And there at the end of the kitchen worktop was a pile of brochures for building materials and workwear. There was a plastic box of unopened post on the sideboard; next to the phone was a big mustard stone pot holding pens printed with logos from construction firms.

So, no evidence of the uber-fit, kayaking partner I had imagined. Unless she was even more minimalist than he was.

There was a fabulous view of a tumbling stream through the windows at the back of the house. Léo had constructed a long, raised veranda to take full advantage of it, furnished with the sort of Adirondack chairs I had always wanted. Down below us, in the dusk, birds fluttered around, dipping their beaks into the water.

'This is lovely,' I said at last. 'What a fantastic spot. No wonder you chose to live here.'

'I love it.' He took a deep breath of the clear air. 'There is nowhere better.'

We stood for a moment and looked out through the trees. Everywhere felt so green and full of energy. Far beyond them I could see the lights of a village beginning to glow, which were comforting in this rather isolated spot.

He turned to go back into the house.

'I can offer you wine, or beer if you prefer?' he said.

'Red wine would be lovely,' I said. 'After all, I'm not going anywhere.'

That came out wrong. I meant to say *I'm not driving anywhere*. I cringed inwardly, hoping he hadn't noticed.

'I cannot offer you the sort of wine you are used to drinking,' he said with a grin, 'but it is very good.'

'Anything's fine,' I said. 'I'm not at all fussy.'

Why did everything I said sound wrong and slightly silly?

'I hardly ever drink white wine; it gives me heartburn,' I added for good measure. Yes, because he needed to know that.

He pulled out two wine goblets, which were the sort of greenish, recycled glass I could have predicted, and poured us two generous measures.

'Come and sit by the fire,' he said. 'It won't take me a moment to get it going.'

He put a flame to the kindling and in a few minutes the fire was blazing cheerfully, a lovely sound of crackling wood and the scent of applewood. I sat on one of the sofas, my head resting at just the right place on comfortable cushions; I really needed to ask where he had bought them. They were so relaxing, not like Sheila's, which tended to repel the sitter and shed cushions in all directions rather than happily accommodate anyone.

'So how long have you lived here?'

'About four years. When my father died I needed a change from the village, more peace.'

He made it sound as though he used to live in the middle of Manhattan, whereas the nearby village was rather a sleepy place. I wondered what he would think of my flat with the traffic streaming outside the front door and cats fighting behind the bins out the back.

'Well, you certainly have it here,' I said.

I sipped my wine, enjoying the rich, fruity taste. I shifted a bit, wincing as my hip twinged.

'Are you not comfortable?' he said.

'Perhaps I overdid it a bit in the garden,' I admitted. 'I should be more careful—'

I didn't add *at my age*, because I didn't want to seem like an old crock.

I didn't feel or think or act my age, as Jenny repeatedly warned me, so I wasn't going to start behaving like an old woman now.

'That is why you are paying Pierre and Sylveste,' he agreed. 'Sylveste is too fond of breaks and cigarettes. You should ask him to help you more. That's what he's there for.'

'You're right. Where can I get some gardening tools? I'm sure Sheila must have had some but I haven't found them and I can't keep relying on Pierre.'

'There are several places nearby, but I can let you have some if you would like that?'

'I can't take yours,' I said.

'Of course you can. My garden is wild anyway; it takes me very little time. I will get them now. Come and see what you want.'

Blast, that meant actually getting up. I shuffled forwards on the sofa and stood up. My hip gave a congratulatory ping and I let out a muffled yelp that I quickly turned into an exclamation of surprise.

Léo turned to look enquiringly.

'I've just seen your – er – wood basket. It's amazing!'

He looked puzzled, as well he might. The kindling was just dumped in a large wooden crate with *Vin Ordinaire* printed on the side.

We went through the kitchen and into the garage. A place of order and neatness, which somehow seemed to convey more personal touches than his house. There was a row of woollen beanies pegged up on one wall, branded with what I assumed were building suppliers. There was an impressive scarlet multi-drawer of tools on wheels and beyond that were ordered racks of shelves and labelled plastic boxes. Plus a long, solid workbench with clamps on the end. I resisted the urge to fiddle with anything; there were a lot of things there that were sharp. I'd be bound to get my finger caught in something or cut myself.

Léo pulled a couple of boxes out. 'Here,' he said, 'help yourself. Or you could just take a box? The bigger tools are here.'

He pointed to a row of hooks on the wall where spades, post-hole diggers and garden forks were neatly lined up.

'Marvellous,' I said.

His garden tools were not like mine had been. They were clean, polished, immaculate and, on closer inspection, oiled. I thought back to the garden shed I used to have back in the day. My gardening equipment had been slung into a broken recycling box any old how. Covered in dried mud and usually rusting. I lost a pair of secateurs once a month on average. I'd have to raise my game.

I chose a few things and he took them straight out to his car and put them in the boot.

'Now, let's eat,' he said. 'You must be hungry. How do you like your steak? I like mine *à point*. Medium rare.'

He pulled a pan out of a cupboard and steaks wrapped in white paper out of the fridge.

'Medium to well done?' I said. 'What's that in French?'

'Perhaps *bien cuit*?'

'Not leather, anyway,' I said, and he laughed.

I think it was probably the first time in my life that a man had cooked a meal for me when he wasn't being employed to do so. I didn't count the barbecues Steve used to do; they were events when I did all the shopping, preparation and clearing up and he took all the credit. And seemed to think that it excused him from any further culinary or domestic efforts for weeks.

This was very exciting. I sat on one of the wooden stools and watched Léo, while I drank my wine. There seemed to be a great deal of butter involved in this cooking process and a lot of flicking and dousing too. And then he put the whole pan into the oven.

'Two or three minutes,' he said. 'Would you like bread? Salad?'

'Bread will be fine,' I said. To be honest, I'd had more than enough salad recently. 'It's the one thing I can't get hold of without a car. It's too far to get to the supermarket. I suppose I could walk into the village, but by the end of the day I'm a bit tired.'

'Well, this is a problem that is easily solved. I can drive you to the market in the village; it's on three times a week and is much better than the supermarket. Fresh things from local people. Wonderful bread. I'm surprised you haven't been there already.'

'I'd like that very much,' I said.

'It's a date.' He smiled, and I could feel my face growing rather warm.

He put the steaks onto hot plates and then whisked up the buttery juices with cream, because it obviously wasn't fattening enough, and a slug of brandy. The smell was wonderful and the whole thing had taken no time at all.

He put a plate in front of me and for a second I probably resembled a Bisto kid, crouched over, savouring the aroma.

'I'm very impressed,' I said as he topped up my wine.

'It's nothing,' he said modestly. 'You can see how easy it is.'

'Trust me, it's not easy; I've never eaten one as good as this.'

We talked over our meal. He told me about Benoît's long-term love interest, Louise, who he was hoping would become a permanent fixture, and about Claud, who had recently broken up with his girlfriend of six years.

'He is *un âme misérable*. A miserable soul at the moment. It's hard to get a polite word from him outside work, always moping and complaining. I wish I knew someone I could introduce him to. He keeps talking about going to Paris; I can't see the point in that. Too many of the young people are leaving the village.'

'You never know who you are going to meet,' I said.

'That's true.'

We grinned at each other.

We chatted quite easily while we ate, mopping up the delicious sauce with French bread, which was of course excellent in its own right. I'd noticed that; French people were either going to get the bread, taking the bread home or eating it. I didn't blame them. No wonder they'd had a revolution over it.

'So tell me about yourself, Kitty. How are you enjoying this adventure?' he said.

We were still sitting at the table, our plates empty, and I was resisting the last hunk of bread left in the basket.

'Oh, there's nothing much to tell,' I said evasively. 'No children, divorced, single now, I live in a flat that I don't like, I work part time as a secretary in an estate agency because otherwise I would go mad.'

God, that sounds dire.

He tilted his head to one side. 'I think that is only part of the story?'

'Well, it's the edited highlights,' I said.

Highlights? Don't make me laugh.

'And your ex-husband?'

Which one?

'Has a new much younger partner and a baby due any time now,' I said. 'I assume he's happy.'

'He cannot be happy,' Léo said firmly, 'not without you. You'll see. He will be back, asking for your forgiveness.'

'I don't think so,' I said, pulling a face at the prospect, 'and if he did, I would have nothing to say to him.'

'So that is that?'

'Exactly.'

'*Quel fou,*' he said. What an idiot.

I sat savouring the compliment, the fact that someone thought the loss of me was a bad thing. It didn't tie in with the insults slung in my direction in the past.

I was difficult and moody and boring (Frank, the barely functioning alcoholic).

I was hidebound by outdated social conventions and worthy of pity (Oliver, the bigamist).

I didn't understand men and everything was my fault (Steve, the serial philanderer).

So, for someone to express approval of me made a pleasant change.

'Thanks for that,' I said. 'That's kind.'

'And do you like France?'

'I love it,' I said, 'what I've seen of it. And I love Sheila's house. It feels so welcoming and friendly. I felt that as soon as I went in.'

'I'm so pleased! But perhaps I can take you out, while your sister is away? Just for a change of scene. For example, Concarneau is delightful. So is Saint-Malo, Dinard. The coast here is dramatic and lovely. Have you visited the Côte de Granit Rose? No? I know several places where the view is wonderful and there is excellent shellfish to eat.'

'But what about the building work?'

He grinned. 'Even I don't work at the weekend, Kitty.'

I smiled back, blushing properly this time. 'Then yes, I'd like that a lot.'

'Good, now, do you need some cheese and fruit?'

Well, of course I didn't *need* cheese and fruit, no one did, but that had never stopped me eating it.

I couldn't resist a ripe Brie in particular, or a salty Roquefort, and he had both.

By the time we'd finished I was full, slightly tiddly because I had drunk most of the wine, and very relaxed. I wondered if Léo was the type to take advantage of this and what I would do if he did.

He stood up and cleared our plates away.

'I must take you home,' he said. 'It's getting late.'

I looked at my watch, rather astonished. It was, too; it was nearly ten o'clock.

'That would be great,' I said, wondering if it was.

Had I been expecting something more from this evening? He seemed to like me, but did he like me *in that way*? Honestly, it felt like the same train of thought that had dogged me since I was a teenager. Why was I always so desperate for a man to like me? Was he just being polite to a customer or did he have another motive?

Hmm. A man with *other motives* was not really something I was comfortable with at the moment, so in the end I felt quite happy to be collecting up my things, wrapping my scarf around my neck and clambering up into his truck to go home. There was always tomorrow. Or the next day.

The night was very black and dark then, the headlights piercing the shadows between the trees. At home, the drive leading up to Jolies Arbres looked rather sinister. I wished I'd left some lights on in the house. I imagined myself walking to the front door, using the torch on my phone to show the way.

'I'll bring the garden tools tomorrow, and for now just see you safely in,' Léo said, 'just to be sure.'

Well, that was nice.

Would he kiss me? Perhaps just in a friendly way? The French went in for pecks on the cheek, didn't they? I wouldn't mind a couple of those.

But all that happened was he waited until I had stepped indoors, and then he called 'Goodnight' as he returned to his truck. So maybe he didn't like me in *that* way. Well, at least now I knew. Which was a relief.

I think.

As I went into the house, my foot knocked against something. A parcel, no, a cardboard box left in the porch.

I picked it up and took it into the kitchen. Inside was a beautiful loaf of sourdough bread and a jar of green jam. Green jam? Unusual. Where had this come from?

15

After I had made sure the house was secure, all the windows locked and the doors bolted, I made a cup of tea and went upstairs to Jenny's room. I'd taken an executive decision to move in there while she was away. Her bed was just as uncomfortable as mine downstairs, but at least there wasn't grit everywhere. For the first few days after the demolition had started, it had been like sleeping in a cat litter tray.

Outside, the night was dark, no car headlights in the distance, no street lamps glowing. The sky was heavy with cloud, no stars or fledgeling moon. I stood at the window, looking out at the black dinosaur shape of Pierre's digger and the trees at the end of the garden. There could be people out there creeping up to the house with ropes and guns. Somehow, I doubted it. If hundreds of pounds' worth of artwork and vintage wine had remained unmolested for a year when the house was empty, I was probably safe. Safer indeed than I had felt at home, where there were always random burglaries, graffiti from the local vandals – who all thought they were Banksy – and the occasional tyre-slashing from someone's rejected boyfriend. Still, I should have left the landing light on.

Ten minutes later, I sat up in bed with my tea and took a moment to enjoy the peace of the place. The occasional creak of the old timbers, and the warmth of the house, shielded by the thick, stone walls. I wondered how Jenny was getting on.

Then I thought about Léo. It was no use; I really liked him. He was tall, handsome and capable. And kind, and generous and thoughtful. And had a French accent that would make a tax return sound interesting.

There must be a *but*. There had to be. I'd married three sociable, good-looking men who'd all had a *but* firmly attached to them. A whisky bottle, a wife and a pregnant girlfriend, respectively.

Léo seemed different. He listened to me as though he was genuinely interested in my views. He didn't roll his eyes at my opinions and try to point out where I was wrong, or glaze over when I was talking. He had laughed at my jokes. He cooked well, his house was slightly spartan but clean and tidy. He hadn't pounced on me. We seemed to like each other.

Thinking about it, I hadn't been pounced on for years. I'd begun to think my best pounce-worthy days were behind me. But Léo had made me wonder. Perhaps they weren't after all. And more significantly, I was beginning to wonder if that was quite so important.

I put my bedside light out and snuggled down to think a bit more. This, predictably, led to me having an exceedingly rude dream about him that involved whipped cream, a hen in a stripy jumper, Pierre's digger and then a distant rattling noise. I woke up in rather a fluster to realise it was my phone, vibrating its way off the bedside table.

'Kitty, is that you?'

'Jenny.' I pushed my hair out of my eyes. 'What's wrong? What time is it? Are you okay?'

'I'm fine. Sorry it's so early. I tried ringing you last night, but you didn't answer. I was worried.'

Hmm. What was the best course of action here? To admit I had been at Léo's house and prompt all sorts of scorn? Or keep quiet about it?

'I had an early night,' I said, chickening out big-time, 'sorry. Are you all right?'

'I'm fine. I'm sorry I haven't been in touch. I'm having such a nice time with Ace. We've been talking non-stop. Except when he has to go and lecture to the students, of course. He's so happy here and he's made loads of friends. He's got a really nice apartment too. Two bedrooms and two bathrooms so we don't fall over each other in the morning, and there are such a lot of really lovely cafés and restaurants nearby, we haven't had to cook at all. And the coffee is really excellent; I don't know how I put up with all that decaf rubbish for so long.'

'That's wonderful. You do sound in good form,' I said, because she did. She sounded really happy. It did my heart good to hear it.

'I'm going to stay a few more days if that's okay with you? I do feel a bit guilty leaving you all on your own, but it's the Easter break coming up, and Ace wants to take me on a little road trip. He says there are some wonderful places to see along the Loire Valley, and Tours is supposed to be nice. He's grown up such a lot; I'm so proud of him.'

'Sounds fantastic,' I said. 'I'm so happy for you.'

'You don't mind, do you? I mean, say if you do.'

'No, I don't mind. Give him my love!'

'And what is happening there? I hope you are behaving yourself?'

This sounded more like the old Jenny.

Thinking of last night's unexpected dinner, chat and resulting dream, I thought it best not to say too much.

'Oh, for heaven's sake!' I said. 'I'm absolutely fine. But just so you know, I've moved into your room because my bed seems to be full of gravel. So make sure you let me know when you're coming back so I can change the sheets.'

'So in fact, at the moment it's helpful if I'm *not* there,' Jenny said happily.

'Very helpful.'

'That's good. I feel better about staying on now.'

'And Paul is managing to survive without you? Microwave still working? Sink plunger run to earth?'

Still not able to find his arse with both hands?

Jenny gave a heavy sigh. 'I think so. He rings me every day, asking what I'm doing, so I've had to make things up. I haven't dared to tell him I'm in Nantes with Ace. He'd probably have a fit.'

I briefly imagined Paul in his new, sludge-green cardigan, rolling on the floor having a tantrum, and shuddered.

'Let's hope not,' I said.

'So if Paul rings you, for heaven's sake don't tell him where I am.'

'He's never going to ring me, I can assure you. But if he did, I'd just come out with it. Why shouldn't you see Ace? You're his mother, Jenny.'

'Well... look, I'd better go; Ace is calling. He's made breakfast. Well, he hasn't actually made it. There is a patisserie just round the corner that does the most fantastic pastries. I could live on them. Much better than a bowl of budgie grit and soy milk like we have at home. He sends his love, by the way. Sorry, I must dash! Have a good day!'

I couldn't have been more pleased for her; she sounded like the Jenny I had known. She was breaking out of her comfort zone, trying to change things for the better, I could see that, and after everything, it must have taken a great deal of courage. And if she could do it, so could I.

Well, that was all very unexpected. She would be casting aside her cardigans next.

* * *

I spent the weekend lazing about and enjoying the peace and quiet. I even managed to read the best part of a book about Brittany, send some emails to friends back in England and do a bit of internet surfing.

Occasionally I watched the little black-and-white television and tried to understand what was going on. There seemed to be a lot of people arguing, whether it was on the news or during dramas. Then I watched a very dark thriller where everyone was smoking, shrugging and snarling. There was a lot of sport, too, and *Tintin*.

On Sunday morning, I went out into the garden and did some pottering about, looking in the battered old shed behind the house, which, disappointingly, was empty apart from cobwebs and dried leaves. There was another little brick building next to the pool, which was full of pipes and dangerous-looking things. I assumed they were to do with the filters or pump or something.

I even hauled myself up onto Pierre's digger and waggled the levers a bit. I wondered how hard it was to drive it, but fortunately he had taken the keys with him so I didn't get the chance to risk it. Probably just as well; knowing me, I would have pressed the wrong lever and crashed into the house or careered off across the garden and into the pool. How would I explain that on Monday morning?

I went to bed early on Sunday night, snuggling down on the twanging mattress with a cup of tea and a couple of reheated crois-sants I'd found in the freezer. And I thought, as I had for a large part of the weekend, about Léo and wondered if he was thinking about me. Probably not; I mean, why would he? But he might be.

We had shared a meal and a pleasant evening, with nothing

terribly remarkable about it. Except Léo had laughed at my jokes and I had laughed at his. But, small as that might sound, I'd come to realise that it was important. Having been married to Steve, a man who'd told me on more than one occasion that I was round the bend, and Frank, who'd found nothing funny until he was several whiskies into the day.

I realised that I was really looking forward to seeing Léo the following morning. I mean, *really* looking forward. Surely, I was too old to have that sort of a crush on someone. And with my lifelong inability to select a decent husband or boyfriend – perhaps 'man friend' was a better term to use – I probably shouldn't even be bothering at all. But I'd never been able to help myself; I just liked men. And they seemed to like me.

Would he say anything about Friday evening? How much he had enjoyed it, how we must do it again some time soon.

What should I wear? Should I try harder for a change? Or should I just stay exactly as I was?

* * *

I woke up early the following morning, showered and dressed. I'd got a bit sloppy about things recently and generally pulled on my shapeless old joggers and various tops to work in the garden. That day, however, after the events of last Friday, and my restless night thinking about what to say to Léo when I saw him, I made a bit more of an effort. I found some reasonably smart jeans and a fairly new T-shirt. Then I tied my hair back and actually put on some mascara. And some of Jenny's organic, fair-trade, free-range moisturiser, which she had left on the kitchen windowsill.

All those hours in the garden meant I was beginning to tan, and thanks to all the exercise the jeans were a bit less tight than the last time I'd worn them. I didn't look bad. All good. Reasonably smart but not like I was making too much of an effort.

I mopped the floor, which was still a bit dust-smeared even after three goes at it over the weekend, and then chucked two more croissants into the oven and opened the pot of green jam that had been left in the porch. I chose to believe it was lime marmalade; it could have been something else. After a few bites I realised I was ridiculously on edge, waiting for the workers to arrive. How old was I? Twelve?

I hoped I wouldn't suddenly remember the rather fruity details of my Léo-based dream of the other night, and if I did, I wouldn't blush too much.

Then, in a gilding-the-lily moment, I went to slap on a bit more moisturiser and, of course, this time I managed to get some in one eye. Flipping heck, it might be wholesome and natural and ethically sourced, but it didn't half sting.

With many loud oaths and much wailing, I stumbled over to the sink, plunging one foot into the bucket full of dirty water I had left in the way and knocking the mop over so it clonked me on the forehead. Then I slapped a handful of water over my face and of course the front of my T-shirt and dabbed at myself with a rather grubby tea towel. As I looked up, bleary-eyed and red in the face, I realised Léo had just arrived and was standing at the door looking at me, his expression horrified.

'Are you okay?' he said. 'What's happened? Are you crying? Have you hurt yourself?'

'No, I'm absolutely fine,' I spluttered.

It must have looked as though I was mad or tearful or both. And there were streaks of mascara on the tea towel, which wasn't a good sign. Who knew where the rest of it was? Everyone knew that an apparently dried-up mascara wand still had the ability to leave a splodge the size of the Isle of Wight where it was not wanted.

'Can I help?' he said, edging towards me.

'No, I'm... I'll just... something in my eye.'

'Let me see.' He held up my chin with one hand and peered at me. 'I can't see anything; does it hurt?'

'Oh it's just... nothing... I'll go and...'

I stumbled off towards the stairs, tripping over a length of wood on the floor and nearly knocking myself out on the fridge. If all else failed after this, I could always get a job in Gerry Cottle's Circus.

'Everything is fine,' I called cheerfully as I made good my escape.

Yes, my effort to look slightly smart and unexpectedly attractive had failed spectacularly. One of my eyes was bloodshot and streaming with tears and my T-shirt was splattered with water. There was also a huge smear of mascara down my cheek. I didn't know why I bothered.

I mopped myself up, changed my T-shirt and started again. Outside, the roar of the digger announced Pierre's arrival, followed by the frenzied braying of Hector, the Trojan prince, as Bertrand rode up the drive.

Honestly, it was like living in the middle of an episode of *Jackass*.

16

I loitered at the sink, doing the washing-up and scrubbing at the wooden draining board. Who knew what lurked in its cracked surface? Plague or botulism, perhaps. I should ask about replacing it.

Just after eight thirty, Benoît and Claud turned up in their van and stood watching the digger, smoking and muttering. Ten minutes later, the triumphant braying from Hector that had announced Bertrand's arrival stopped, and shortly afterwards I could hear Bertrand laughing.

By then my heart was thumping with anticipation and I was cleaning the hob, after first making the mistake of spraying some kitchen cleaner onto a lit burner. The resultant steam was akin to tear gas and I had to go back out into the hall to have a choking fit.

After the air had cleared, I composed my face into a welcoming expression and opened the kitchen door.

'Oh. Has Léo gone?' I said airily, looking around.

Sylveste flicked his cigarette butt into the rubble bucket.

'No, he has gone to Morlaix. A pick-up. *Il cherche des carreaux.*'

He pointed to a box by the door. 'He also left you this – for the garden?'

Cue disappointment. Pick-up of what? I didn't like to ask in case it was something embarrassing. Haemorrhoid cream or new underpants.

'Oh, I see. Well, never mind. I must get on. How is your leg, by the way?'

With a mournful face, Sylveste pulled up his trouser leg and showed me the same bandage that I had put on last Friday. It didn't look quite so impressive. In fact, it looked as though he might have used it to clean his car over the weekend.

'Well, that's no good, Sylveste,' I said. 'It's filthy; you should have changed the dressing!'

He turned the corners of his mouth down like a sulky child. 'Jeanette was going to get some plasters, but she forgot. And she doesn't like the injury. The blood. *Une phobie du sang.*'

He looked up at me with tragic puppy eyes.

'Oh, for heaven's sake. Well, you could have got some. Men are allowed into shops to buy things too, you know. Come into the kitchen,' I said, 'and we'll look at it.'

With all the enthusiasm of a dog going to the vet, he followed me.

'Should I take...' Sylveste motioned towards his belt.

Take his trousers off?

'No, absolutely not!' I said quickly. 'Just roll the trouser leg up.'

We spent the next half an hour removing the dressing, which of course had stuck to the graze. I didn't know the French equivalent to 'big wuss', but that was what Sylveste was. There was a lot of wincing and protest from him before we eventually got it off. Underneath there was an unremarkable and scabby wound. I gave it a wash with some disinfectant, provoking another bout of whimpering and flinching from Sylveste, and 'Don't be such a baby' from me, which made the other three, who were clustered around the kitchen door snort with laughter.

'You need a new dressing,' I said, 'because it's healing okay but it needs some protection from all the dirt and mud. I'll get the first aid kit.'

I went upstairs to find it, and when I came back downstairs the three of them were all standing around, peering at Sylveste's shin and tutting.

They sprang away like naughty children when I appeared.

Then there was more fidgeting and gasping from the patient while the other three, round-eyed, sucked in their cheeks and winced in sympathy.

When I'd finished, they all clapped Sylveste on the back as though he'd had his appendix out on the kitchen table. It was rather endearing, actually; men might be able to build patios and land a man on the moon but nearly all of them were fazed by the sight of blood, especially their own.

'*Dis merci, Maman,*' Pierre said in a silly voice as Sylveste pulled his trouser leg down over the new bandage. 'Thank you, Mummy.'

Mummy?

Sylveste aimed a punch at his brother and said something that sounded rude.

Still no Léo. I wondered how long it took to get to Morlaix and how long it would take to get back, but I could hardly ask.

'Off you go then,' I said briskly, washing my hands and chucking the old bandage into the bin.

'Thank you, Keetee,' Sylveste said sheepishly.

So, I was even Kitty to them.

It was by then nearly ten o'clock and no one had done a stroke of useful work, me included.

Pierre started up his digger again and the noise mercifully faded as he trundled off down the garden towards the thicket around the pool. It took him no time at all to rip up huge chunks of brambles and add them to his growing bonfire. Underneath, the earth was riddled with all sorts of stuff. Spindly grass, some bulbs pushing optimistically through, several empty wine bottles and a pair of sunglasses.

I wondered about the story behind these things. Had Sheila been in the habit of lazing beside the pool in her sunglasses with Léo's father on the next-door sunbed, both of them knocking back wine and chucking the empty bottles into the shrubbery? It didn't seem likely. Had it been some of her students enjoying a lazy afternoon in the sunshine, their sketches forgotten?

There was a huge hydrangea bush, just starting to bud, struggling under the brambles and bindweed. I'd noticed a lot of similar bushes in the area; I hoped it would have blue flowers. Pierre declared it would. *À cause de la terre*, which I think meant the soil was the right acidity.

I could now see the neat area of paving stones surrounding the pool, which were in good condition but green with algae and very slippery. I was exonerated; it was no surprise I had fallen in. Perhaps Léo had a pressure washer I could borrow. Then, of course, I wondered where he was and pretended to be stretching out my back so that I could sneak a look at the driveway. Perhaps he wasn't coming back today at all? Maybe he had been uncomfortable on Friday evening although I couldn't imagine why he should have been. Not many people could be offended when someone admired their home, complimented their cooking and laughed at their jokes.

I messed about for a bit with some of the tools Léo had lent me, digging up roots and moving broken branches, which I added to Pierre's bonfire. It was going to be like an Armada beacon by the time he lit it. I really could see I was beginning to make progress. The stone flower beds by the house were cleared and ready for something to go in them. By lunchtime I could see the whole pool for the first time and Pierre stood admiring it and then going to appreciate his bonfire. It was very exciting, even if the pool was still filled with lumps of mud and dead leaves.

I could almost imagine myself in a new, slightly retro swimming costume, possibly with polka dots, walking into the shallow end and swimming up and down, doing an elegant crawl like something out of an Agatha Christie episode. Looking at the pool then, the prospect seemed a long way off. I would have to remind Pierre about the person who could sort it out. Surely it would need some sort of chemical additives to stop it from turning into a swamp.

Almost as though he had read my mind, Pierre turned, held an imaginary phone to his ear and shouted across at me.

'*La piscine* – I will ring my friend Hugo. I will ask him to call.'

I gave him a thumbs-up sign. 'Excellent!'

It was nearly lunchtime by then and I was getting a bit bored, if I was honest. There was so much to do and no one to chat with, no one to admire my work. I could have done with a dip in the pool, too; I was hot and tired, my hair sticking to my face. I was probably red-faced and sweaty. I needed a break.

Happily, at that moment, my phone rang.

'Kitty, it's me. You'll never guess!'

'Jenny, how are you getting on? What won't I guess?'

'I'm in Angers!'

'No, I wouldn't have guessed that. Is it nice?'

'It's glorious,' Jenny said. 'Do you know it's the seat of the Plantagenet dynasty? There's a massive castle.'

'Fabulous,' I said, pulling a bit of bramble out of my hair.

'We are going to have lunch in a minute. Ace has found a really wonderful place, and, great excitement, a *special friend* of his from the university is going to join us. Her name is Marie-Odile. I think she might be French. We are right by the castle, sitting outside under a parasol, and I'm drinking wine! At lunchtime! Ace sends his love, by the way; he's looking forward to seeing you again soon. He said to tell you to gear up. I'm not sure what that means but he said you would know. Ace says his friend teaches at the university and they often meet up. I can't wait to meet her.'

'How exciting,' I said. 'Give him my love.'

By then I was perched on a low garden wall overlooking the pool, wondering if I had perhaps overdone things. Blanche the hen wandered out of the hedge, pecking and clucking, and was swiftly followed by five others. This wasn't the plan. I would have thought Mimi would have put them into detention at least.

'And the wine is really lovely, too. I feel quite spoiled. And Ace loved the snow globe; you were right to suggest it. We are staying in Angers tonight and then you'll never guess where we are going tomorrow!'

'Probably not,' I said, trying to sound jolly.

Two of the chickens had a brisk fight over a bug in front of me. I flapped a hand at them to be quiet.

'Azay-le-Rideau! Isn't that amazing? Ace says he's always wanted to go there. He has booked us a beautiful hotel, with a spa. And he says if I want a massage, I can book one – his treat – to make up for missing my birthday last year, although he did send a nice card.'

'That's marvellous.'

'You were so right when you said I should come and see him. It's like a dream. We get on so well, he's such good company and I understand now why he fell out with Paul. Honestly, that man has a lot to answer for; he said some terrible things, really upsetting.'

I gave a silent, triumphant fist pump and did a silly little sitting-down dance. At last she was seeing things differently. And I knew from personal experience that having realised your husband was a nasty piece of work, it was impossible to unthink it. There was always that little tic at the back of your mind that said, *Ah yes, but remember when...*

'Well—'

'I think Ace plans to stay here for the foreseeable future. He's really enjoying it and his French is brilliant, of course; it makes everything so much easier.'

'Yes, I bet it does—'

I made shooing motions with my free hand as Blanche came over to peck hopefully at my shoelaces.

'He's really spoiling me, not that he has to, of course, but it's so relaxing and just what I needed. He's so thoughtful and kind.'

I stood up, my spine and my hip twanging away like 'Duelling Banjos'. I needed a drink of water if nothing else. Benoît and Claud were rummaging for something in their van, which meant I could get into the kitchen without falling over someone.

'And then after that Ace has suggested we go to La Rochelle, which is on the coast, of course. It's Easter this weekend, don't forget! Ace says that Easter eggs are delivered by the church bells, not by the Easter bunny. And traditionally they eat lamb, which will make a change because Paul has always refused to eat it. Talking of which, you haven't heard from him, have you?'

'Paul? No, not—'

God forbid.

'Thank heavens for that. Anyway, I'd better go, I think Ace is coming back. I'll send you some pictures if I remember. I'll be in touch!'

And with that she ended the call.

Yes, lovely, glad you're having a great time, being spoiled and having massages and posh meals. The hens send their regards. Me? Oh, I'm fine. I may get the mud out from under my fingernails in time for Christmas. And the scratches on my arms will heal eventually. Don't give me a second thought...

I was being mean. And grumpy. I was genuinely glad for her, but it was a little difficult to bear, imagining her wearing smart clothes and proper shoes, sitting at some chic bistro knocking back the wine and eating exciting meals when I was contemplating left-over something for my evening meal and the remains of some vegetable soup I'd made three days ago for my lunch. Jealous? *Moi?*

Not a bit.

The kitchen was still in a right state and, of course, as Léo still hadn't returned, the downstairs bathroom was still literally a building site. The familiar film of dust was settling over every surface and the water was turned off so I couldn't fill the kettle for some reviving tea without going upstairs to the bathroom. I grabbed a hunk of cheese from the fridge and some dusty grapes from the fruit bowl that were beginning to look a bit wrinkled and went upstairs to eat. Then I went back downstairs to find the rest of the bottle of Château Léoville Poyferré 2012 I'd been drinking last night and brought that back with me.

I was definitely feeling a bit sulky for a moment. Yes, of course I wanted Jenny to see Ace and reconnect, but I would have liked a bit more help here, if I was honest. But on the other hand, there was time for that; there was always time to weed flower beds and mop the floors. There was not always time to make amends for past wrongs, to rebuild a parental connection or a sisterly bond. That was far more important.

Actually, I didn't care how long Jenny stayed with Ace; I was getting on well, the exercise was doing me good and I was feeling better about myself and my future than I had in years.

I sat back on the bed, the springs plunking underneath me. I bounced my way into the middle of the mattress and wondered if I would ever get back out again.

Outside, through the open window, I could hear Bertrand talking affectionately to Hector while he had his lunch.

'*Quel bon âne.*' Which I think meant 'good donkey'.

Hector responded with his usual trumping noise.

I could hear the young men laughing somewhere.

I munched on my cheese lunch, admiring the bite radius my fangs had left in the block. Disgusting, really. I'd have to cut that bit off before Jenny saw it. I wished I had some bread. Then I swigged some wine from the bottle because I'd forgotten to bring a glass upstairs. Classy. I hoped it wasn't one of those seventy-euro posh wines. If it was, I was probably guilty of breaking several ancient French laws. If the gendarmes heard about this, I would almost certainly be arrested. They would use my bite marks in the cheese as evidence of something. English depravity, probably.

I hadn't intended to eat all the cheese, but I did. I hadn't intended to drink all the wine either, but I did. And then I had a little nap, waking a couple of hours later to find I had squished all the grapes into the bedspread.

17

Léo didn't come back at all that day or the next.

Benoît thought he was working somewhere else, some sort of emergency involving a faulty something in a house near Ploudalmézeau. Claud just shrugged his shoulders and didn't have much to add to the conversation. My word, he really was miserable.

I reverted rapidly to my usual slovenly appearance, jogging pants and sweatshirt as I continued my cleansing of the garden.

One morning, I woke up to find another present on my doorstep: four eggs in a shoebox and a paper bag filled with asparagus spears. Now that was nice of my mystery caller. I made plans for eggs Benedict, which, thinking about my recent eating habits, seemed like the height of sophistication.

Pierre lit his bonfire with great enthusiasm and that was a good excuse for us all to stop work and stand around it, watching, and in Sylveste's case, helpfully flicking cigarette butts into the flames. Then he pitchforked some more dead wood onto it and we watched that too until the wind suddenly changed and blew all the smoke towards us and we all had to stagger away, choking.

Still, in between all that excitement, I managed to finish clearing the flagstones around the pool, and then I borrowed a pressure washer from Pierre, which provided another distraction for the workers. They all stood watching me as I scoured the green slime off the stones, resisting the impulse to write rude words as I did so.

Eventually, after they had all had a turn with it – and I think *they* might have written rude words in French because there was a lot of sniggering going on – the novelty wore off and they all went back to work, leaving me to carry on. I was out there pressure-washing for the rest of the day, and it was a very mucky job, particularly when the angle of the blaster caught on a stone and flicked mud over me. Still, it was a satisfying and mindless way to spend the afternoon and there was clear evidence of my hard work to admire, which was very pleasing. I'd nearly finished and was thinking about stopping for the day when my phone rang.

I wiped some mud out of my eye and answered before I had thought about it.

'Is that you, Katherine?'

No one ever called me Katherine. The voice was vaguely familiar.

'Yes, hello. Who is this?'

'It's Paul Batty. Your brother-in-law. Jennifer's husband.'

No!

I almost dropped the phone.

Was it too late to pretend I was a wrong number, or that I couldn't hear him properly?

Could I do that sort of broken-speaking trick to convince him I had poor reception and then hang up? Could I put on a strange accent?

Difficult, as the reception was annoyingly clear. He could have been in the next street. Horrible thought.

'Where are you?' I said, dreading the prospect that he might be at the ferry port in Roscoff waiting to be picked up.

'I'm at home, of course. And you are the last person on this earth I wanted to phone but I couldn't think of anyone else. What's that awful noise you're making?' he said irritably. 'I can hardly hear you.'

I turned the pressure washer off and dropped the blaster on the ground where it took its revenge and spurted water over my feet. I should have worn wellingtons. My trainers had been a silly idea.

'That's better,' he said. 'I'm trying to contact Jennifer, but now her phone seems to be off. She's always allowing it to run out of charge; it's very annoying. Can I speak to her?'

Um.

'Not at the moment,' I said, sinking down onto the little wall with a sigh.

'Why not?'

I resisted the urge to tell him the truth.

'She's gone out,' I said.

'Where?'

I gave a nervous laugh. 'What is this, the Spanish Inquisition?'

'Spanish Inquisition? I thought you were in France?'

I'd forgotten just how lacking in humour Paul was.

'We are, that was – never mind. Jenny has gone out to – buy bread.'

'Well, when she gets back, tell her I want to speak to her. It's urgent.'

'Can I help?' I said, wondering if perhaps I should be more accommodating.

After all, he might be in hospital having an embarrassing emergency operation or been the victim of a scam raid on his bank account. Or maybe he had been arrested for being in possession of an offensive personality?

'I shouldn't think so, unless you know where she keeps the printer cartridges. I have some very important accounts to print out.'

'Near the printer?' I said. 'Hazarding a guess.'

'I've looked there.'

'Under the bed? In the greenhouse? In the messy drawer in the kitchen?'

'We don't have a messy drawer in the kitchen,' he said.

Don't be ridiculous. Everyone has a messy drawer.

Even at this distance, I could tell he was talking through gritted teeth.

There was a long pause when I thought perhaps he might have rung off, except I could still hear his breath whistling down his nose. I'd forgotten about that.

'Look, I realise you are attempting to be funny, but I need to talk to Jennifer.'

'I've told you, she's gone out,' I said, doing a bit of teeth-gritting myself.

'Well, when will she be back?'

'I don't know; when she gets here, I expect,' I said, my irritation levels rising.

'Why can't I ever get any sense out of you?' he grumbled. 'I'm going to try her phone again. She's all right, isn't she? I mean, there's nothing wrong? And while we are at it, why is my bank statement showing transactions in Quimper and Lorient? That's miles away from you. I looked it up on the map.'

I sent up a silent prayer that Jenny hadn't used her bank card in Nantes.

'Absolutely nothing wrong,' I said, 'and we are allowed to go out sometimes, you know. Getting to know the neighbourhood. And Jenny's doing great work here. She's...'

He made scoffing noises. 'What exactly is she doing, anyway? She's useless at decorating and DIY.'

'Well, that shows what you know. She's been up and down ladders, painting walls, putting up shelves and all sorts of stuff.'

I heard him tutting and breathing heavily with annoyance.

'She couldn't put a shelf up to save her life,' Paul sneered.

'Well, you're wrong there. The builders were very impressed.'

'French builders, maybe,' he said.

He really was the pits.

'Oh, last year these builders worked on rebuilding...' Where had she said she was going? '... the chateau at Azay-le-Rideau,' I said, 'when some of the battlements fell down. I believe an English tourist was killed. He was an accountant, too. Crushed by a Plantagenet cannon.'

'Really?'

'Oh yes, it was very sad. No one ever claimed the body. Someone said his wife just went into the cathedral and lit a candle of thanksgiving, walked away and went home. I could be wrong.'

'Good God!'

'Yes, I think in the end they just walled him up in one of the oubliettes.'

There was another long pause while Paul presumably tried to get his head around this and decide if I was serious or not.

I watched as Bertrand emptied his latest barrow-load into the skip and then on his way back shared an apple with Hector. Hector brayed loudly and appreciatively.

'What on earth was that?' Paul said. 'That terrible noise?'

'The sirens from the prison,' I said. 'I expect someone's escaped again. It's always happening. We don't take any notice any more. Unless they run across the garden and then we fire a warning shot with the rifle.'

'Rifle? You have a rifle? That's sheer— Prison? There's a prison? I don't remember that.'

'Built only recently,' I said, 'with EU money. Designed by Sir Norman Foster. There's a swimming pool and a spa.'

'How absolutely typical!' he snorted.

At that moment a flatbed lorry backed up the drive and parped its horn very loudly, which made Hector ring out his usual challenging reply. This was followed by Bertrand shouting at him to shut up, and then the roar of Pierre's digger trundling across towards the drive.

'What the hell is going on over there?' Paul shouted over the noise.

'I'd better go, Paul, I have lots to do and you can get back to your tax returns.'

'I will. And tell Jennifer I want to speak to her urgently,' he said. 'I shall ring back, and don't think I won't.'

'*Ma pauvre sœur!*'

'What does that mean?' he said suspiciously.

'Oh, and by the way, *va te faire foutre*. Have a nice evening,' I said sweetly.

I'm sure it didn't mean that at all, but I'd seen Sylveste writing it with the pressure washer, and it seemed appropriate.

Just after lunch, Hugo the Pool Boy arrived in a rusty VW camper van that probably would not have passed its MOT in England. Hugo himself was a revelation. He was probably about fifty with a grizzled beard and matching shock of hair that was held back with a pink unicorn hair band.

'The pool, I look,' he said, and he trudged off down the garden to do just that. Then he got a load of stuff out of his van. Something that looked like a bigger pressure washer and another thing I assumed was some sort of vacuum cleaner.

As he trotted past me, he pointed at the little brick shed that contained all the mechanics of the pool. 'I will check if you need a new pimp.'

I didn't know that was necessary. Not that I'd ever had a pimp, and I was mildly offended that Hugo thought I had, until I realised he meant a new pump.

A man of few words, which under the circumstances was just as well.

He was jolly good too, very efficient and he hardly spoke to anyone, me included. By the end of the first day he'd completely drained and pressure-washed the pool, only packing up to leave when the sun was setting.

He shouted at me as he passed, something about the pump, that he would talk to someone.

As Hugo's van left the driveway and I was about to lock up, Léo came back.

I stood by the front door as he pulled up and got out of his van.

'Where have you been?' I said, rather more resentfully than I had intended.

He grinned. 'An emergency, but here I am and I have a present for you. I hope you will like it.'

My heart lifted. A present? What would that be, then? Flowers? Champagne? A cashmere wrap in palest blue? Jewellery?

He went to open the back doors and lifted something out; it was obviously very heavy.

'Tiles, for your bathroom,' he said.

'Oh, lovely,' I said, forcing myself to sound pleased.

'I hope you will like them; I had to search for the right ones, based on your picture. Everywhere I went they didn't have them.

And I knew the right one was out there. A friend of mine tracked them down.'

He lugged several boxes into the house and piled them up on the floor.

'Where did you get them?'

'Orléans,' he said.

'But that's miles,' I said, having thought about it.

He nodded happily. 'Seven hours. I slept in the van.'

'But that's ridiculous. Fourteen hours driving for tiles! And sleeping in the van? You didn't have to do that!' I felt bad now that I hadn't been more appreciative.

'I didn't mind; I wanted you to be pleased,' he said. 'Let's take a look.'

He took a penknife and cut through the tape fastening the boxes closed.

It was exactly as I had hoped. From the tiles I could see, it would form a really gorgeous picture.

'I don't know what to say,' I said. 'It's fabulous! Thank you!'

He grinned. 'Then it was all worthwhile. You have been working so hard, I thought it would cheer you up. Ah, I was almost forgetting. I have brought you something else.'

He went back to his van and returned with a huge, golden, beautiful, crusty, gorgeous loaf of bread. I greeted it with a cry of joy and hugged it to my chest.

'That pleases you more than the tiles, I think,' he said, laughing.

'Oh my God, I have been dreaming of bread,' I said, 'thank you so much! You must have a glass of wine.'

'If you aren't busy?'

I laughed. 'No, I'm not busy. Jenny is still away and I've been gardening all day so it will be nice to have a sit-down.'

'And you thought I had abandoned you,' Léo said with a twinkle.

I suddenly remembered I was expecting to feel embarrassed, seeing him again. Oh well, it was a bit late for that now. I hadn't blushed, stammered or said anything foolish. And I was still in my gardening clothes, which were filthy and a bit damp and I wasn't sure if at any point that day I had brushed my hair.

'Let's stay out here,' I said. 'It's still a bit dusty inside. I'll get the wine.'

He pulled out a chair and sat down with a happy sigh.

I pulled out the first bottle I found, which had a jolly flag on it. Château La Fleur-Pétrus 2007.

Léo looked at the bottle and shook his head.

'You are doing it again, Kitty. This was my father's favourite wine; I know how much it costs. This is worse than the other bottle.'

'Worse?'

'More expensive.'

'Well, the cork is out now,' I said, 'we might as well enjoy it.'

He tutted a bit and laughed.

'You have been busy. You are like your aunt, a hard worker, I can tell,' he said, waving one hand towards the garden. 'What a fine place this will be again.'

We clinked glasses.

'To your garden, *madame*,' he said, and looked straight at me.

Then I did blush; I blushed horribly.

'When is Jenny back?' he said. 'Is everything okay?'

'Yes, she's having a great time. They are off on a road trip over the Easter weekend.'

'Oh yes! Easter? That's this weekend? Is it really? I'd forgotten.'

'Apparently.'

He looked thoughtful as he sipped his wine. 'Why don't you come to my house, for Easter lunch. My sons and Louise are all going to the beach as the forecast is so good. So I will be on my own and need you to help with the lamb I will cook. With rosemary and garlic. And I think *pommes dauphinoise.*'

Considering I had been having snatched meals and snacks and leftovers all week, this sounded like my idea of heaven.

'Don't think about it, don't look for excuses, just say yes. You will be doing me a favour,' he said.

'Well, if you put it like that – I'll bring the wine,' I said, and we grinned at each other rather foolishly.

'Nothing less than Château Rothschild,' he said. And laughed.

My heart did a little flutter; I hadn't realised how much I had missed him. That was a bit worrying, wasn't it?

18

On Friday the builders had the day off, so I was left on my own to enjoy the peace for the first time in ages. It was really rather wonderful, and a shame that the pool – now cleaned and refilled – was still too cold. I'd been watching it with all the obsessive care of a first-time mother, checking *le pH* and scooping out leaves on a regular basis. Perhaps it needed a cover?

There had been some phone calls from Paul, which I had ignored, and then one from Jenny to tell me she would be back after the Easter weekend.

'You don't mind, do you?' she said.

'No, I'm enjoying the peace and quiet,' I said.

'Ace says he wants to stay in France forever, and I can't say I blame him. It's such a lovely country, the people are nice and I've had such a great time with him. You were right, absolutely right.'

'Can I have that in writing?' I said. 'People don't say that very often.'

'Any more news about Paul?' she said. 'I know he'll be expecting me back home soon. I don't think he imagined I was going to be away for so long.'

'Well, we have been going as fast as we can,' I said rather tartly.

'I know, I've been no help at all, have I? Chocolate teapot, that's me.'

'Oh, don't worry, there's still plenty more to do when you get back. Léo says we can make a start on the painting after the weekend. When are you going to get here?'

She made a few vague noises. 'After Easter. I promise.'

I thought about saying, *Take as long as you like,* but I didn't. In truth, I was feeling pretty tired after all the activity and needed her back to share the work. Or at the least do something. And from a purely personal point of view, I had missed her. I wanted to hear all her news.

No, I wouldn't get resentful. After all, seeing her only son after a break of two years was far more important than pulling up weeds.

'That's great. Bring some bread,' I said, 'and croissants.'

'Okay, I'll try to remember,' she said. 'Right, Ace is waiting; we are going out for dinner. It's a place that specialises in seafood and lobster. What are you having?'

I thought about it. The asparagus was long gone.

'Leftover pasta, leftover cheese and whatever else I can find in the freezer.'

'Perhaps I'd better pick up some supplies on my way back?'

'Great idea. I'm going to do some lolling about by the pool with a glass of wine. There's plenty of that,' I said, hoping to make her jealous.

Actually, thinking about it, I had found something to enjoy every day that didn't rely on vintage wine. The sight of the cleared flower beds, the progress on the renovations, the sound of the builders laughing, talking to Léo about what they were going to do next. Even Hector made me smile. And better than all that, my mobile ringing and seeing Jenny's name on the screen.

I was changing; inside, my thoughts were untangling. I didn't need to plod on with my unexciting life; it wasn't too late. I could do this: go somewhere new, talk to people, make new friends, make decisions and accept challenges. I had a little jump of happiness inside, knowing that Jenny could too.

'Oh well, I must go, see you soon!'

She rang off with a jolly laugh and I limped upstairs to have a shower. The prospect of a couple of days off and someone else cooking for me again was very, very appealing.

* * *

I was up before dawn on Saturday and started making a half-hearted attempt to finish clearing the sitting room, ready to start redecorating. The builders had already taken two of the three decrepit sofas out of the house and dumped them in the new, empty skip. Inspired by this, I had been through the house, finding all sorts of old, rusty and broken things stored away. The attic in particular had been rammed full of junk that no one could possibly want. Holey buckets, broken chairs, moth-eaten blankets – they all went into the skip. It was a very liberating feeling.

I had already packed away some of the many books and pushed everything into the middle of the sitting room so the walls were clear. Then I realised the four wall light shades were full of dead flies and dirt so I took them down, retching delicately as I washed them out. I carefully dried them on a tea towel and was busy inspecting them, wondering how old they were and where Sheila had bought them, when someone knocked loudly on the kitchen door. I did a startled juggling act and succeeded – with a loud scream – in dropping one on the floor. I stood and looked at the broken glass, which seemed to have spread itself over a far wider area than I would have thought possible. Oh, great.

The kitchen door opened.

'Are you all right? I heard you shout. Are you hurt?'

It was Léo, looking both concerned and disarmingly handsome in jeans and a chambray shirt.

'Just me being clumsy,' I sighed, looking down at the shards of glass. 'I'll never find one to replace it.'

'I'll find something,' he said. 'It was my fault anyway. I startled you.'

'I'm easily startled,' I said.

He laughed. 'I'll bear that in mind.'

I swept up and then hoovered. Perhaps I shouldn't walk around barefoot for the foreseeable future.

'I was thinking you might like to visit the Easter market? And then it's time for you to go into the storage facility,' Léo said.

'I don't want to go into storage,' I said.

He laughed again. 'I don't mean you; I thought it would be a good idea to get the paintings out of the house, now that the door into that room is clear. Before we start any more work.'

'Good idea,' I said without much enthusiasm.

Yes, I knew it needed doing but I'd been hoping for a day slobbing around doing nothing and perhaps watching television. Very excitingly I'd found a tin of biscuits in the cupboard I'd forgotten about, too.

'It won't take long. And then I will take you out for a celebration meal?' he said. 'If you would like that?'

Ooooh!

'That's an excellent idea,' I said, perking up.

He smiled and looked relieved, although why he would imagine for a moment that I would refuse, I had no idea.

'What are we celebrating?'

'Easter, the spring, friendship. Who knows,' he replied.

He had cleared his van and between us we took all of Sheila's paintings out and stacked them in the back. There were about thirty middle-sized canvases and ten smaller ones. I took a look at some of the ones that weren't packaged up. Watercolours, a few oils and some small unfinished sketches. I picked out the four that I liked the best, with some idea I would hang them up once we had decorated.

'Your aunt painted my father's portrait a few years ago. I wonder if it is here?' Léo said. 'I'd like to see it. Let me know if you find it.'

'Of course.'

Empty, the room looked even more dismal than it had before. It was dark, musty and cheerless.

'No need to look so worried; I am going to change this, remember?' Léo said. He sketched it out with his hands. 'A new window there and one there. Some shelves, perhaps? Sheila had the idea it would make a pleasant dining room. But you could do anything with it. An office or even another bedroom? It's up to you.'

'I wonder what would appeal to buyers?' I said thoughtfully.

His mouth turned down. 'I can't imagine what it would be like not to have you living here, even though it's only been such a short time. You seem comfortable here.'

'Yes, it's strange, isn't it? I like it. I'm happy here. It's beginning to feel like home.'

He grinned. 'Well, we must go, and take these to the storage unit. You will have some paperwork to do when we get there, so perhaps bring your passport? And then we can go to the market in the village.'

We got into Léo's van and edged down the driveway. Two chickens were having a dust bath in the drive, beaks open in ecstasy. Léo tooted the horn at them, and they scurried off round the back of the house.

After a ten-minute drive, we passed through the village and turned off into a small industrial estate where *les formalités administratives* were dealt with. We were processed in double-quick time by a sulky-looking girl with *droite* tattooed on one hand and *gauche* on the other, who obviously thought it was unfair that she was expected to work on Easter weekend. I had to pay for three months in advance and buy a flimsy-looking padlock for an exorbitant price before we could offload our loot.

My questions and objections to this were met with a shrug and 'Ce n'est pas moi, ce sont les règles.'

It's not me, it's the rules. Well, yes. I'd heard that many times before.

Still, then we were free of official duties and Léo drove us to the centre of the village, which looked very attractive with strings of bunting across the town square. There were stalls and little gazebos all along the main street and there were people everywhere. It looked a completely different place from the quiet, down-at-heel place I had seen when we arrived.

Léo found somewhere to park, which didn't seem to be particularly organised, as there were vehicles everywhere and I was sure I saw the gendarme who probably should have been directing traffic sitting at a pavement café with an espresso.

Léo was right; it was a brilliant place. I bought some bread from a cheerful woman in a tie-dye skirt who shook my hand and introduced herself as Francine. She knew exactly who I was, too; I supposed the word must have spread. I chose sourdough and something covered in seeds and grains that was almost beautiful enough to photograph and put on Instagram if I'd known how.

There were stalls filled with wonderful wheels of cheese and glorious vegetables. Jars of honey and chutney, fruit and garden plants. It was a good job Léo was with me because he ended up carrying all my purchases, leaving me free to keep on scooping up new treats. There was even a *chocolatier*, with a stall filled with chocolate truffles and the most enticing-looking shards of broken chocolate, arranged casually but beautifully in straw baskets. There were gorgeous herbs potted in little tin buckets and a stall with the most appetising-looking charcuterie and pâtés of every variety. I could have stayed there for the rest of the day.

Léo had to take my shopping back to the truck at one point because I had bought so much stuff. Several times, people came up to shake my hand and ask how the building work was going. A couple even wanted to talk about Sheila and tell me how much they had liked her. It made me feel as though I was part of the place already.

Unwisely, Léo had left me unattended, so when he returned, I had another load, but this time I had found a stall selling baskets. There was nothing there I didn't like. Baskets for shopping, for bread, fruit, picnics, wine bottles and laundry. Some of them had fabric linings; some were painted. I mean, who wouldn't want a gorgeous wooden bread box with *M Gustav, Baker au Roi* stencilled on the side? I did, so I bought one. Also a grey wooden egg cupboard with wire mesh sides and *Merci mes Poules* in white.

'You are going to fill the truck up at this rate.' Léo laughed when he finally found me.

'How did I not know about this place before?' I said. 'It's all my shopping dreams come at once. And everyone has been so nice, asking how things are going.'

'I told you, everyone liked your aunt; they have been wondering about her house. Several people have been keeping an eye on the place while it was empty. Now then, perhaps we should take this back to the house before we go out?' he said, taking my shopping bag from me and sagging under the weight. 'What have you got in here? Rocks?'

'Vegetables and fruit,' I said, 'and the most beautiful bottle of olive oil.'

'Well, you've had fun,' he said. He bent and kissed my cheek. 'I'm glad to see you so happy.'

My cheeks were aflame. Did women my age still blush in situations like this?

* * *

Later that evening, he drove us to a restaurant on the coast where we were able to sit next to an open window with the most marvellous view over the water. The sun was dipping low over the sea; there were little boats everywhere and families looking cheerful and happy. It was like something out of a tourist brochure.

'This was always one of my favourite places,' Léo said, 'but I haven't been here for years.'

'Oh? Why ever not?'

He shrugged. 'It's more pleasant to eat with company.'

'We were lucky to get this table,' I said.

'I have a confession,' he said with a guilty look. 'The owner is a friend of mine; I reserved it, in case you agreed to come here with me...'

'Really?'

He looked down. 'I wasn't sure. I hoped you would.'

Impulsively, I reached across the table and put my hand over his.

'I'm glad you did,' I said.

He smiled and took hold of my fingers. 'So am I.'

We just sat there, both of us looking a bit – well, dazed, I suppose.

I wondered how long it had been since he had taken a woman out like this. How long was it since I had spent time with an attractive man who liked me? Probably several years. That might have been depressing not so long ago, but why would I feel like that now when Léo was sitting in front of me? We had a beautiful sunset developing over the sea to share and I was already feeling happier and more confident than I had in a very long time.

Behind him, the waitress cleared her throat and tapped a pencil on her notepad.

Well, I couldn't think about anything sensible then. We both scrabbled at the menus, which we had ignored, and I tried to make a sensible choice. From a cursory glance I just knew I wanted *frites* and, at some point, one of the huge crepes that were being carried past our table.

It turned into such a lovely evening. No one hurried us, we ate seafood and drank local wine and talked. My word, we talked about so much. I didn't think I'd talked to a man like that for years, and Léo was a man who listened. He didn't interrupt or argue. It was very refreshing after years living with Steve, who would argue to the death about trivial things like the correct way to peel potatoes, but not actually do it himself. Just stand over me criticising. I remembered a particularly vicious row about the recycling too and the provenance of a Pringles tube.

'By the way, have you got a preferred way of peeling potatoes?' I blurted out.

What was I thinking?

He laughed. 'No. Why – do you?'

'No, not at all. I've been told my potato-peeling is quite random, though.'

'You can show me tomorrow if it will make you happy to have a second opinion?'

I grinned. I was already very happy.

19

We got home quite late. The night was dark and the light shining from the window was welcome.

He came with me to the front door to see me safely in.

'Thank you for today,' I said.

'My pleasure, Kitty. I had fun.'

'Me too.'

We stood and looked at each other in the gloom. He bent and kissed my cheek.

What did I want? What did he want?

Was I going to do what I had so often done in the past – act impulsively, make the wrong move? But this didn't feel like the wrong man at the wrong time.

'Come inside, Léo,' I said softly. 'It's cold out here.'

* * *

He stayed with me that night. It seemed absolutely the right thing to do. Until we actually got into bed and the noise from the sagging springs set us both off into hysterics.

He was propped up on one elbow, his arm around me.

'You have to do something about this bed, my Kitty,' he said between kisses. 'I cannot concentrate.'

'Really? You seem to be coping.' I giggled.

I was no stranger to French kissing, but I had to say, French kissing with a Frenchman in France was something else. Quite a different matter.

That night reinforced my conviction that some people knew what they were doing in the bedroom and others had no idea and never would. Perhaps it was a talent that couldn't be learned. I certainly went to sleep with a smile on my face and I think he did too.

* * *

We woke up late on Easter Sunday morning, and for once I made an effort with my appearance and didn't do anything foolish while I was waiting for him to finish his shower. I think I looked quite presentable in my one smart, pink dress, flat ballerina pumps and some make-up. I was having a good hair day too, which was always welcome, if unexpected.

Léo's face lit up when he came downstairs and saw me.

'*Joyeuses Pâques!* Happy Easter! You look *charmante*, Kitty,' he said, and he held both hands out in appreciation.

'Happy Easter to you too! Thank you,' I said, thinking, *Well, you look pretty* charmante *too, actually*. He did too, very handsome.

I turned a few lights on before I left this time, in case it was dark when we returned home, loaded the wine into the back of the truck (two red, two white because one of each seemed stingy) and hauled myself up into the passenger seat as elegantly as possible.

I wasn't sure how much actual help he needed from me when it came to our lunch because when I went into the house everything seemed to be ready. In no time there was a delicious smell of lamb roasting, with garlic and herbs. The *pommes dauphinoise* were assembled with no help from me, ready to go into the oven and very good they looked too, smothered in cream and cheese. He put a match to the fire, and we set the table with cutlery and white linen napkins and silver napkin rings, which he'd pulled out of a drawer. There were glasses at each place setting and he even put some flowers in the middle of the table.

'You are very organised,' I said. 'You didn't need my help peeling the potatoes after all.'

His eyes twinkled at me.

'I was warned you might be a bit – hmm – random in your peeling skills. But I did need something,' Léo said more seriously as he put a dish into the oven. 'I needed your company.'

Crumbs.

'Now tell me, how is it all going? Living in the middle of the house when there is so much going on all around you.'

'Oh, I'm managing. It was Jenny who found it a bit difficult. She'll be back soon.'

'That's good; you will have company again,' he said. 'Now, would you like a gin and tonic?'

'If you are having one?'

'I certainly am.'

He settled me next to the fire in a chair with a view of the valley below the house, and I sat watching the trees waving in the breeze, the sunlight filtering through the branches. I wondered what it would be like to live in a house like this, with such peace and relative isolation. I tried to imagine him here on his own day after day, going through his routine, cooking for himself, reading or watching television on his own.

Perhaps his life had been more like mine than I realised. Maybe people of our age, whether we had children or not, eventually became more isolated unless we did something about it. The new branches of every family tree spread out wider with time. They had families of their own to preoccupy them, their own lives to lead. People moved to a new town or a different country. I couldn't wait for my future contentment to find me; I had to make it myself.

I kept having rather unsettling flashbacks to the previous night – the look of him, his face in the shadowy light above mine, the sound of his breathing, the feel of his hands.

'Do you have family apart from Benoît and Claud?' I asked, trying to think about something else.

He handed me my drink. 'I have an aunt and uncle in Rennes, cousins in Paris. A sister in Italy. She lives near Milan with her husband and four children. So I am an uncle. How about you? Apart from your sister?'

'Not really. I mean, there's her husband, Paul, and their son, Ace, in Nantes, but we are a pretty small family – that's about it.'

He sipped his gin. 'I think you do not like this Paul? Your face always shows that.'

'I don't like him,' I said. 'He's a – a nightmare.'

I sipped my gin, it was lovely – not too strong, and it even had ice and lemon in it. Impressive. Perhaps I'd been wrong about men and my ice-cube trays assumption.

'So we should think about decorating soon. You and Jenny need to consider colours. Perhaps you have some ideas? Your aunt said for a long time that when the renovations were finished she wanted to bring brightness to the house but she needed time to think about it, and then of course nothing happened.'

That was a sad thought, that a woman who seemed to love colour and nature had lived out her last years in a house that was dark and rather gloomy.

'Cheerful colours, I think,' I said, 'in her honour.'

'I think she would like that.'

'Jenny probably won't,' I said. 'Her husband only likes magnolia.'

'Hmm, we will not ask him; we will ask her, shall we? And try to persuade her to agree with us.'

That felt nice all of a sudden – that we were in cahoots, working towards something a bit more personal than just bathroom tiles.

'Surely there is something I could do towards lunch?' I said. 'I feel a bit of a fraud just sitting here drinking gin.'

'You can open the wine,' he said. 'I will find you a decanter for the red. Have you brought something terribly expensive? I hope not.'

'I've no idea,' I said. 'I just pull out the nearest bottle and hope for the best.'

He shook his head. 'I remember Sheila sitting in the garden with my father, drinking red wine and laughing together. They were good friends. I didn't realise she had such a collection.'

'Perhaps she swapped paintings for wine instead of selling them?'

'Perhaps. Do you paint?'

'No.' I laughed. 'Not since school. I don't think I had any talent at all. My art teacher once held up one of my paintings to the class and said it was a waste of paint.'

'That's a terrible thing to do!'

'Well, it's stopped me wasting paint since.'

Mrs Brown, that was her name. What a strange thing to remember.

He shook his head. 'You are divorced, like me?'

Not quite like you; I've been a bit more profligate.

I'd realised recently that all three of my marriages had been based on deceit.

Frank had lied to me about being an alcoholic, Oliver had lied about being single and Steve had just – well – lied. The common denominator had been me. Not that I thought it was my fault, because that was an easy road to take. Too many women did that, blamed themselves when it was obvious to everyone else they weren't responsible.

If I was ever going to take myself or any man seriously ever again, it would have to be on an honest basis. On both our parts.

I took a deep breath and plunged in.

'Married three times, divorced three times. Although you can't really count the middle one because he was still married to someone else. Obviously, I didn't know about that at the time, or I wouldn't have gone near him with a bargepole. He told me he had been widowed. But I suppose with the benefit of hindsight I should have been suspicious that he was usually away during the week, working in Glasgow. In fact, he was living five miles away in Martin Hussingtree.'

Léo's eyebrows registered his surprise at this nugget of information. 'And Martin Hussingtree? He is another—'

'Oh God no, it's the name of a town. Near Worcester.'

'I see. So what happened?'

'Oliver's actual wife found out and came to my house while I was out at work and smashed in the front door with a sledgehammer.'

'*Mon Dieu!*'

'He – Oliver – tried to tell me it was just kids messing about, because it was Halloween, but then a few days later she came back and left the top tier of their wedding cake on the front doorstep. They'd only been married for about a year and she'd been saving it for the christening of their first child. Which didn't arrive, I should add. Of course, the local foxes got to it first, so there was fruit cake and icing all over the drive, and some fox vomit over the side of my car, plus a plaster model of the bridegroom with its head bitten off. I'm not sure if she did that or the foxes... well, anyway, it probably doesn't matter. Why am I telling you all this?'

Léo put his hand over his mouth and was spluttering with laughter. 'I'm sorry, it's not funny at all.'

I grinned. 'Well, it is, actually, looking back at it. Not at the time, of course.'

'No, of course not. And the other two husbands?'

'The first one, Frank, was married to me and also to a certain Lady Glenfiddich – I mean whisky. She won in the end; her charms were greater than mine. And the third one, Steve, had several affairs while we were married, which I never knew about until much later. His new girlfriend was expecting a baby when I found out about her. She came to the house too, to beg me to sign the divorce papers. At the time I didn't even know we were getting divorced, and Steve had hidden all the documents addressed to me in the bottom of a chest freezer we kept in the garage. Let's be honest, I would have had to have eaten a lot of fish fingers before I found them.'

By now, Léo was almost weeping with the effort of trying not to laugh. He'd stuffed his knuckles into his mouth.

'I'm sorry, I'm sorry, I know it's not funny. It's just the way you tell it,' he gasped.

I pulled a comical face. 'If I didn't laugh, I'd cry. But what's the point?'

'You are marvellous,' he said, wiping his eyes. 'I've never known anyone like you. How do you stay so positive and optimistic?'

'Well, my attitude is you can either get depressed and wallow in misery or pick your life up and keep going. I know some people thought I was very casual with my reaction, particularly my sister and her husband, but inside I wasn't. I'll admit I was absolutely devastated.'

It felt strange to be talking like this, but it was also liberating. Perhaps I had been maintaining a stiff upper lip for long enough; maybe I needed to confront my past mistakes and learn from them.

I knew now what it felt like to be happy with myself, properly happy, and I liked it.

'Truly, I'm sorry,' he said.

'Well, some of it was a long time ago. Some of it wasn't.'

I bit my lip, remembering some of the distress and the many arguments I'd been a part of over the years. And then I'd fallen out with my sister too, and for the most ridiculous of reasons: trying to defend the indefensible. Perhaps I'd just got into the habit of arguing. After all, none of it had been Jenny's fault. I needed to do something about that. It wasn't only Jenny who needed to wise up and apologise; it was me, too.

'Anyway.' I finished my gin and put the glass down on the table.

He reached across and put his warm hand over mine.

'You're a great woman, Kitty, never forget that,' he said.

'And how about you?' I said. 'Tell me about your divorce. I mean the edited version, of course. Not the full horror.'

He was thoughtful for a moment and looked puzzled.

'These things happen. And if I am honest, we had nothing in common other than the boys, and eventually she wanted someone else, not me. She wanted excitement and glamour and the sort of life in the sun that didn't appeal to me. She thought she had those things with him, but I don't think it worked out the way she had hoped. Knowing that man, I'm not surprised. I assume she is happy now. I don't ask. I think we were as civilised as it is possible to be.'

'I admire you for that,' I said.

I hadn't been nearly so easy-going. My marital history was peppered with arguments, disappointment, disbelief and occasionally incendiary rage. There had even been an incident in Steve's golf clubhouse involving a Pringle sweater and some HP Sauce that still made me blush with embarrassment when I thought about it.

'How is lunch coming along?' I said brightly, wanting to change the subject to something easier.

A kitchen timer pinged and Léo went to take the lamb out of the oven in a marvellous fat-splattering moment that filled the kitchen with a delicious aroma.

'I'm really looking forward to this,' I said. 'I don't think I've had a proper home-cooked meal like this since I was last here.'

'I was like that for a long time when the boys left home,' he said, 'and then I realised I was depriving myself of two of life's greatest pleasures. Cooking and eating.'

'You're right,' I said, watching, mesmerised, at he took out the dauphinoise potatoes, a golden, bubbling cauldron full of gorgeous, cheese-crusted calories. I could have demolished the lot on my own.

All my life I'd wanted to have a meal like that. Not just because the food was so good and someone else had prepared it, although that was brilliant too.

Too many times in the past when family dinners were an actual thing, I spent hours cooking a meal – Christmas dinner being the extreme example. I would be in the kitchen for most of the day, juggling saucepans and burners and dishes, testing and tasting and keeping things warm while everyone else lolled around with sherry and a tub of Quality Street. Then the whole thing would be demolished in a matter of minutes, cutlery flashing, as though there was a time penalty, and someone was going to blow a whistle. The dirty dishes cleared away, dessert dispatched with equal speed and people complaining they didn't really like Christmas pudding, then a quick trawl through the nuts and After Eight mints and everyone back to the television with the rest of the Quality Street, complaining there were only toffee pennies and coconut left.

This, on the other hand, was one of those long, drawn out,

relaxing meals for which I had always yearned: no rush, and time to talk and appreciate the food and the occasion. Then he brought out some cheeses and we spent another hour over that. Occasionally he got up to put a log on the fire; later on he even lit some candles on the table and still we sat there, chatting and relaxing, drinking wine and enjoying each other's company.

'So what next for you?' he said. 'When the house is finished and you sell it?'

I sighed. 'I really don't know.'

'You dislike the place you have chosen to live now?'

I sipped my wine and thought about it. Perhaps 'dislike' was too harsh. My flat was big enough, easy to look after and convenient but it lacked the heart that Jolies Arbres had. I didn't get the same feeling of contentment when I went through the front door or unloaded my shopping into the modern kitchen units that I did when I opened the rough, wooden door to Sheila's pantry. Even if the bed jangled every time I turned over, I had never slept as well in my flat as I did here. The flat was mine; I had bought it without a mortgage, but I'd never felt it was my sanctuary, not like I did now. In Sheila's house.

I tried to explain.

'I had to buy somewhere in a hurry and it was a bad choice. I made the mistake of viewing it during the day, when I should have gone there at midnight. If I had I would have heard the neighbours, the noise from the street below, realised the difficulty parking. Still, it keeps the rain off.'

'I would hope so! And what do you think of France?'

I had a little flutter of excitement. Was he just making conversation or was he asking me these questions for some deeper reason?

I would just be honest.

'I love it,' I said. 'I'm happy here. I love the space and the peace.

I'd love to be able to get out and see more of it; I've been a bit stuck for the last couple of weeks, with no car.'

'I've told you I will take you to see some places,' he said. 'I'd like to,' he added.

He had been sitting opposite me; now he picked up his wine glass and came to sit next to me.

'I'd like to,' he repeated. And he kissed me.

It was the sort of kiss that made me feel as though I *mattered*. It wasn't the sort of kiss that was a greeting or a *thanks for getting the dry-cleaning* sort of thing. I couldn't remember the last time another man had made me feel like Léo Bisset did. It must have been years. How sad.

But on the other hand, it wasn't sad at all, because I felt sort of lit up inside, excited, pleased. He wanted to kiss me last night, he wanted to kiss me again today, he'd come around the table to do so, quite deliberately. And I liked it. A lot.

He kept an arm around my shoulders and smiled at me.

'This is using up a lot of my courage, Kitty.'

'Really?' I said, a bit light-headed. Did he have feelings of insecurity, just as I did?

'Oh yes, I have wanted to do that for quite a long time before last night, but I wasn't sure if you would slap my face.'

'I've never slapped anyone's face,' I said. Because I hadn't.

'You should have told me,' he murmured, and he kissed me again.

'You didn't ask,' I said, coming up for air.

'Forget all this,' he said with a nod at the dirty dishes. 'Come and sit by the fire with me. Bring your wine; perhaps we could open another bottle?'

'Good idea,' I said.

We sat together, snuggled up on the sofa and drank our wine. We watched the flames and kissed each other a bit more. He murmured things in French in my ear that I didn't properly understand, but they turned my insides to water.

Where was this going? Was there something more to this weekend and this evening that I hadn't expected? I mean, I'd thought about it, of course I had. Wondered if he felt the same way I did.

It seemed he did.

Which was just the perfect end to the perfect day.

I meant perfect in the absolute sense of the word.

20

I woke up the next morning with another extremely pleased smile on my face. None of that *goodness me, where am I* business. I'd woken a couple of times in the night and looked over at him, his face deep in the pillow, his lashes long against his cheek. What a thoroughly marvellous way to spend a weekend.

This then made me wonder if he had woken up at some point and looked over at me. I have been known to snuffle and drool in my sleep, so I hoped not. How would we both feel when we woke up? What was going to happen next? What did I want to happen next? What was I doing? Where was the bathroom? Could I get there and back without waking him up? And what was he doing? Shouldn't one of us have a plan, or some idea of where this was all going? Or perhaps I was over-analysing; perhaps it wasn't actually going anywhere. Maybe this was just a 'thing' like lots of other things in life.

In the end I went to the loo and went back to bed. And then I went back to sleep; after all, it was Easter Monday and another bank holiday. No builders were going to turn up at the house; no deliveries of pallets of bricks were arriving. Hector would not be braying his flatulent way up the drive. It was a proper day off.

When Léo woke up, he put an arm around me and pulled me in for a cuddle. I'd always loved morning cuddling almost as much as I liked sex. It was more intimate in many ways. Both of you were awake, aware, sober, and the cuddle was a thing in its own right, not just a prelude or an epilogue for something else.

'Good morning,' he said, and he dropped a kiss on the top of my head, 'did you sleep well?'

'Mmm,' I said, still drowsy.

'Me too,' he said, and he hugged me. 'My bed is quieter than yours.'

I laughed and draped one arm over him. I could feel the muscles in his chest under my fingertips, and it was very exciting.

Then I think we both dozed off again because when I woke up and checked my watch it was ten thirty.

This never happened. Ever.

To sleep until the middle of the morning wasn't something I'd done since I was in my teens.

And Léo was still there too. I was warm, rather pleased with myself and after a couple of weeks of sleeping on such an uncomfortable mattress, this bed felt like heaven. He was right; I really did need to get a new bed. What I really needed now was a cup of tea.

'Shall I make you a cup of tea?' Léo said.

I grinned at him. 'Yes please. You read my mind.'

He kissed the tip of my nose. 'Stay there, I'll return *tout de suite*. Here, you can use this if you like?'

He gave me a freshly washed and *ironed* dressing gown.

I did stay there. And then I pulled on the dressing gown and nipped to the bathroom and tried to make some sense of my hair. And he did bring me a cup of tea and he got back into bed and we sat up, propped up against the pillows, which were the big square ones that the French seemed to go in for. So sensible. There was a wonderful view of woodland and birds busy in the branches. Nesting, perhaps, which, thinking about it, was what I had been doing too.

'Today, do you have any plans?' he said after a while.

'Nothing planned at all,' I said happily.

'Marvellous. What shall we do?'

So, we were 'we' now? He wasn't rushing me out of the house and talking about having to go over some invoices.

'Breakfast?' I said hopefully.

After all the fun and games of the last couple of nights, I was starving.

He grinned, as though he was thinking much the same thing. 'Of course.'

* * *

We had a leisurely breakfast: croissants, raspberry jam and coffee. We sat outside on the veranda, the sun warm, the sky blue, the sound of distant church bells drifting across the valley.

'I'm enjoying working on your house,' he said, 'and that's not always the case with these jobs. But I have fond memories of your aunt. She was very good company for my father during his last months when he was ill. Did you know she gave me a drawing just before she went into hospital? It's in my study.'

'You must show me before I go,' I said.

He put his cup down on the table and went to fetch it. This was a pencil sketch, absolutely lovely, of some birds on a bird table. I was unreasonably excited to recognise it as the same bird table I had washed and repainted. It made me feel a sudden connection with Sheila, and gratitude that her generosity had brought me to this place and this moment.

I think the birds were long-tailed tits, but I didn't volunteer the information. For obvious reasons.

He stood behind me with his hands on my shoulders and reached down to kiss my shoulder. I shivered with delight.

'I'll let you know when I find that portrait of your father.'

'Please do, I would love to see it again. Now, before I drive you home, I'll take you on a little detour,' he said, after a while. 'Then I can see what it is you have been doing in your garden, and maybe the pool will be ready for your first dip?'

'The water has been too cold up to now. I'm not that brave.'

'Pools are a nuisance,' he said. 'A lot of work and a great deal of trouble.'

We finished up and I collected my belongings, which somehow had been scattered around the house. Hmm, how did that happen?

We drove to the coast in time for lunch at a small, rather tumbledown shack that he said served wonderful seafood. There were half a dozen tables outside under a yellow canopy, and the air was heavy with the scent of herbs and garlic. We had passed some bigger places where people were crowding into the car parks and beaches but he had found us somewhere special, as I knew he would. We had a platter of *fruits de mer*, which came on a stand, layered with ice and wedges of lemon. I wasn't very used to seafood, cracking shells and that sort of thing, but he helped, showing me the best way to do it. We washed it down with cold cider in frosted glasses while Monsieur le Patron stood on the other side of the lane, smoking a cheroot, making phone calls and looking at the huge, pink granite boulders that littered the beach below.

All too soon it was time to go.

Léo helped me into my coat, leant over my shoulder and kissed my ear.

'When can I see you again, Kitty?'

'Tomorrow, I expect,' I said. 'I hope you will be turning up for work? I really need that bathroom.'

'I didn't mean that, and I think you know it,' he said.

I grinned up at him, delighted. 'Soon? You were going to take me to Saint-Malo.'

'I will, perhaps next weekend?'

'I'd like that,' I said.

And then, as we reached the car, he turned, took me in his arms and kissed me again.

He drove me home; I'll admit I was a bit fuzzy with all that had gone on. I was remembering the touch of his hands on me, his breath on my skin. Did men remember things like that too? Or was sex something that they processed in a different way? Perhaps he was quiet because he was thinking about more prosaic things like the wiring and grouting the tiles.

He reached across and took my hand, kissing my fingertips.

'Nearly there,' he said.

'Come in for a glass of wine? And then we could look around the garden.'

At last, just before three o'clock, he drove through the gates and up the driveway towards Jolies Arbres, which actually was beginning to look rather pretty, now that the trees were coming into leaf, and there was a flash of primroses in the grass. I looked with affection at the house, the wisteria meandering its way across the front of the house and...

We both spotted it at the same time.

'Ah,' he said.

'Oh God,' I said.

It was Jenny's car. She was back.

As the truck pulled up, the front door flew open and Jenny came rushing out.

'Léo! Do you know where—'

Then she saw me getting out of the passenger seat and her mouth actually dropped open with shock.

'Kitty! *Kitty?*'

'Hi,' I said, trying not to sound as embarrassed as I felt.

'What the... who... why... where the hell have you been and what have you been doing?'

'Auntie Kitty!'

It was only then that I registered another car parked around the side of the house.

'Hello, Ace,' I gulped.

'This is Marie-Odile,' he said, as a tall, gorgeous looking brunette came out of the front door behind him. 'She's been looking forward to meeting you.'

There was a horrible silence as we all looked at each other in turn.

'Gear up, we've got a dead marine,' Ace murmured.

'*Enchanté*,' Marie-Odile said, coming forward to look me up and down. She was glossy and groomed with tumbling chestnut hair and wonderful blue eyes. What must she think of me, turning up with some random man? What had Jenny told her?

Oh God.

'We wanted to surprise you; we arrived last night,' Ace said.

Last night?

From his expression, he was finding all this rather amusing. From the look on my sister's face, she wasn't.

'I didn't think to see you today, Léo,' Jenny said rather pointedly.

The air temperature dropped several degrees.

'Perhaps you should go, Léo,' I said. 'I'll see you tomorrow.'

'If you're sure?' he said.

We stood watching as Léo drove back down the drive.

Ace took Marie-Odile back into the house.

It took a few seconds before Jenny found her voice.

'You're doing it again, aren't you? What the hell are you playing at?' she hissed.

'I'm not playing at anything,' I said, 'and if I was...'

'Please don't tell me you have slept with that man?'

I shrugged. 'Okay, I won't tell you.'

'Kitty, are you completely mad? Good God, I can't turn my back for five minutes!'

'No, not at all. And you've been away a lot longer than that. Did you have a nice time with Ace?'

'Ace wanted to see you; we talked so much about you and how... then he said he wanted to come back with me and why didn't Marie-Odile come too? And when we got here the lights were on and nobody was in.'

I held out my hands in a gesture of agreement. 'As is so often the case with me.'

'Don't make a joke of this! I was worried sick; I tried ringing you but your phone was off. I thought something might have happened to you.'

Well, it did, actually, but that's for another discussion.

'I'm sorry you were worried; I would have left you a note if I'd known. Although I didn't know I was... well, I didn't know I wasn't going to be back.'

'So you just did what you always do, leapt into bed with some man at the drop of a hat.' She made a strangled noise. 'Have you learned nothing at all? Honestly? What exactly did you do over the weekend?'

'Why, what did you hear? Has the news reached as far as Nantes?'

'*Oh, Kitty!* Just when I thought you were starting to see sense.'

'Look, I'm sorry, Jenny. I didn't mean to worry you; Léo asked me over yesterday for lunch. Today we went out for some seafood. One thing led to another.'

'One thing always seems to lead to another with you,' she snapped. 'That's the story of your life. You've done so many really irresponsible things as a result, haven't you?'

I felt myself begin to bristle with annoyance.

'Look, Jenny, I'm old enough to make my own decisions; I haven't done anything illegal. I don't have to ask your permission before I do something or go somewhere. And a lot of the stupid things you're talking about me doing were done before the internet was invented so there's no actual proof.'

Jenny thought about this for a few minutes, pushing her spectacles up her nose, always a familiar gesture, a sign she was nervous. She brought out the worst thing she could think of.

'You're reckless and thoughtless. I bet he will run a mile when he finds out your marital history.'

'I've already told him,' I snapped back, 'before you take it on yourself to enlighten him.'

'Have you? Good grief. Everything?'

'Everything. I told him about me and he told me about him. He's a really great man, Jenny. I like him and he seems to like me.'

'Exactly! That's the problem. He *seems* to like you. He probably thought all his Christmases had come at once. Him on his own, you at a loose end, with the emphasis on *loose*.'

I held up a hand. 'Let's not do this, Jenny. Let's not fight.'

Things had been going so well; I'd dared to think we might be mending old bridges and building new ones.

'What will Ace think? And Marie-Odile? I could die of embarrassment. And now they have to go back. So you've missed your chance.'

She turned and went back into the house and I followed her. I think we were both equally annoyed for different reasons.

The kitchen was empty although there was the scent of croissants in the air. She picked up a cafetière of coffee and poured out a mugful, took a sip and pulled a face.

'Do we have any sugar? I couldn't find it.'

'You never have sugar!'

'Well, I do now,' she shouted. 'If I'm not allowed to criticise your hopeless relationships, then you're not allowed to criticise my sugar intake.'

I went and fetched the packet and she doled out a spoonful into her mug, then stirred it noisily. I could hear Ace and Marie-Odile moving around upstairs.

'So? Marie-Odile? Do you like her?'

'Very much, actually. French, of course, but you can't have everything.'

'Xenophobe,' I said.

Jenny's head jerked up. 'I am not and never have been a xenophobe!'

'But you'd prefer it if she was English?'

'Well, of course I would. It's easier.'

'I'd agree with you, if she had been a Martian or a werewolf.'

'Oh for heaven's sake, stop being so tiresome. Really, Kitty, I do wonder if you have ever had a sensible thought in your entire life. Or voiced a sensible opinion.'

'I have lots of sensible opinions; you just don't agree with most of them. Which makes me wrong, doesn't it?'

'Usually. The facts speak for themselves. Dipping in and out of marriages, changing jobs on a whim—'

'While you are the paragon of virtue when it comes to life, aren't you?'

The momentary ceasefire in our argument was over. I felt a familiar stone drop into my stomach.

'Well, anyone with any sense would prefer my way of doing things,' she said furiously.

I wasn't having that.

'Oh yes, married to an anally retentive bully for thirty-some-thing years, that's a great way to spend your time. Allowing him to cut your only son out of your life. If this trip hadn't happened, when do you think you would have seen Ace again? I'll tell you, it would have been *years*. He could have got engaged, married, had children and Paul would have kept him at arm's length because his feelings, *his feelings* were hurt. Paul wouldn't have thought about what you were feeling, or Ace for that matter. You would have lived for years just the two of you fossilising away in your beige house with your bloody slippers and microwave meals without any possi-bility of Paul relenting.'

'Oh shut up, you're giving me a headache. And I've sorted things out with Ace; I've met his girlfriend.'

'But it was all a deathly secret, wasn't it? And when do you expect to see him again?'

Jenny didn't answer. I looked over at her. Her face was white with fury, her mouth pinched into a sharp line.

'And as usual, all this upset is because, even now, you can't keep your knickers on,' she said at last. 'Paul was right, you are a...'

She stopped.

'A what?' I demanded.

She threw me an angry glare. 'Never mind. Your whole life you have been like a man magnet; heaven knows how, because you've never been anything special to look at. Paul says I was always better-looking than you, and yet you got all the boyfriends. And even now, when you are sixty-bloody-two, you still manage to find a man to seduce.'

I was speechless with shock. Partly because of the *never been anything special to look at*, which might be true but she didn't have the right to say it, and partly the inference that I had taken advan-tage of Léo.

'Could I first point out that I don't give a tiny rat's arse what Paul thinks of me, and secondly – seduce? How dare you. I can assure you there was no seducing going on, not on either of our parts, just very enjoyable sex between two consenting and single adults.'

'So you *did* sleep with him! I knew it! I bloody knew it! You never did have any self-control, and the reason for that is because you were the one that always got away with *everything*. All your life. You were the younger one and Mum and Dad spoiled you. I wasn't allowed mascara till I was fifteen, I wasn't allowed flares, and *you* never got acne. Do you know, Mum was always asking me if I thought you were pregnant, and that's when we were still at school. It could have been the length of your skirt, the fact that you used to smoke on the train home, that you got drunk nearly every time you went out and thought no one would notice. Why – even now – can't you act your age? What is your *problem*? What is the *matter* with you?'

'Nothing is the matter with *me*; everything is still in full working order and I've had no complaints from anyone up to *and* including now! And what has age got to do with enjoying life? I'm not the one married to a man who has the humanity of a cockroach, zip-up slippers *and* a comb-over, whose greatest enjoyment in life is probably going to the doctor to have his prostate checked!'

There was a horrible silence.

I wished I could take the words back; I wished we both could.

Jenny picked up her coffee mug and then put it down again. I wondered if she was thinking of chucking it over me and I leaned back a bit in case she did.

'Right,' she said, her voice very tight and angry, 'you've managed to make everything horrible and difficult again. And I'd had such a lovely time with Ace—'

'Well, I'm so bloody sorry. Poor Jenny. Poor you. Having a lovely time driving around from one chateau to the next. I genuinely do hope you had a great time. All those meals out and spas and massages. Good for you, I really am pleased it went so well. But to be honest, I *haven't* had quite such a brilliant time. I've been left here on my own for days on end, working myself into the ground, dealing with the various workmen who have turned up, sorting out all the decisions and problems. Living in the middle of noise and chaos and mess and muddle. No, don't give any of that a thought.'

Jenny stood up and I watched with a sinking feeling as she stalked off upstairs, her footsteps heavy on each step.

21

I sat there, my hands around my cooling coffee mug, wondering what Jenny was doing. She'd said some nasty things and so had I. Did that make us even? Was there even such a thing? Probably not. She always had been the one with the forensic memory. I was the one who operated my mouth before my brain was properly engaged.

Blast and damn, why had I risen to the bait? I'd honestly thought we were starting to get on better, that she was finally out from under the thumb of her domineering husband. That our argument all those years ago could be overcome. She had been to see Ace, eaten seafood, been to a spa; she'd been drinking wine at unspecified times, and adding sugar to her coffee.

I wanted to run upstairs and say sorry, tell her I was wrong, that I'd been thinking about things and I owed her an apology. But I didn't. Because I didn't think I'd done anything wrong. Impulsive, crazy, impetuous, perhaps, but not wrong.

So what should I do now? Perhaps I should have a look through the fridge and see what I could conjure up for our evening meal, not that I was very hungry. I'd leave her to think about it. I hoped she might take on board some of the things I'd said.

Half an hour later, Ace and Marie-Odile came back downstairs with their overnight bags. I followed them out to their car.

'I'm sorry about all this, Ace,' I said.

He came over to give me a hug. 'No worries, Auntie K. I wish we didn't have to go; we can catch up another time. If it means anything, I think Mum is over-reacting. If he makes you happy, then go for it.'

'Thanks, Ace, I appreciate that.'

'Just a bit of a heads-up before we go. She's been getting a lot of calls from Dad. And every time she does, she's upset. I think that's part of the problem. I've told her what I think, but it's difficult, isn't it?'

'What did you say?'

He stuck his hands in his pockets. 'I've told her she needs a life of her own, whether it's with him or without. I'm not sure if she understands that.'

'You're very wise, Ace,' I said.

He gave a wry smile. 'I'm not sure about that, but I do know a bit about self-preservation.'

We spent the last few minutes chatting about nothing in partic-ular while Marie-Odile smiled and nodded and asked polite ques-tions about the garden and the pool.

Jenny came out to say her goodbyes and I tried to be tactful and left them to it.

Back in the house, I cleared up the coffee things and put some laundry on. It looked as though Jenny had been sleeping in the cheerless bedroom behind mine while Ace used her room upstairs.

I heard the car pull away and the cheerful toot of its horn and then there was silence. I peered nervously out of the window to see what Jenny was doing. She was standing in the drive, on the phone. Not saying anything.

A few minutes later the front door slammed, and I heard her going upstairs. Perhaps I should make some fresh coffee, and maybe she would have cooled down enough for us to have a talk. She was bound to be upset, especially with Paul badgering her. He knew exactly which buttons to push. But there was hope for the future, surely? Now that she had connected with Ace again. And had some time to herself. Perhaps I could help her see her way through this and decide what she wanted to do next? I didn't want to see her disappear from my life again. She was my sister; she was someone who mattered to me, who I loved.

I would apologise, explain – explain what? That, yes, once again I had allowed my feelings to get the better of me. But what feelings? The fear that I was facing the future alone? There were worse things. Being with the wrong person, for one. I'd found that out the hard way.

I jumped as I heard Jenny's bedroom door slam.

Then the sound of her coming down; she was dragging her case behind her, the wheels banging on the stairs.

'What on earth are you doing now?' I said.

She flared her nostrils at me like an outraged horse.

'Not that it's any of your business, but I'm going home, to my husband. The man I've made very happy for many years, the man who has been a good husband to me while you have spent your life rattling chaotically from one disaster to another, and now you're doing it again. And you've been sneering at me and my boring life when yours is no better. Which of us can claim to be the success, I wonder?'

'You're going *home*? But—'

'I am. I have my passport. I've tried to ring Paul but he's not answering.'

'But—'

'You can do what you like; I'm not going to be here to cramp your style any longer,' Jenny added, 'and I've got one more thing to say to you before I go. *Jimmy Ormond*.'

'"Long Haired Lover from Liverpool"?' I said, confused. What did he have to do with all this?

'That was Jimmy Osmond. Jimmy Ormond was my boyfriend, when I was nineteen. He worked in the optician's in the High Street. He was forever bringing me spectacle cases and glass-cleaning cloths.'

'The tall, stringy bloke with halitosis? Yes? Are you planning to make a point any time soon or is this just a random rant?'

'When we broke up, Jimmy Ormond told me he had only been going out with me because he fancied you,' Jenny spat out.

'Well, that's not my fault!'

'You used to flirt with him when he came to the house.'

'I never did,' I said furiously.

'He said you made a suggestion to him.'

'I might have suggested he clean his teeth more than once a fortnight...'

'There's no talking to you.' Jenny did a magnificent flounce and turned to the door.

'And if you go now, how am I expected to get home?' I asked rather icily.

Jenny shrugged. 'I don't know. I'm sure you will find a *man* to help you out.'

And with that she left, the front door banging behind her.

* * *

I sat back down at the kitchen table and stayed there for a while, mechanically eating a few biscuits although they were like cardboard in my mouth. I wanted to cry but I didn't seem able to. I wanted to run down the road after her car and bring her back.

I didn't know what I thought was going to happen next. Would she return? Would she admit she too had been unkind, that she wanted us to try again?

Well, she didn't.

There was a horrible sort of finality to this moment. It was like the prequel to one of those television programmes where long-lost families were reunited and everyone cried and apologised, even though they had probably forgotten what it was they argued about.

I didn't think I would ever forget and, knowing Jenny, she wouldn't either.

I cleared up, wiping down the worktops and wrangling the hoover around so that everywhere was clean and tidy for when Jenny did come back. Then I went upstairs and changed the sheets on her bed and cleaned the bathroom. I kept looking out of the window to see if there was any sign of her car, but the day wore on and Jenny didn't return.

She must be at Roscoff by now. Maybe the ferry had been full and she hadn't been able to get on? Knowing Jenny, she wouldn't turn around and come back; she would sit on the quayside and wait. In her own way she was equally as stubborn as I was. I felt terrible. I wondered if she did too.

I spent the rest of the evening wandering about, tidying up, doing some laundry and then, as the sun was setting, I sat out in the garden with a glass of wine and at last did a bit of hopeless sobbing. It was horrible crying like that, on my own with no one to talk to. No one to reassure me or rub my back, tell me it wasn't my fault and everything would be okay. Eventually I got fed up with it and just concentrated on slugging back the wine and feeling sorry for myself. And then I started to feel sad for Jenny. It couldn't have been much fun going back to Roscoff, boarding the ferry, driving on her own. I could so clearly imagine her pulling her case, finding a seat, looking out of the grime-splattered window, watching the water, just as we had done when we'd come here. Was she okay? Was she upset? Was she too crying?

I felt absolutely awful. All the excitement and joy of the last forty-eight hours lost.

And apart from that, on a practical level, how would I get home?

* * *

The following day the men were back again, and the work continued. Léo wasn't with them and I spent the morning wondering if he had thought better of our weekend of frolicking. Perhaps he regretted it? Perhaps I did too if this was the result.

But then, just after lunch, his truck came up the drive, pulling to a halt next to Hector and the fresh, steaming pile of donkey business recently deposited.

'Hello,' he said, his eyes twinkling at me. He dumped a new bag of plaster on the floor, and a beautiful bunch of flowers on the kitchen table. 'Just been to pick up some more materials. And bring you these.'

'Hello,' I said, 'thank you so much. They are lovely.'

There was a little catch in my voice.

He put a hand on my shoulder. 'What's wrong?'

I was aware that Claud and Benoît, while apparently in the new bathroom, wrestling with the pipework for the new shower, were shamelessly earwigging.

'Oh, you know,' I said. I had the horrible feeling I was going to cry again.

He took hold of my arm and pulled me out into the garden.

'What's happened? I can see you have been crying. Jenny's car has gone.'

'She's gone home, back to Roscoff, to the ferry,' I said.

'What? Why? Is there a problem at home?'

'No. Jenny and I had a row after you left. A really bad one.'

'Because of me?' He was horrified.

'Because of lots of things,' I said. I took a deep breath. 'We fell out a few years ago, and it seems things were far from settled. She said some awful things and to be honest, so did I. I said stuff about her life and her husband, and there was an old boyfriend, and oh, I don't know, once we got started it all came out; it just went on and on, round and round in circles like some Pink Floyd thing on a loop.'

'My poor Kitty, I'm so sorry,' he said.

He rubbed my arm gently, in sympathy, I suppose.

'Please don't be nice to me,' I said, biting my lip. 'I don't deserve it; it was my fault too.'

'When is she coming back?'

'I don't know. I don't know if she's ever coming back.'

I sank down onto the little wall that seemed to have become my preferred perch and kicked at a tree root. The tabby cat edged out from behind the pool house and looked meaningfully at me.

'But she's your sister, your blood. That means so much. I'm sure you can mend things?'

I sighed. 'I don't know. I can't seem to think straight at the moment. I haven't really had the time to concentrate.'

'What can I do to help?' he said.

'Nothing,' I replied, 'I can't think of anything. I suppose we both need time to calm down.'

We sat there in the sunshine in silence, while Léo held my hand and rubbed his thumb over my knuckles.

'My advice would be to keep busy. Don't sit and brood, keep busy. Unless of course you want to go home too?'

I thought about this option. Of all the things I could do, this seemed the least attractive.

The cat came to wind itself around my feet, miaowing. Perhaps this was what happened when you were my age and alone. You spent a lot of time crying and thinking. Other people's cats sought you out.

'No, I don't want to go home,' I said at last.

'Home' suddenly felt a strange word. Where did I think of as home now? My heart was being won over by this place; even the earth it stood on was embedded under my nails.

'I'm glad,' he said. 'I'm glad you won't be going. I see the pool is cleaned and full again.' He didn't sound very approving of this; in fact, he sounded rather annoyed.

'Yes, but it needs a new pump. Someone is going to come and fit a new one. Soon, I hope.'

Léo shrugged. 'These engineers can be very unpredictable.'

There was a long silence, which was rather uncomfortable.

I slapped my hands down on my knees.

'Right. I think I've had a good idea. I've been meaning to weed the drive. There are some prize-winning thistles coming up there; perhaps Hector would like them.'

'I'm sure he would. And, Kitty, if there is anything I can do, anything at all, you must tell me. I would like to give you a hug but I'm sure my sons are watching, and it might give them some silly ideas.'

'Of course.'

What sort of silly ideas? Pleased or critical?

'Can I come around this evening? I don't like to think of you unhappy and alone.'

I thought about this for a long time, which was very unlike me.

Yes, I wanted him to come around this evening, of course I did. There was nothing I would have liked better than to have him here, to spend more time with him, to eat and drink wine and go to bed with him again. Enjoy the comfort of his arms. But on the other hand, I didn't want him to be here if Jenny suddenly came back. How would that look?

I could so clearly imagine the fuss that would cause, and then we would be back to square one, bawling and shrieking at each other like a couple of cocktail-laden bridesmaids on a hen night. But even more unexpectedly, I wanted some time to myself.

Perhaps I should wait and see if she would let me know that she was actually home. And theoretically at a safe distance before I did anything more about Léo.

'Not this evening,' I said at last. 'I think I need time to think.'

'Of course you do,' he said. 'I'm so sorry you are unhappy.'

'Right,' I said, taking a deep breath, 'I'm going to start that weeding; at least then I will have something to show for my day.'

'That's the secret, *chèrie*, keep busy. I am going to go and get that bathroom finished off. Because that will make me feel better. And please forgive me for causing so much trouble.'

'Oh Léo, it's not you; you're coming in at the end of a very difficult few years.'

We stood up and I saw Benoît and Claud standing, quite brazenly watching us from the kitchen doorway. They both darted back into the house like a pair of naughty children. What must they be thinking?

We walked back to the house together, the tabby at our heels, miaowing all the way.

Léo reached out and brushed my hand with his. Just a feather-like touch.

'I'll be thinking of you,' he said. 'I'm here if you need me.'

I gave him a small smile and went to collect my gardening tools and a green waste bag. Then I began at the far end of the driveway and started digging up the weeds and grass and even what looked like a few sprouting trees. It was a good thing to have chosen. Mindless, tiring and productive, and quite vicious at times. It was therapeutic. I kept at it all afternoon with just a couple of short breaks for orange squash, some chocolate and a few biscuits – still a slave to that healthy eating regime. Not.

By the time the workers were finished for the day I was about halfway through my task. The vans left, kicking up dust and loose stones in their wake. Driving over my hard work. Léo came to see if I was okay, asking what he could do to help. There didn't seem to be anything.

I went into the house and had a shower and pulled on my pyjamas and dressing gown. It might only have been six fifteen, but I wasn't expecting visitors and certainly wasn't in the mood for any sort of formality. I came back downstairs to find the tabby sitting on the kitchen table, licking the butter. It looked fatter than ever. I shooed it out and locked the door.

As I turned off the lights in the kitchen I saw, on a shelf above the sink, Jenny's faience café bowl. We'd bought one each that day we had gone out together to Quimper. Matching patterns. With our names on the side. And she'd left hers behind.

It was the saddest thing I'd seen for a long time, and I felt the tears prick behind my eyelids.

22

I sat up in bed with a large glass of Château Pape Clément 2017 and sent an email to work telling them I wouldn't be back any time soon, that things were taking longer than I'd anticipated and I would understand if they wanted to replace me with someone else. I'd been on a zero-hour contract anyway.

Somehow, I knew I wouldn't go back to my old life, whatever happened. How could I when my head was full of other things? When I now felt so differently inside? The last few weeks had shown me I could be independent, that I could cope with life on my own terms. I could make decisions and changes. I didn't need to stick to the well-worn path of getting older and more invisible. My happiness mattered to me.

I thought about this for a while, sipping at my wine. It wasn't because of Léo either, this change in me. Yes, I was enjoying his company and his friendship, and maybe there was something more to this relationship. Time would tell. But it wasn't the prospect of that which had caused this shift in me. For the first time, I was enjoying being me. I didn't need anything or anyone else to validate me and my choices. Yes, I liked Léo, but I didn't need to hand over all my problems for him to sort out.

I sent a group email to my friends, one that glossed over the truth quite successfully, I thought. Finally, I sent Jenny a text that evening too, asking if she was safely home, apologising for my part in the argument, and asking if she was okay. I think I must have re-worded it about a dozen times before I sent it, and I added a kiss at the end.

She replied almost immediately.

I'm back, I'm not okay.

No kiss at the end.
I sent a reply.

I've weeded half the drive x 🙂

I waited to see if she would respond, but she didn't.
I turned the light out shortly after that, riddled with guilt.

* * *

I lay awake, thinking about that afternoon all those years ago, when everything seemed to have gone wrong forever between me and my sister. But it hadn't been just that, I realised that now. Our relationship had been going wrong for years, as Paul gradually launched his campaign to wean Jenny away from her friends, her work and from me.

Invitations were in short supply, even after Ace was born and I was one of his godmothers. I couldn't count the number times they had cancelled visits to my house. There was a work thing or Ace was unwell or they'd decided to go away for the weekend on the spur of the moment. As though Paul ever did anything on the spur of the moment. And then Jenny's solo visits stopped too. There was always something happening; Paul needed her to type out some reports or Ace needed to be taken to a school event, although why both parents needed to take him every time to every football practice, I wasn't sure.

The last time we met up was at the Old Duck and Trumpet, a rather dull pub on the outskirts of a dull village halfway between our homes. It was the anniversary of the day our mother had died and perhaps we were both rather raw.

I'd been there a few minutes early for once and sat at the slightly sticky table with a rising feeling of dread. They arrived bang on time, half past twelve.

'Here comes the Old Duck,' I muttered under my breath as Jenny came in. Paul, looking very beige in a zipped-up anorak, was a few steps behind her. 'And here comes the Trumpet.'

'Nice to see you,' I said, getting up to give Jenny a hug. I didn't hug Paul; I didn't think he would risk coming too close to me anyway, in case some of my badness transferred itself to his important person. They sat down. There was a great deal of fussing with his anorak zip.

'Can I get you a drink?' I asked.

'We'll both have mineral water,' Paul said, 'no ice.'

Fair enough; the atmosphere was icy enough already in my opinion.

'The carvery is open – they have pork, beef, lamb or chicken,' I said a few minutes later when Paul had finished polishing his cutlery on his handkerchief.

'We'll both have chicken,' he said, looking suspiciously at the serving counter over the top of his glasses.

'You always used to love lamb, Jenny,' I said encouragingly. 'Why not have that for a change?'

'We'll have chicken,' Paul repeated.

They had chicken. It took a lot of fussing about at the counter as Paul selected the right vegetables, even scooping one of Jenny's roast potatoes off her plate and back into the serving dish.

'You haven't got any gravy, Jenny. Would you like some?' I asked, holding out the metal gravy jug towards her.

'We don't have gravy,' Paul said. 'It's full of fat.'

'Don't you?' I said, sloshing half a pint of the stuff onto my lunch.

We went back to our table and the meal progressed in uneasy silence, Paul dissecting his food into small shreds before he ate it with no obvious pleasure.

'So, how's Ace?' I asked. 'Everything okay in Edinburgh?'

'He's doing well,' Paul said, and gave a nasty little laugh. 'Not taken to wearing a skirt yet.'

'Kilts? Very sexy, I always think,' I said, trying to be jolly, 'especially on a hunky crofter with muscular calves.'

'He's enjoying life,' Jenny said. 'He's very busy.'

'Post-grad life, eh? How marvellous for him.'

'A waste of time,' Paul said firmly, examining a carrot baton for signs of tampering. 'He'd be better off getting a proper job now he has his degree. Though what he will be able to do with it who knows?'

'Perhaps he'll be a teacher?' I said. 'Then he could work anywhere.'

'Those who can, do; those who can't, teach,' Paul scoffed predictably.

I was rapidly losing my appetite. I put my cutlery down.

'That's a strange thing to say, Paul. Even you must have been taught at some time. I mean, it wasn't as though you were born with the ability to do spreadsheets, audits and end-of-year accounts, was it?'

'Those are important things; teaching French isn't,' he said.

'Of course it is,' I said, now thoroughly annoyed. 'We can't expect everyone to speak English. I wish I'd kept up with my French. I used to be okay, actually. What about foreign trade or diplomacy or politics? Languages are incredibly important.'

Paul gave a dismissive snort.

'So how's work going?' Jenny said, obviously trying to change the subject.

'Work? Yes, what exactly are you doing now? Still working at that *clinic*?' He managed to make it sound rather disgusting, as though people were creeping in under cover of darkness to let me deal with their hideous diseases. 'I expect you could do with some foreign languages there.'

'Do you always have to be so nasty?' I said at last. 'I'm enjoying my job. Ace is enjoying university. Those are good things, aren't they?'

He breathed heavily down his nose at me as he finished chewing his mouthful. 'You see life as somewhere sprinkled with glitter, don't you, Katherine? Hopping from one job to another, like a frog negotiating a pond. Hop, hop, hop, there you go. While the rest of us do something meaningful; we stick at things. We stick at our marriages.'

'So why did you make Jenny give up her job at the library? Aren't books and reading important?'

He adopted an expression of outrage. 'I didn't make Jennifer give up her job. She was too busy, that was the problem. Looking after the house and me and being a mother. Something you wouldn't understand, of course.'

'Ace left home years ago, and how much looking after does a grown man need? Perhaps if you did something to help, she would be able to have a life other than looking after you?'

'I don't think that's any of your business,' he said.

'It is when it means she's not allowed out to see any of her friends or me.'

'Perhaps she doesn't want to see her friends – or you.'

No one was eating now.

'Just stop it, Kitty,' Jenny said. 'How I live my life is up to me. I'm perfectly happy.'

'I bet you're not,' I said.

'How would you know? And why are you seeking to interfere yet again? Oh yes, Katherine knows best, doesn't she? The world's expert on life and relationships,' Paul sneered.

'I was trying to talk to my sister, but as usual you are butting in, interrupting and stopping her. Is Jenny even allowed a view on anything any more? She isn't even allowed gravy. Or her choice of food. You're a bully, Paul. Everyone knows it.'

Things were getting heated now; voices were being raised.

'Here we go, she's off on one yet again. That didn't take long,' Paul chortled, leaning back in his chair.

'I just wanted us to have a quiet lunch and time to talk about Mum,' Jenny said sadly.

'So did I. But you won't be allowed to do that,' I said, 'I guarantee it. Paul never could stand talking about someone other than himself. Let's talk about you, shall we, Paul? Let's all agree how wonderful you are. Let's talk about tax returns and the budget and VAT. Then we can all sit in silence and worship at your feet.'

Jenny's mouth tightened. 'Just stop it, Katherine.'

'*Katherine?* Since when was I Katherine to you? I've always been Kitty.'

'Kitty is a young woman's name,' Paul said with a smirk.

'Oh shut up, no one asked you.'

'Don't tell my husband to shut up,' Jenny said.

She put her cutlery down with a clatter and Paul raised his nose and looked offended.

'I wish just for once I could talk to you on your own. Can't you see what he's been doing ever since you married him? Alienating all your friends, your work colleagues, me, even your son, for heaven's sake. Controlling every bloody thing you do. I was hoping we could meet up on our own just for once, and remember our mother, and have a nice lunch together but he won't even let you do that. He's a narcissist, a control freak, an albatross.'

'*Caw caw*,' Paul said, flapping his elbows.

From his expression, he was thoroughly enjoying himself.

'I'm just trying to help,' I added.

'The day Jenny needs help from you when it comes to relationships is the day I give up,' Paul said.

'Yes, I'm the first to admit I've made some mistakes, but at least I don't have to dress like an old woman. At least I have friends and I have fun. When was the last time you had fun? A girls' night out?'

'Girls,' Paul laughed, 'spare me!'

'Oh shut up, just for once, Paul. You patronising know-all.'

'Don't speak to my husband like that,' Jenny said, chucking her napkin down on her dinner plate.

'Why, will he take it out on you later?' I said.

'How dare you!' he shouted.

I saw Jenny flick him a glance, and it confirmed all my suspicions.

'More than one way to punish people, though, isn't there, Paul? Without leaving bruises. What about sulking? Not speaking?'

'You are and always have been a disaster. A joke,' Paul said, pushing back his chair.

I realised that a lot of people had stopped eating and were openly watching us.

I could just imagine them later on, telling their friends all about it.

Three people arguing and carrying on, it got really nasty. And we only went there for a quiet lunch. You don't expect that at the Old Duck and Trumpet. There was a coach party in, too – what they must have thought of it!

'We're going, Katherine,' Jenny said. 'You've embarrassed me in a public place, and I would have thought you would have had more respect than this, particularly at this time. I wanted to remember Mum.'

'So did I!'

'I think you've finally lost the plot, Katherine.' Paul rummaged in his pocket for a handkerchief and wiped his nose. 'Come on, Jennifer. I've heard enough,' Paul said, zipping up his anorak with a decisive movement.

I stood up as well.

Even the people in the queue were watching us now, plates held out in front of them, mouths open.

'Trust me, you haven't. You're a contemptible little woodlouse, Paul Batty. A coward. A self-obsessed blot on the escutcheon of men everywhere.'

'And you're a meddling witch with the morals of an alley cat,' he fired back. 'No man is safe within fifty yards of you, are they?'

'Well, you bloody are, Paul! I can reassure you on that point.'

Jenny grabbed her handbag and stalked out, slamming the door behind her so that Paul, hot on her heels, almost banged his nose on the glass.

No, that hadn't been a good day, all things considered. And they had left me to pay the bill.

* * *

I spent the rest of the week weeding the drive. After the first hour I had attracted an audience. I looked up at one point to see four white chickens watching me. I mean just standing there, in a line, watching what I was doing.

'What?' I said, pushing my hair out of my eyes.

The largest and boldest of the hens – Blanche – stood on one leg and gave a cluck.

'I'm weeding, not that it's any of your business. And by the way, you don't live here.'

I sat back on my heels and Blanche darted forwards with an amazing turn of speed, pecking up a bug on the ground in front of me that I had unearthed.

'Help yourselves,' I sighed. 'Fill your beaks up. There's plenty for all.'

They stayed there all afternoon, watching me and occasionally snaffling up a worm or a grub from the earth. I even had to lift one of them up and shove it out of the way a few times as it gained courage. Not something I had ever expected to do – shove a chicken aside. It felt warm and very soft but solid too underneath all the feathers. They were obviously used to being around people.

Half an hour later Mimi arrived with her pram, and without any preamble, gathered the hens together.

'*Ce ne sont pas vos poules,*' she said rather angrily.

Well, no, obviously they weren't my chickens; it wasn't as though I had lured them away with tasty treats, compliments and affection. I felt quite annoyed at such an inference. Perhaps Mimi should look to her own security and have a stern word with Blanche, who seemed to be the ringleader. Unfortunately, O-level French had not prepared me for such an exchange, so I didn't say anything. I just smiled rather maniacally and tried to help. I didn't think she was at all impressed. Then Mimi took them away again.

By the time the workmen left on Friday afternoon, the new downstairs wet room was finished, along with a power shower, toughened glass screens and the rather gorgeous wall-tile picture. It really did look lovely in there; it was almost a shame to use it.

Still no news of Jenny, what she was doing or how she was feeling. I was going through the days on autopilot. Getting up, working through my tasks and then going to bed; it was almost like my old life, before I came here. I hated that feeling.

The following Monday, Léo took me out to buy paint so I could start decorating the sitting room. We went into a home decor place too, and I ordered two giant sofas that were in the sale and some new curtains patterned with leaves and birds. I felt pathetically glad that he was there to sort out firstly the delivery of the sofas and secondly what size curtains to pick. I didn't think I had ever, not even once, known how curtain sizes worked, or what to buy.

I'd decided to keep the walls pale yellow with white woodwork, hoping to bring some light into the gloomy room. I hoped Jenny would approve of my choices – that was if she ever saw them. Would she remember what she had said to me? That whatever I decided would be okay? Somehow, I doubted it. I could just imagine her mouth puckering in disapproval.

On Tuesday, while Claud and Benoît started knocking the storage room about – cue more foundation-rattling blows accompanied by their radio turned up to warp factor 5 playing French punk/grunge interspersed with machine-gun-style interviews with angry people – Léo and I started painting.

We hadn't really talked properly after all the chaos and upset of the last few days. In fact, the more time went on, the more embarrassed I became. We'd had sex, I had confided all sorts of things about my past, my insecurities, my hopes for the future. He knew about my appendix scar and the fact that one of my boobs was very slightly bigger than the other. Okay, it was very common, and he hadn't said anything at the time, so there was always the possibility he hadn't noticed, but I knew he knew.

At the time it hadn't seemed to matter; now I wondered if he was looking closely at me to try to remember what the difference had been. I started wearing a baggy sweatshirt.

We worked on opposite sides of the room, almost on a parallel orbit, like two space stations. We didn't talk much, other than to occasionally compliment the other's work. Although how much damage could I do with uneven walls and new paint? I made coffee; he brought a box of pastries from the local patisserie. One evening after work he took me out to the market to restock the fridge and when we got back, I didn't ask him in. I just wanted to be on my own. We looked at each other as though we were almost strangers, talking about nothing in particular. Commenting on the weather, how the grass would need mowing again soon.

Everything between us seemed to have gone off the boil. One day we were looking at each other, talking, flirting, having a romantic meal together and having very enjoyable sex. The next we were behaving like polite strangers in a lift. Not making eye contact, talking about the weather.

I was distracted by the Jenny thing, the possibility that our relationship really had hit the rocks this time. Maybe that was more important to me than anything else. My sister, lost to me for so many years, was lost again.

Every night, I fell into bed exhausted; even the discomfort of the mattress and the melodic jangling of the bed springs didn't stop me from falling asleep. And it rained for a week, which meant the weeds were making a break for it all over again.

Léo suggested the proposed trip to Saint-Malo one weekend. I wanted to but I put him off; I was tired and unsettled and I was anxious that we might be getting into deeper water than we were already. It was really depressing. Jenny and I had found each other again; we had begun to regain our trust in each other. I'd seen glimpses of how we used to be, friends and allies. And now all that had gone. I didn't think I could bear it.

Life continued along these lines for another week. My mind was busy with things I could possibly do to repair the relationship with my sister, wondering if I would ever see Jenny again. I just wanted another chance.

* * *

That night, I was up in the bedroom that had been Jenny's. I'd had my shower and was in my pyjamas, sitting up in bed with the remains of a bottle of Château Talbot Saint-Julien 2016 and some salt-and-vinegar crisps, which seemed to complement it nicely. I had been trying to read the book Jenny had left behind. I'd just read the same paragraph three times because my brain kept alternating between thinking about Léo and wondering if we would get the carpet down before the new sofas arrived, when above the din of the rain against the window I heard a strange noise outside.

I closed the book and listened more intently.

Was this the arrival of the battalion of thieves and crooks that Jenny had predicted? The weather was pretty wild out there; personally, I would have gone out robbing on a night when the rain had stopped.

I got out of bed, pulled on my dressing gown and tiptoed to the top of the stairs. The familiar smell of dust and old bricks drifted up to meet me. Someone tried the door handle.

I could feel the hairs on my arms, my legs and the back of my neck stand to attention; I felt like a large but inadequate hedgehog.

I needed a weapon.

I crept into the bathroom. All I could find was a handbag-sized can of hairspray that might have contained enough product to spray in one eye. I'd have to aim carefully.

Then I went down the stairs, each one creaking disloyally under my weight.

Someone tried the front door again. I held my breath.

Then, the cheek of it, *someone knocked.*

Burglars knocking on the door to be let in? That didn't sound right.

Bravely, I cleared my throat.

'Who is there? I warn you, I have a gun and if you don't go away, I'm going to set the...' What was a deterrent sort of dog? '... the Alsatian on you. And the Dobermann.'

'Let me in!' someone said.

I moved closer to the door.

'I'm warning you.' I crouched down to dog height and made some quite convincing growling noises. 'Down, Brutus, down! Bad dog!'

'Who the hell is Brutus?'

I stiffened with shock. 'Jenny? Is that you?'

'Of course it's me. Let me in. It's chucking it down out here.'

I dropped the hairspray and wrestled with the door bolts, eventually sliding them back with a crash. Jenny fell in, dragging her case behind her.

'Thank God for that. I'm soaking,' she said.

She was, too; the water was dripping off her hair and her raincoat was clinging to her legs.

'What are you doing here?' I said.

She shrugged off her coat and pulled her case into the kitchen. She looked at me in my pyjamas and dressing gown.

'Why are you dressed for bed? Do you know it's only eight thirty?' she said. And then, barely pausing to draw breath, 'Can I have a very large, very cold glass of white wine? I'm absolutely gasping.'

'Of course,' I said, going to the fridge while still keeping an eye on her.

She rubbed at her wet hair with a tea towel, slugged back half the glass of wine in one go and held it out towards me for a refill.

'I've come back,' she said unnecessarily.

'I can see that,' I said. 'What's happened? How are you?'

She took another gulp of wine and then looked down at her hands.

'I'm exhausted, I'm furiously angry and I'm rather shocked,' she said at last.

'Not as shocked as I am,' I muttered, carefully sitting down opposite her.

I wanted to sweep her up in a big hug, but I didn't want to make any sudden moves; she looked as though she might either burst into tears or make a lunge for the knife drawer.

'Is everything all right?' I asked at last when the silence had dragged on for too long.

Jenny tossed her head stiffly. Her eyes looked different behind her glasses, as though she hadn't slept for a long time or had maybe been crying or both. I wasn't sure if my sister cried much; she was usually too busy being angry or frustrated with me when I saw her.

'No, actually. No, everything is far from all right. Everything is completely wrong. As wrong as it could be.'

There was another long silence.

Jenny looked up at me and her bottom lip wobbled. We stared at each other for a moment; I felt as though something momentous and unexpected was coming.

'Oh, Kitty,' she said at last, and she put her head down on her arms and burst into noisy sobs.

I went to her side of the table and put my arm carefully around her.

'What's happened? Come on, Jenny, this isn't like you.'

I did a bit of comforting back-rubbing and then while she wasn't looking, I reached across for the wine bottle and took a swig.

'What am I going to do?' she wailed at last.

'Well, I don't know, what's happened? Why are you so upset? Is it me? Have I done something? I mean, apart from the other stuff, and the comment about Paul's prostate, which of course I didn't mean.'

Jenny did some sniffing and nose-blowing and straightened up. 'Oh, don't be so silly, Kitty. It's not always about you, you know.'

'Most things are, or they can be traced back to me,' I said, resuming the back-rubbing.

'It's...' Her lip wobbled again.

She took another gulp of her wine and a deep shuddering breath.

Then she put on her *I'm trying to control myself* expression, which I had seen many times over the years.

She raised one finger. 'I have something to do.'

I watched as she went up to her room and then came back downstairs. She was holding her knitting bag in her hand, the sludge-green wool sticking out from the top.

Without a word, she went outside into the rain.

I waited; I didn't have a clue what she was going to do.

A few seconds later she returned without the knitting bag.

'I've chucked it in the skip,' she said. 'The whole damn lot.'

* * *

'So?' I said at last.

'It's Paul,' she said. Her face tightened, her mouth a little button-hole of anger. 'He's an anally retentive, stinking, lying hypocrite,' she said.

I gasped in utter shock. 'And you came to this realisation because...?'

Jenny ran her hands through her hair and some bits stuck up at the sides, giving her the look of a rockhopper penguin for a moment.

'Oh, I know. You've been saying this for years. I've never had a kitten because of him. I've never been allowed in the greenhouse because of him. I didn't have another baby because of him. I've missed out on so much of Ace's life because of him. And now...'

'Yes? Now?'

Jenny took a deep breath and her hands hovered over the top of the table.

'Right. I don't want to go over this more than once so you might like to get yourself a drink,' she said.

I did as I was told, scurrying into the wine cupboard, grabbing a bottle of red, wiping the dust off with my sleeve and pouring myself a generous glassful. I didn't take my eyes off my sister for a second. I had the feeling something earth-shattering was coming.

She cleared her throat as though she was going to make a speech.

'Right. I got a space on the second ferry out of Roscoff the day I left here. People were still coming out to France, not going home, so there was plenty of room. When I got back to Plymouth, I even bought Paul an Easter egg, at the Exeter services. A Kit Kat one with a mug. I knew he wouldn't like it, he'd probably throw it away, but I wasn't thinking straight. Anyway, I got home and I was feeling quite good about things. And then, when I got back to Little Croft, there was a strange car in the driveway. One of those stupid little electric things with no room that looks like it's made out of Lego. Paul always laughed at them when we saw one. Anyway, there it was. I wondered if it was perhaps a doctor and Paul was ill.'

'And was it? And was he?'

Jenny snorted. 'Neither, but there was a woman in the kitchen, in a nightdress, making free with my Le Creuset milk pan. Making Horlicks, if you please. All that nonsense about being pre-diabetic.

What are you doing? I said and she looked at me like a startled cat. And then Paul came downstairs, in his new pyjamas and dressing gown. And it wasn't even ten o'clock.'

I gasped and put my hands over my mouth, releasing slightly so I could have some more wine.

'And Paul said, *It's not what you think, Jennifer.* Just like that. *It's not what you think, Jennifer.*'

'And was it? I mean, was it what you thought?'

Her face twisted up into an angry grimace, and her hands twisted together in two furious little fists. 'Of course it was. It was exactly what I thought. The woman was apparently *Alison from work.* Now, I've heard all about *Alison from work.* Paul said she was elderly, fat, with a dodgy hip and nut allergy. Well, she wasn't. She was about fifty, bottle-blonde, and a face like a slapped arse with lipstick. Quite brazen about things. Looking at me as though I had no place there and what was I making such a fuss about?'

'What did she say?'

'She gave me this look, and she said, *You must be Jennifer. Perhaps I'd better go,* and I said, *Yes, I think that would be wise, before I smack you around the head with this milk pan.* And then she laughed. She actually laughed at me and said there was *no need to be aggressive; you must have known this was on the cards.* Then she said she'd better get her stuff from upstairs, by which I think she meant her clothes, and I said no, and I shoved her out of the kitchen door and then chucked her handbag after her.'

I put my hand over hers. 'Jenny, I'm proud of you!'

She allowed herself a cold little smile. 'And then Paul and I had an argument that made our row the other day seem like chicken feed. And at one point he told me to calm down and would I like some Horlicks to settle my nerves.'

I gasped. 'I would have chucked it over him!'

'I did,' she said with an air of pride, 'and it went in his slippers, too. The ones with the zips. They'll be ruined.'

'Good. And what happened then?'

'Then we had another row, which went on for hours because for once I wouldn't let it drop, and he said I was only behaving like that because I had spent too much time with you.'

'See? I *knew* it would be my fault,' I said.

'And he wanted to go to bed and we could discuss it in the morning, and I said, *Not a chance, Casanova*. And we were up until four in the morning and eventually he admitted he had been having a *special friendship* with Alison from work for some time. And I poured myself a large gin and he made that prissy face he does when he's going to be patronising, and said, *Alcohol is a harsh friend, Jennifer*, so I chucked that over him as well. For a bit I was sort of amazed that none of the neighbours had even said anything but then I realised none of them speak to us anyway.'

'Bastards! All of them!'

'Well, to be honest, in their defence, life in the cul-de-sac has never been the same since he complained to the council about the Olympic torch going past the end of the road in 2012, and then there was the business with the recycling, which rears its ugly head every few months. And then I went to bed and when he tried to follow me, I threw my glass of water over him. So that was three things. And he said, *These are new pyjamas, Jennifer*, so I chucked the glass at him too.'

I spluttered a laugh. 'You didn't! Well done!'

'And then a couple of days after that when I couldn't stand him either creeping around me as though I was a grenade with the pin out or pretending nothing had happened and could he make me a cup of tea, I told him I was coming back here, and when I returned, I expected him to be gone because Mum left the house equally to me and you, although very generously, you've never pressed for anything, but now you wanted it sold.'

'That's right, blame me,' I said with a grin. 'So how do you feel now?'

Jenny slumped. 'A bit drained, actually, and rather flat if I'm honest. But on the other hand, glad that I said all the things I said. And for good measure, I did bring up his prostate.'

'Oh, Jenny!'

She heaved a huge sigh. 'Done now.'

'It must have been awful.'

'It was, but at the same time I suddenly felt like I was escaping. That I was suffocating. I feel better and yet worse at the same time. Quite sick. And for the first time I really realised just how awful it must have been for you. Because you're right. Frank wasn't your fault. Oliver wasn't your fault, and nor was Steve. So the only thing I wanted was to get away from Paul and to get back here and apologise. To you.'

I held my breath for a moment, absolutely shocked to the core. I hadn't been expecting any of this.

'Oh, Jenny, honestly, I'm the one who should be grovelling. I'm sorry,' I cried, 'I know you're right. I have been a disaster; all my life I have careered around from one man to the next. And I don't know why.'

'Well, better that than be stuck with...' She struggled for an appropriate word. 'With *him*.'

We sat and drank wine in silence for a few minutes, both of us deep in thought.

Jenny took a deep breath. 'I've had a lot of time to think about it. I could see things were changing for you and something was going to change for me too and I was scared. Better the devil you know, I suppose. But it was seeing Ace again and seeing how lovely he was with Marie-Odile. So kind. Considerate. He wanted her to be happy, that was the thing, and if she was, then he was happy too. Paul was only ever concerned with himself. I suddenly realised that I didn't matter to him, not really. I can't tell you what an awful thing that was. I felt second-rate, a fool.'

I went and put my arms around her. She was shivering.

'Oh, Jenny, you're not second-rate. And you're certainly not a fool. You've had decades of this. You deserve better.'

Jenny closed her eyes and slumped a bit. I hugged her even tighter and she patted my arm.

'I'm so tired. Tired of worrying, of never having an opinion, of not mattering.'

We sat with our arms around each other, and I felt a massive surge of relief. Jenny had come back to me. She needed me again. I was going to be there for her.

'You matter to me, Jenny, and you matter to Ace. I'm sorry for the things I said, for not being more understanding. I'll always support you, whatever you do, you know that, don't you?'

Jenny nodded. 'And I'm sorry I left you with all this to sort out.'

'Do you want me to show you what has been done while you've been away?' I asked after a while. 'I mean, the shower room is lovely; we won't need to share a bathroom any more. And out in the garden – well, it's dark now, of course, but the pool will be ready when the man fixes the new pump. Which reminds me, I must have a word with Pierre.'

Jenny sighed heavily and reached for the wine bottle.

'Tomorrow,' she said. 'For tonight, for the first time for a very long time, I just want to get sloshed.'

'Jenny!'

I reached for the bottle and topped up her glass.

23

'So what are you going to do?' I said at last.

By then it was nearly eleven thirty and the pair of us had been chugging wine back like there was no tomorrow. And eaten all the emergency chocolate sardines, which had been jolly expensive – I'd bought them as a treat for when I finished the driveway.

'No idea,' Jenny said, stifling a yawn with her hand. 'The one thing I do know is I've had enough. I'm not going to go back to how things were. When I was staying with him, Ace told me some of the things Paul had said to him and done over the years, absolutely unforgiveable things. Telling Ace to move out when he was choosing his A levels and refused to do applied maths. He wanted to do languages, of course. But Paul had some prehistoric idea that they were *girls'* subjects. That boys should do manly things like science and maths and engineering.'

'That's r-ridiculous,' I said, slurring a bit.

'Isn't it?' Jenny said, smoothing out the last chocolate sardine wrapper with her thumbnail. 'And he said if Ace didn't go to Oxford or Cambridge, he was a failure. And Paul went to a bloody polytechnic, if you please! So of course, unknown to either of us, Ace applied to universities as far away from home as he could, which is why he ended up at Edinburgh.'

'Poor Ace,' I murmured, slumping across the table. I'd known that was what Ace had planned, but perhaps this wasn't the time to remind her.

'And I swear I had no idea. And then the last time Ace came home after he finished his PhD, they had a massive argument that I *did* know about. That Ace might call himself *doctor*, but he wasn't really. I never told anyone; I think I was in denial for months afterwards. When Ace said he was going to work in France because he had been offered a job at a university, it all kicked off; they were at it for hours. The next day, Ace left.'

'How did you stand it?'

Jenny held her hands up. 'I don't really know. You and I had already lost touch, and then Ace was taken away from me as well. I think I was in shock for weeks, and then Paul started making some sort of pathetic attempts to be nice to me; he even unloaded the dishwasher a few times without being asked.'

'Oh, big wow,' I said sarcastically. 'I wish you'd told me; I would have understood. What a bastard he was.'

Jenny nodded her head. 'I know, I know you would have. We always stuck together through thick and thin, didn't we?'

'I don't remember the thin,' I said. 'I was the one on a diet all the time.'

Jenny gave me a friendly shove. 'You are daft.'

'Look, you need to think about what you're going to do.'

'I will – not now,' Jenny said. 'I s'pose we should go to bed.'

We sat there for a few more minutes and then Jenny got up, with some effort, and wobbled a bit.

'I'm not picking you up if you fall over,' I said warningly. 'I'll just leave you there.'

'Cow,' she said, stabilising herself against the table.

And then she leant down, put her arms around me and kissed me on the cheek.

We looked at each other, both of us rather emotional for a moment. I was so happy I wanted to cry. But at the same time, I had an almost crazy desire to laugh.

'I am going up,' Jenny said, rather grandly. 'It might take a while.'

'Take your time,' I said, 'and don't fall down the stairs.'

She flapped a hand at me in farewell and staggered off. I sat and listened to her footsteps thumping slowly up the stairs and then I went to bed too, the springs jangling away like a Salvation Army tambourine as I did so.

In the few minutes before I fell asleep, I thought about what it would be like to be married to someone like Paul. What an absolutely ghastly thought. If it had been me, I would have been arrested for assault and battery after a month. Heaven knew how Jenny had put up with him for thirty-something years. I had a short, but very satisfying mental argument with him, organising the insults for the next time we met up, and then I realised I probably never would see him again and felt very pleased.

Poor Jenny.

And that was the unexpected and truly great thing to come out of this. She had come back. She was here, in this house, asleep. This time we really had made up. And tomorrow was a new day. It hadn't been too late after all.

* * *

The following morning, I woke early with an aching back from the terrible mattress, a dry mouth and badger's breath.

I went into the kitchen to make tea and looked hopefully in all the drawers for some aspirin. Of course, there wasn't any; it was all upstairs in Jenny's Médecins Sans Frontières first aid kit. On the kitchen table were three empty wine bottles, which the two of us had demolished in about three hours. Good grief, no wonder I had a headache.

I sat at the kitchen table listening to my head pounding and drank my tea, wondering what time the builders would arrive. Was it possible to ask them not to make too much noise in case they woke Jenny up? Probably not. Still, it was a new day; my sister was back with me; we were talking again; we had another chance to build bridges. And perhaps this time we would do it properly.

Time passed while I tried to work out how I should behave when Jenny woke up. Which was odd, as I'd never been particularly conscious of such things. Perhaps it would be best if I was soothing and calm, not add fuel to the flames by carrying on the assassination of Paul's character and behaviour.

Should I be anxious? Sympathetic? Supportive? Make a joke of it? No, definitely not that last one; even I could see that wouldn't work.

I made myself some more tea and laid the kitchen table with the things she might like for breakfast. I took our matching café bowls that we had bought in Quimper and put them side by side; it was lovely to see them there together. I had some eggs, some croissants, the giant box of chocolate milkshake powder and the heel of a stale French stick. Not exactly much of a celebration. Perhaps I needed to go out and restock? It would be exciting to go back to the market with her and show her all the lovely stalls. It appealed to think of spending time wandering around with Jenny, picking out unusual condiments and perhaps even laughing about odd things. My spirits lifted.

Perhaps when we were out we could buy some champagne and rejoice?

No, maybe not. Not with the way my head was feeling this

morning, and perhaps that would be tactless? To raise a glass and cheer because my sister's marriage had fallen apart. Although I had heard of people having divorce parties. Maybe that was a step too far.

* * *

There was a familiar noise outside as the workmen's vans came up the driveway, followed shortly afterwards by a bang on the kitchen door.

I opened it, and Bertrand held out a large loaf of bread wrapped in crinkly Christmas wrapping paper and a jar of jam.

'*Ma femme*, she sends you gift,' he said. '*Un cadeau.*'

'A present? Really? How kind. *Très gentille*,' I said, '*merci beaucoup*, Madame Bertrand.'

Bertrand was convulsed with chuckles at this, one calloused hand held over his mouth.

'*Mimi est une terreur*,' he said when he finally caught his breath, 'but she is jam person. Very good.'

I assumed from this that Mimi had made the jam, which was a luminous purple and possibly beetroot. Beetroot jam didn't sound too good to me, but it was a kind thought. Had she been responsible for the green one too?

'Excellent, *merci*, Mimi!'

'And *ma fille*, my daughter, Colette, she is returned. She looks after her friend and the new baby; she is a good girl. Very kind.'

'That's nice. You'll be glad to have her back.'

Bertrand pulled a face. 'Yes, but she is twenty-seven. She is not mother of any children. Mimi *ne comprend pas*.'

'There's still plenty of time, Bertrand,' I said encouragingly.

His expression showed me he didn't agree.

Behind him I could see Léo standing in the driveway, talking on his phone. He looked grim.

'Is everything all right with him?' I asked.

Bertrand glanced at Léo.

'Not good, *le patron* not happy today,' he muttered, his mouth turned down, 'Mimi not happy, Claud not happy, Benoît not happy. No one is happy.'

I went outside and walked over to Léo, arriving at his side as he ended the call.

'Ah, good morning,' he said.

He certainly didn't look very cheerful.

'Everything okay?' I said. 'Jenny came back last night.'

'So I see.'

'I've been telling her all the things we have been doing while she was away.'

'Good, good. I hope she is pleased.'

He was obviously uneasy.

I'd had enough men in my lifetime getting funny with me and not telling me why. That was the sort of thing women did too, being cross about something and then getting even more annoyed when people didn't understand why. I wasn't going to put up with it.

'Look, I know I've been a bit preoccupied for the last few days, but that was because I was worried about Jenny. Have I annoyed you too? Have I done something?' I said.

'It's not you,' he said.

'Then what is it?'

'The damned pool. I knew it would cause trouble. That man...'

I frowned. What man? Why was he so bothered?

'Hugo is supposed to be—'

'It's fine, it's your pool; I must get on,' Léo said. 'It's none of my business. I need to get Claud working, and not sulking.'

He stalked off, still stabbing at his mobile.

At that point I heard noises from upstairs and Jenny's bedroom window opened. Some thumping about and a groan. Jenny was awake.

'I must go, Bertrand,' I said. 'Please thank Mimi for the presents. *Ma sœur*, Madame Jenny. She has *mal de mer*. She needs some *petit déjeuner*.'

Bertrand looked a bit puzzled at this but shuffled off to find his trusty wheelbarrow. It was only then I realised I'd said Jenny was seasick. I drew breath to shout something after Bertrand but then realised I couldn't think of the word for hangover anyway, so I didn't bother.

* * *

'Are you okay?' I shouted up the stairs.

I heard a muffled groan as a response. Perhaps I'd leave her to it for a bit.

I fired up the infernal coffee machine and hacked some wedges off the loaf, which was still warm and a thing of great beauty. It took all my willpower not to stuff it straight into my mouth. I looked at the beetroot jam and then decided to just put it on the table without explanation. Then I hid it behind the milk jug. Perhaps it would be better if it didn't announce itself too soon, but just crept up on Jenny.

'Good morning!'

Through the open kitchen door I could see Benoît and Claud approaching the digger and looking it over rather carefully, as though they thought I had been messing about with it again. Apparently last time, Pierre and Sylveste could tell. I'd left some lever in the wrong position. Boys and their toys.

'Good morning,' I shouted back.

There was the usual thunderous roar as Claud started up the

engine and then trundled off, presumably to start digging the foundations of the new dining room around the other side of the building.

'Is there any coffee?' said a weak voice behind me.

'Morning, Jenny. Sleep well?' I said cheerfully.

She made shushing sort of gestures with her hands. 'Coffee?'

'Just ready,' I said as the coffee machine started erupting behind me.

She slumped into a chair and looked thoughtfully at the beetroot jam, which was peeping shyly out from behind the milk jug.

'What's that?' she said at last.

'A present from Bertrand's wife, Mimi. Isn't that kind?'

Should I mention the return of the chickens? Perhaps not.

Jenny nodded very slowly but didn't say anything.

'Scrambled eggs? Toast? Mimi sent some lovely bread too.'

I was so happy to see her that I would have done anything. Even made her lasagne for breakfast if that was what she wanted.

Jenny shook her head very slowly.

'Headache,' she said.

'Hangover,' I replied. 'You'll be fine when you get some food down you. That jam is probably just the thing. A local remedy for all sorts of ills.'

Jenny looked doubtful.

'Just coffee,' she said again.

I pushed a mug over the table towards her. Jenny nodded her thanks and then winced as the noise from the digger outside hit a new crescendo of power.

'What on earth are they doing now?'

'Digging the foundations of the new dining room,' I said.

'My teeth are rattling.'

'Come out into the garden; we can sit under the pergola. The clematis has started to flower. And I'll show you the pool. You could have a dip if and when the man comes to fit the pump. That would be nice, wouldn't it?'

'No swimming costume,' Jenny answered.

'Knickers and bra then. Skinny dipping? Under cover of darkness?'

She stood up and gave me an old-fashioned look.

'Okay then, we will go to the supermarket and buy you one. A chic French bikini with ruffles.'

'I don't think so.'

I put my arm around her shoulders and led her out into the garden.

'Okay, a knitted stripy one down to the knees. With a matching hat.'

Jenny laughed and then clutched her head. 'Ow.'

24

We took our coffee and sat by the swimming pool under the shade of the pergola. I fussed around her, making sure she was comfortable and not too cold. I liked the feeling of that, of looking after her. She had always been the one who had looked after me when we were small.

I had already dragged a couple of chairs up there, and the little ironwork table, and it was very pleasant. Until Blanche poked her head out from the hedge.

I held my breath and waited for the screams from Jenny, but none came.

'Oh God. That hen is back again,' she said.

'I'm afraid it's not just Blanche—'

'You've given her a name?'

'She has quite a few friends, too. Dotty, Clucky, Frilly Drawers. Bertrand's wife, Mimi, had to come twice and get them. She stuck them all in an old pram. It was quite funny; I wish you'd seen it. Well, the way things are going you still might. She seemed to think I had been luring them away.'

'You haven't, have you?'

'Of course not,' I said. As this was a moment for confession, I added, 'There's a cat, too, that seems to think this place is her territory. She belongs to Bertrand's daughter, Colette, but she's quite friendly. I keep trying to get rid of her, but she keeps coming back.'

Bang on cue, the tabby appeared from behind the pool house and, predictably, Blanche squawked off in the other direction. The cat ignored her and came towards us, miaowing all the way.

'Chatty,' Jenny said.

'Bertrand called her Gigi,' I said.

To my amazement, Jenny put her hand down towards the cat and twitched her fingers. Obligingly, Gigi thrust her head under Jenny's hand and allowed her ears to be fondled.

'I like cats,' Jenny said. She looked rather flushed. 'I've always wanted one but—'

'But Paul said no?'

'Of course.' She dropped her face into her hands. 'Oh God, Kitty, what am I going to do about Paul? My life, my marriage!' she wailed, exasperated.

Every fibre of my being wanted to scream out, *Divorce him, start enjoying life, never speak to him again, put all his beige slacks and acrylic cardigans on a bonfire*, but instead I tried to be the rational and supportive sister Jenny needed.

'Well, you need time to think,' I said. 'What's best for you and of course for Ace. Take your time. Have you told him about all this?'

Jenny shook her head. 'Not yet. I suppose I should. I've just not mentioned it. And then, of course, I didn't get the chance.'

'*Of course* you should tell him! He must have loved having you to stay, to see you again after all this time. He'll want to know that you are all right, that he can see you whenever he wants to.'

'Yes. But it's so *embarrassing*.'

'For Paul, maybe, but not for you,' I said. 'You've done nothing wrong.'

We sat and thought about things for a while, while Gigi's purrs rose to epic levels and at last she threw herself on the ground and rolled over, all four paws in the air.

'I never believed it would come to this,' Jenny said, and she slumped a bit. 'I suppose I just assumed we would plod on forever if I thought about it at all. I'll be honest, I was secretly dreading Paul getting really old. He'd be impossible if anything was ever really wrong with him. The thought of having to *nurse* him or give him a *bed bath*. Am I an awful person?'

'No,' I said firmly, 'you're not an awful person. He's behaved like a tyrant for such a long time. I'm proud of you for walking away from it all. That must have taken a lot of courage.'

'But how will I cope? I mean on my own?'

'Like most people,' I said. 'Like I did. Day by day until you get your life back into some sort of order. Make a list of all the things you want to do. If you want to get a divorce, then speak to a solicitor. Do something nice for yourself every day. Even if it's just having lasagne. Go through your wardrobe and chuck out all the things Paul liked. Because they will be the things that make you feel all beige and depressed again.'

'When did you get so wise?' Jenny sighed.

'I'm not, but I know what it feels like to start again.'

I did, too; I couldn't count the number of times I had separated my possessions from someone else's. Gone through the bathroom cabinet and thrown away aftershave and razors. Chucked out magazines about football, cameras or worse.

'I suppose you do. But at my age, I'm going to be on my own *forever*,' she wailed.

'You don't know that,' I said, rubbing her arm, 'and I can tell you from personal experience, there are sadder things.'

'I'm not brave like you,' she said at last. 'How do I go about rebuilding my life at my age? How do people do that, anyway? What am I?'

'You're you,' I said. 'You don't need to be brave; you're great and that's what matters.'

There was a long pause while Gigi, her eyes narrowed with concentration, crouched at Jenny's feet and did some exaggerated bottom wiggling before leaping onto Jenny's lap.

'See,' I said, 'I love you; Ace loves you; the cat likes you.'

* * *

Pierre and Sylveste arrived after lunch with the tractor lawn mower and this time Sylveste took his turn while Pierre collected up a few things he had left behind on their last visit. It looked as though they were just about finished in the garden, and I was going to miss them. Pierre then went to look at the swimming pool. He felt the water, which was still very cold, although I was being very disciplined about *le pH*.

'No good?' he said. 'Too cold.'

'Still no engineer,' I said. 'Hugo was supposed to be contacting an engineer to fix a new pump and check the heater. And that was ages ago. Can you chase him about it?'

He nodded and pulled his mobile out.

'No answer,' he said. '*C'est typique*. I don't know this person, the one Hugo said to use.'

He then left a long message for Hugo and put his phone away.

'Thank you,' I said, 'and it looks like you are packing up. You are leaving.'

Pierre stuck his lower lip out.

'*C'est dommage*,' he said. 'I have liked it here. Nice garden. We will come back to lay new turf when the building work is finished over there.'

'You are welcome back any time,' I said, 'especially if you want to mow the grass.'

'You pay me, I will do it for sure,' he said with a grin. 'Sheila did that.'

Jenny wandered out to join me. 'Are they going?'

'Well, they have just about finished. Pierre is going to come back once a month to cut the grass. Are you feeling better?'

Jenny yawned. 'I'm just tired; perhaps it's a reaction to all this? I don't seem to have thought about anything else for a long time.'

'Well, there's plenty to do here to take your mind off things,' I said. 'Léo and I have finished painting the sitting room and the new carpet is going in soon, then the new sofas should be arriving any day, I hope.'

'Do you think—' Jenny stopped.

'What?'

'Do you think we could get some new beds? Mine is like sleeping on the Ukulele Orchestra of Great Britain.'

'We can go and do that tomorrow,' I said. 'And when we decide what we want, Léo can go and pick them up in his truck.'

'Ah yes. Léo,' Jenny said. 'What's happening there?'

'I think it's all gone a bit quiet in that direction.'

'You like him, don't you?'

Yes, it was true, I did like him, and I missed him, too. I missed him being there, his smile, the clever way he dealt with things, the way he never seemed to let anything get him down.

'I do, I like him very much,' I said, forcing a smile. 'Come on, let's go and see what the workers are doing.'

25

The following day, Jenny drove us to a furniture warehouse nearby where we wandered around looking at beds. And rugs and occasional tables and lamps. I didn't think either of us had forgotten that we were planning to sell the house once it was finished, but perhaps we could make it as attractive and comfortable as we could while we were there. It was especially great to see Jenny start to express an opinion again.

We chose a couple of bed frames and mattresses in no time and arranged for them to be delivered. I thought about phoning Léo up and asking him to help out, but at the last minute I didn't. Anyway, it would be good for Jenny to see there was nothing wrong with being independent women sorting it out for ourselves. And for me too, actually.

We had lunch in a ramshackle café in the village, where several spotty youths were logged on to the internet, that Bertrand had mentioned the day we arrived. Then, with incipient indigestion from the paninis we had eaten, we went to the supermarket where we stocked up before going home.

* * *

A colourful blue and green van had preceded us up the winding lanes that led to Jolies Arbres, and as we neared the gateway, it too turned in and parked behind the truck that was already there.

'Who is that?' Jenny asked. 'Have you seen that one before?'

'Never,' I replied.

We pulled up behind it and a man got out and looked around him with a sweeping glance. He pushed his cool sunglasses up onto the top of his head and fiddled with his mobile phone for a few seconds before stretching out his back as though he had been driving for hours.

'Now, he really does look like Sacha Distel. I thought all that stuff about French men was a myth,' Jenny said.

The Sacha Distel lookalike glanced at us as we got out of the car and his face creased into a lopsided and very attractive smile.

'*Bonjour, mesdames,*' he said, favouring us with a flash of very white teeth.

'*Bonjour,*' Jenny replied, which was a surprise.

'I have the honour of meeting Madame Price or Madame Botty?'

'Batty,' Jenny said quickly, 'Jennifer Batty.'

'*Enchanté,*' he said, bowing over her hand.

Jenny gave a funny little squeak. Oh, for heaven's sake.

'I am Dominic Delors,' he said smoothly. 'Please call me Dom; I am here to make all your dreams come true.'

As far as I was concerned, he was oil in human form.

'The new pump for your pool,' he said, 'the heater.'

Ah.

A dull-looking chap who had been smoking in the front of the van opened the passenger door and slid out, standing exhausted on the gravel.

'This is my son Denis, who will be working with me,' Dom said with enthusiasm, as though to convince us that Denis wasn't as gormless as he appeared to be.

'Excellent,' I said, 'I'll take you to see the pool.'

'First we will get our specialist equipment,' Dom said, managing to make it sound slightly saucy.

Jenny snorted. I sent her a hard look.

'What on earth is the matter with you?' I hissed as we led them across the lawn towards the pool.

'Nothing,' Jenny said, sounding shocked.

'Stop behaving like a teenager, then.'

'I'm not. I'm just being pleasant.'

'Ah, here we are,' Dom said. 'What a perfect spot.'

Denis dumped the boxes he had been carrying on the flagstones and pulled out his cigarettes.

Dom went into the brick hut where all the equipment was housed and came back out. Denis opened one of the canvas bags and pulled out a saw, which he waggled in the air, making the blade hum.

'Quite right, Denis,' Dom said. 'Always so keen, aren't you? Are you not thirsty after the drive?'

'Coffee?' Jenny said, right on cue.

'How kind, if it's no trouble,' Dom said as though it was her idea.

I followed her back to the house.

'What are you doing?' I asked as she clattered about with mugs and a plate for some biscuits. 'You've never once made coffee for the other builders.'

'Nothing! For heaven's sake,' she said. 'Look, you can start unpacking the groceries while I take this out.'

'Well okay, but just leave them to it,' I said. 'You know what you said about workmen.'

'Of course I will,' she said. 'I'm just trying to be nice.'

'You were never this nice with Bertrand,' I said.

I watched as Jenny opened a glossy packet of French biscuits – langues de chat – which had been expensive. I'd thought we were saving them for a special occasion and to my mind this wasn't it.

I unloaded the shopping from Jenny's car and lugged it into the kitchen. I started putting it away in the pantry, while also keeping an eye on my sister, who was still out there in the garden, chatting away to Dom and even laughing. She was still holding the plate of biscuits in front of her as though she was a waitress. This was very odd.

Then I went to see how the builders were getting along with the new dining room. Claud was alone, happily laying bricks, the radio turned up to warp factor 5.

'No Léo,' I asked airily, 'or Benoît?'

'They will be here,' Claud said, turning the radio down a notch.

'There is a man putting a new pump in the swimming pool,' I said, 'in case you were wondering what the new van was. If it's in your way I'm sure he can move it.'

Claud went off to have a look around the side of the building and came back looking grim. He muttered something, obviously not happy.

'No! *Ce n'est pas possible*,' Claud said. He rubbed a hand over his face. '*Quelle sont les chances?* This man, what is his name?'

'Dominic something,' I said. 'Delors.'

Claud's face darkened and he dropped his trowel into the pile of cement.

'*Ce bâtard*,' he growled.

'Do you know him?' I said rather foolishly. It was obvious he did.

Claud wandered off to make a phone call. I watched him for a moment, standing with his back to us, head down, speaking very fast.

'What is it?' I asked Claud when he returned.

'Yes, I know him,' he said at last. 'We know him. I knew it. *Mon pauvre père... ce ne sera pas bon. Benoît sera furieux.*'

'What is it?' I asked. 'Why will Benoît be furious? What's the matter?'

Seconds later I heard the sound of a truck pulling up to a skidding halt on the gravel outside and a car door slam shut.

The two of us hurried around to the back garden where we saw Benoît striding away from us across the lawn, his face like thunder.

'*Mon Dieu...*' Claud muttered, 'my father and my brother are back.'

It all happened very fast after that. One minute Dom was talking to Jenny, a coffee cup in his hand, his sunglasses parked on top of his head like some sort of Olympic rower. The next Benoît had lunged at him with a furious roar and Dom flew back into the pool. Which must have been unpleasant on many levels, not least of which because the water – although *le pH* was acceptable – was freezing.

Léo ran towards his son, shouting something, and I followed, while Benoît stood on the edge of the pool, his hands clenched into fists. Jenny was twittering away in distress like a distracted owl and Dom, minus the sunglasses, was floundering about, trying to get to the side of the pool. His cool linen jacket ballooned around him; he was gasping and spluttering.

'What on earth are you doing?' I shouted. 'Are you crazy?'

'This man, I have been waiting a long time for this,' Benoît shouted.

Dom finally found a handhold on the side of the pool and Benoît stepped forward to deliberately tread on his fingers. Dom fell backwards with a yelp and what sounded like a fruity French oath.

Wailing in distress, Jenny clutched the plate of langues de chat against her chest and they all fell on the ground. Like a streak of lightning, Blanche and her feathery accomplices raced out of the hedge and fell on the biscuit shards with enthusiasm and a lot of squabbling. Jenny screamed, standing with the empty plate above her head, while the hens clustered around her feet in a very pecky and clucky way.

'Kitty! Do something!'

'Benoît! Stop,' Léo shouted.

Benoît turned away, snarling and obviously furious.

Father and son had a rapid, angry exchange and then Benoît stomped away across the garden.

The rest of us stood and watched as Dom dragged himself to the steps and clambered out. He didn't look quite so polished now.

'*Imbécile*,' he snarled. 'How was I to know?'

'You saw the trucks; you must have known,' Léo shouted at him.

He looked and sounded furious, his voice bitingly cold.

At this point the hapless Denis came out from the pool shed, still holding the saw in his hand.

'*J'ai coupé les tuyaux*,' he said proudly.

'He's sawn off the pipes to the pump,' Léo said, wiping one hand across his face.

'Is he supposed to do that?' Jenny asked, yelping as a hen pecked at the laces of her trainers.

Denis looked around, obviously rather confused. '*Tu vas nager, Papa?*'

'No, I'm not going for a swim; I fell in, you idiot,' Dom snapped as he stood shivering on the side of the pool, trying to wring the water out of his jacket.

'*Mes poules. Ne pas nourrir mes poules.*'

It was Mimi, back again for the third time to rescue her flock with her empty pram. She had a face like thunder and her woolly hat was pulled even lower than usual over her eyebrows. Behind her was Bertrand, astride Hector the Trojan prince, who suddenly bolted unsteadily across the lawn.

This time, the hens, distracted by the unexpected biscuit feast, ignored Mimi, much to her fury.

'*Cotcotcot*,' she called encouragingly, but to no avail. She sent Jenny a black look of resentment and fury. '*Tu voles mes poules.*'

'We are not stealing your hens!' I shouted above the general mayhem.

Out of the corner of my eye I saw the tabby cat lurking behind a recently planted shrub, with the distracted expression cats always had when they were having a wee. She did a bit of perfunctory earth-scraping before launching herself at Blanche, who flew up into the air with a lot of loud and heart-rending cackling. Mimi, outraged, took off one of her fur-lined boots and slung it at the cat, missing by miles of course, but landing a hefty whack on Dom's forehead. He staggered back with a shout and fell into the pool. Denis took a hesitant step towards him, saw still in hand.

Bertrand and Hector had by now overshot the mark several times and bolted past us towards the end of the garden. Hector's hooves were churning up great divots of mud, and his muzzle was held skywards, nostrils flared. He let out a challenging bray, as though he was a war donkey, plunging into the skirmish.

Bertrand's hands and heels were very high as he tried to regain control of his overexcited steed. As he careered past us, Hector was as flatulent as ever. It was *Don Quixote* mixed with *Blazing Saddles*.

'*Mes poules! Mes jolies poules!*' Mimi wailed.

Unconcerned, the hens carried on pecking away at the biscuits with evident enthusiasm, until Mimi began scooping them up and depositing them into the pram. An activity that, of course, was a complete waste of time. As soon as she put them in, they hopped out again with a lot of furious clucking.

Then Blanche, keen to assert her authority in the actual pecking order, started a squabble with the hen I had called Dotty, beaks and feathers everywhere, and in the middle of the altercation, Bertrand and Hector careered through again, scattering the flock all over the garden. Wisely, the cat made a break for it, and shot towards the house, her tail fluffed out like a loo brush.

'Do something!' Jenny screamed at me.

'What do you suggest?' I yelled back.

We looked at each other for an agonised moment and then, unexpectedly, Jenny started giggling. She clutched the empty biscuit plate to her chest and roared with uncontrollable laughter until she wept.

Well, of course this set me off, and the two of us staggered towards each other, the tears running down our faces as we propped each other up.

'That's the funniest thing I've seen in years,' she gasped at last, wiping her eyes with her sleeve.

Having done two circuits of the garden, Bertrand and his excited steed had now veered off back across the grass and down the drive, and distantly we could hear Hector's excited neighing and Bertrand shouting, '*Hoo, hoo, hoo, Hector! Hector!*'

'God, I hope they are going to be okay,' I gasped. 'I hope Hector stops eventually.'

Dom squelched out of the pool again and stripped off his jacket, trying to once again wring the water out of it while Denis played with the edge of his saw. I saw Denis flinch slightly when predictably he drew blood, and then with a feeble cry he fainted. He actually went down like a sack of potatoes, crumpling from the knees down. Obviously, someone else with *une phobie de sang.*

'Right,' Léo said, as calm was at last restored, 'perhaps we should get on?'

He took a few steps towards Dom, who stepped back. I could see him falling into the pool for a third time, but mercifully he stopped himself.

'Whatever you are doing, you'd better get it done and leave,' Léo said, with none of his usual good humour. 'We have work to do.'

'*Me va bien*,' Dom muttered, which I took to mean 'fine by me'.

Satisfied she had collected all her hens, Mimi pulled her missing boot back on again and stamped off. Then she returned, pulling something out of her coat pocket, which she handed to me. It was a large Kilner jar of bright orange jam.

'*Merci*, Mimi. Marmalade?' I said, trying to speak normally.

'*Confiture de carottes*,' she muttered.

Carrot jam – mmm, delicious. You don't see that very often.

Jenny and I limped back to the house, still chuckling.

'What was all that about?' she said at last.

'I have absolutely no idea,' I said, 'but I wouldn't have missed it for anything.'

26

Very kindly, under the circumstances, Jenny took a couple of towels out to Dom and a plaster for Denis, who had recovered from his faint and was sitting miserably on a chair with his head between his knees.

We stayed out of the way after that. Dom and Denis did whatever they had to do with the new pump and the heater, and the noise from the builders was happily low-key as they were building, not demolishing. Claud had turned his radio down to a reasonable volume, too, so after all the excitement it turned into a quiet day.

Happily, it was also warm and sunny; we hoped Dom had dried out reasonably quickly.

Later that afternoon, Dom came back up to the house, looking around him as though he was expecting an ambush from the builders on the other side.

'All done,' he said conspiratorially as though he was afraid someone would hear him. He messed about with some paperwork, ripping off the top sheet with trembling fingers and handing it over.

'Did you find your sunglasses?' Jenny asked Dom politely.

Dom's mouth tightened. 'No, and they were Vuarnet.'

'Well, when we find them, we'll send them on,' I said.

Dom gave a disbelieving pout, a bit of a head toss and said '*Pfft*' in a very French way.

I was glad he had been able to fix the problem, but now I just wanted him to go. Jenny kept catching my eye and I was afraid I was going to start laughing again.

At last, still a bit damp in the trouser department by the looks of it, Dom got back into his van and they reversed down the drive and away. I heaved a sigh of relief.

'Well, we weren't expecting that, were we, boys and girls?' I said.

'What was all that about anyway?' Jenny asked. 'I mean, can you find out?'

'I'll die trying,' I said, 'don't you worry. What's the time?'

Jenny looked at her watch. 'Quarter to five. Sun's over the yard arm somewhere, isn't it?'

'Damn right,' I said. 'Listen to you! I'll get the glasses; you get the bottle. We'll go down the garden, out of the way.'

* * *

We sat there chatting about nothing in particular and working our way down an excellent bottle of Louis Latour Corton-Charlemagne Grand Cru 2014, which we paired with some breadsticks and a pot of salsa. A fine accompaniment.

The colours were beginning to bloom in the flower beds; the lush leaf cover overhead from the clematis was thickening up. Between the branches, the Paris to Atlanta jet left a trail across the blue sky. We kept an eye on the house, but as the workers were out of view on the other side of the building, there wasn't much to see.

'Shall I cook something this evening?' Jenny said at last.

I did a double take. 'Really?'

'I always quite liked cooking; I just haven't done any for a long time,' she said.

I waved one hand towards the open kitchen door. 'Please feel free.'

'It might not be a success. I mean, not as good as what you do.'

'Whatever you do will be fine by me,' I said encouragingly, 'and I don't care if you lick the spoon. Watch out, Léo's coming.'

Léo came across the garden, looking rather embarrassed.

'I have come to apologise,' he said, waving one hand towards the pool, 'for that.'

'That's fine,' I said, 'we haven't seen anything so funny for a long time.'

At the same moment, Jenny said, 'What was all that fuss about?'

Léo shuffled his feet. 'I think it was unfortunate. I can only apologise.'

He obviously didn't want to discuss it.

'Well, is Bertrand all right?' I said.

'Oh yes, he is unhurt and so is Hector. He just came up to the house to keep Mimi company.'

'That's good.'

Next to me I could feel the pulses of curiosity emanating from Jenny like radio waves. I nudged her with my elbow.

'I must get on,' Léo said. 'I have just had a message from the carpet firm, to tell you they will be here tomorrow to fit the new carpet in the sitting room.' He gave a tight little smile and flicked me a look.

'Sorry again,' he said.

Don't be like this, I wanted to shout. *Be like you used to be. When you were all friendly and relaxed.* What had I done? What had happened? Had he – as we used to say back in the day – dumped me? I'd never been dumped, but I had occasionally been the dumper. It was a horrible feeling.

'You obviously know Dominic Delors,' I said, hoping to encourage some of the facts out of him.

'Oh yes, I know him. I met him many years ago.' He nodded slowly and thoughtfully.

'So, he's not a particular friend of yours?'

'Not a friend at all. If I had known he was going to be here I would have said something. Or made sure Benoît was out of the way... well, never mind. I'm sorry.'

He gave a tight little smile and wandered back across the garden.

What was the full story here and how could I find out?

Next to me, Jenny started going on about what she was going to cook for our evening meal and getting rather excited at the prospect. She was wavering between a ham salad and chicken salad, neither of which would need much actual cooking. But I didn't say anything – baby steps, I suppose.

Just after five o'clock, the workmen left with jaunty waves out of their windows, their vans barrelling off down the drive in a cloud of dust.

'I'm going to make a start on dinner,' Jenny said.

I got up and followed her into the house, my feet dragging.

'What about Léo anyway?' Jenny said in a rather distracted voice.

She started getting everything out of the fridge, even the things she couldn't possibly need unless she was planning to put a pot of custard in the salad.

'Oh, you know,' I said, fidgeting.

'No. What do I know about Léo?'

I was aware this was going to be a pathetic moment, and something I hadn't done for decades. Ask my sister for relationship advice. When my sister was probably as qualified to give it as Hector.

'I think he's gone off me and I don't know why,' I said.

Jenny stopped washing the lettuce and looked at me. 'Léo?'

'Yes, it's not as though I have a crush on Bertrand, is it?'

Jenny snorted. 'Knowing your eclectic taste in men, I wouldn't put it past you. I expect it was all the stuff, you know, the fight and Dom and all the shouting.'

'I suppose so,' I said.

Jenny looked thoughtful, waving the chopping knife in her hand around. I stepped back a bit.

'Or perhaps it's got nothing to do with you at all? Perhaps he's worried about work, or he's ill or broke or maybe the work has dried up and he's facing financial ruin?'

'Or perhaps he has been abducted by aliens, or maybe it's not him at all but his identical twin brother?' I suggested.

'Has he got an identical twin brother?'

'No, Jenny, I'm just saying. He seemed keen and now he's not; we seemed to have a connection and now we don't, and I don't know why.'

'Then ask him,' Jenny said. 'Do I slice these tomatoes or leave them whole?'

'*Of course* I'm not going to *ask him*. What sort of sad sap would I look like? *D'you still like me? Have you gone off me?* Absolutely ridiculous. I do have some dignity. Not much, I'll agree, but a bit nonetheless.'

Jenny sighed and looked at me.

'When did you get so timid? You've always been the one who said and did what you thought without any hesitation. And yet now you're like a silly teenager. Perhaps I should pass Léo a note at playtime. *My sister really likes you...*'

'Oh, I don't know,' I muttered.

At that moment I was just suspecting a problem; talking to him might have confirmed something I didn't want to know about.

'Look, the carpets are coming tomorrow; I'll sort that out and you can go and have a quiet chat with him. Pretend you're having a catch-up.'

'*No!* That would be so obvious!'

Jenny's eyes brightened. 'Here's a good idea: why don't you ring him, ask to meet up somewhere. Tell him you need to talk about – ooh, I don't know – the window shutters? Or the new dining room. You could say you're not sure where the radiators should go. And if you met in the village, you could go into that wine bar we saw the other day. And you could have a glass of wine and maybe one thing would lead to another...'

This sounded exactly the sort of thing Jenny might have said to me in our shared bedroom forty-five plus years ago. We would have been sitting on our beds, me hugging a pillow and looking anguished, her being the sensible older sister who – as far as I was concerned – knew more than I did about boyfriends and how to handle them. That was ironic considering how her romantic life had turned out.

Quite often she would have her hair in heated rollers, always wanting to have the sort of curls that nature had given me for free. Sometimes she would have a face pack on and would dole out advice through stiff lips so she didn't crack it.

'What if he says no? What if we have nothing to talk about?' This too was something I could have said all those years ago.

Jenny gave me a look. 'I've known you all your life and you have *never* had nothing to talk about. Are we having ham or chicken with this?'

'Either. Both. You do know this isn't really cooking, don't you? It's just putting things onto plates.'

'It's the best I can offer under the circumstances,' Jenny said. 'I am dealing with my own problems, you know, not just yours.'

'Sorry.'

The only sound was the noise of Jenny's knife on the chopping board as she destroyed some spring onions.

'I just had an email, from Paul,' she said a last.

'Why didn't you tell me instead of letting me moan on about Léo? What did he say? I mean, you don't have to tell me, obviously it's private. Sorry. Unless you want to tell me. But you don't have to...'

'Of course I'm going to tell you if you will let me get a word in. He said he wants us to try again. That we have too much to lose. All those happy years, all those happy memories. He was going through a mid-life crisis and I wasn't there for him because I was too wrapped up in my own life.'

'I didn't think you had a life?'

'I didn't.'

'Right. Okay then. What else?'

'He said Ace wouldn't want us to split up, that he was at a difficult age.'

'Difficult age? He's not exactly a kid any more. How old is he?'

'Thirty-three.'

'I thought so. So did you reply?'

'No, not yet. I need time to think. This is my life,' Jenny said.

I need time to think.

Well, that was what I was supposed to be doing, but I hadn't managed any serious thinking at all. I just kept remembering Léo, the way he had looked, what he had said, how he had made me feel, the way his eyes sparkled when he laughed. I needed to actually plan my future, where I was going to take my life, not just keep going over our conversations and analysing them.

She pulled some more things out of the fridge and then put them back.

'I thought we had some ham?'

'We do.'

'Well, I can't find it. I thought it was on the table. I'm sure it was. I remember taking it out and putting it here.' She put the flat of her hand onto the far end of the table.

Then she bent down to see if it had fallen on the floor.

Jenny went into the hall and I heard her exclaim.

'The paper bag is here at the top of the stairs. But it's empty. How did it get there?'

I listened as her footsteps clomped about overhead for a few minutes and then there was a shout of alarm. I dropped the bread on the table and hurried upstairs.

'What's the matter? Are you okay?'

Jenny was standing in her bedroom, her eyes wide with shock. There were shards of our ham on the floor.

'What's the matter? What's happened? Where did—'

Wordlessly, she pointed to the open airing cupboard door.

'What?'

She pointed again.

I peered round the door, wondering what on earth had shocked her so badly.

Inside, on a pile of vintage blue-and-white towels, was the cat. And four teeny tiny kittens.

The cat was licking a front paw and looked exceedingly pleased with herself.

I dropped to my knees, enchanted.

'Oh look,' I whispered, 'I told you she liked you.'

27

'Kittens,' Jenny said faintly, 'in my cupboard.'

'They are so sweet,' I said, leaning forward a bit to see better. 'Four tabbies.'

'What should we do?'

My voice went all squeaky. 'Aw, look at them. Their little paws. Their little noses. Nothing. You can't move them. Not when they are so little. They'll be out and about in no time. One morning you'll wake up and all five of them will be pushing you out of bed.'

Jenny blinked. 'Really? I'm not sure I like the sound of that. Surely they live somewhere else? I swear this place really is turning into a zoo.'

'It's called the country,' I said. 'I think it's great.'

'Well, you have them in your wardrobe, then.'

'Ah no, Gigi has chosen you,' I said. 'It's an honour.'

Jenny wasn't convinced. 'It won't be when they are all clawing up my leg and miaowing all night.'

'You'll love it. I mean just look at them.'

'Blooming cats. You do know she's had all our ham?' Jenny muttered, but her face had softened.

'Come on, let's leave her to it,' I said, tugging her arm. 'We'll have chicken.'

* * *

Two days later, the sitting room was finished, and we put all the books back on the shelves. And the new curtains up. And it looked fantastic. We had turned a dark and cheerless room into somewhere we wanted to sit, to relax and read. We still didn't have a decent television, but that didn't seem to matter.

Our success gave Jenny a new lease of life when she saw how things could turn out. She had plans to start on the other rooms that needed decorating, but with the house still full of builders' stuff it didn't seem sensible. She started by clearing out all the junk from the third bedroom we didn't use. Then she did some glossing of the skirting boards before looking at the wall colour charts Léo had left for us. After two days she had narrowed it down to five possible choices. I left her to it. It was great to see her doing something that she enjoyed, having a new interest.

Meanwhile, Claud and Benoît worked on, plastering the new dining room and fitting the new electric sockets and two radiators but, disappointingly, there was no sign of Léo or Bertrand. Claud thought they had gone off to work on another job on the other side of the village, and that he had left this one to them. I couldn't believe that perhaps he was avoiding me, although that was how it felt. Ever since the episode with Dom Delors and the pool pump. But then again, Léo was working; he needed to spend his time profitably. My thoughts went round and round in unsatisfactory circles.

Meanwhile, I took the opportunity to have a chat with Bertrand when he returned.

'I think we have your cat,' I said, 'upstairs, and she's had kittens in a cupboard.'

Bertrand's face softened. '*Les chatons?* Ah, *j'aime les chatons.* I love them. 'ow many?'

'Four. Their eyes are still closed.' I did a lot of blinking to emphasise this.

He was clearly delighted, clasping his cloth cap to his mouth in his excitement.

'Ah, *je les bénis,* bless them! I may send Colette to see them? Gigi is her cat. That will make her so happy.'

'Of course,' I said.

'I will ring her now.'

I didn't have to wait long. About ten minutes later, a young woman came down the drive on a bicycle, skidding to a halt and rushing to the kitchen door where I was washing some apples to put in the fruit bowl.

'Gigi!' she called. 'You have Gigi? I've been so worried about her!'

I stared at her for a moment, speechless. She was an absolutely glorious creature in the mode of a young Audrey Tautou. I knew about her because I'd seen *The Da Vinci Code.* She was tiny, with a short, glossy bob and sparkling dark eyes. She was dressed in a simple blue T-shirt under some rather stylish linen dungarees. She was everything chic and attractive that French women were rumoured to be. She was definitely not what I had been expecting.

So Mimi couldn't be as old as I'd first thought; she must be much younger. And presumably Bertrand was too.

'Colette?' I said at last, in case I was mistaken.

She smiled, a perfect white smile that gave her fetching dimples.

'You are Kitty?' she said.

We shook hands and then she threw her arms around me and kissed my cheek.

'I was sure something bad had happened. Gigi, she is okay?'

'She's fine,' I said, smiling back. 'She has four of the dearest little kittens. You must come upstairs and see them. Perhaps when they are a little older you can take them home with you.'

Colette followed me upstairs, tiptoed into Jenny's bedroom and knelt at the shrine of kittens in the cupboard.

'My little Gigi,' she murmured, stroking the cat's head.

Gigi purred contentedly.

'You naughty cat,' Colette said, 'you worried me. And here you are!' She looked up at me. 'Thank you so much for looking after her.'

'It's a pleasure,' I said. 'Actually, I haven't really done anything.'

'Oh, but you must be so busy. Papa has told me how hard you have been working in the garden. And you have the builders here? Léo Bisset? And his sons? Benoît and – and Claud?'

Something in the tone of her voice and the way she ran her slim fingers through her hair made me interested. And then a brilliant idea occurred to me. 'Come and see what they've done.'

'Oh no, I couldn't possibly, I don't want to get in the way,' she said, flushing rather pink.

'I insist,' I said. 'It would be my pleasure.'

We went back downstairs, and I took her on a brief tour of the new sitting room, which she said was *elegant and beautiful*, the new bathroom, which she said was *merveilleux*, and then out to the garden to look at the pool and the new shrubs. Then on to where the builders were working and the new dining room. All the time she was slightly on edge, fussing with her necklace, smoothing down her hair.

My plan worked beautifully. I knew I was right. I should do it for a business.

Claud and Colette took one look at each other and I swear the sparks flew across the piles of electrical cable, wooden flooring and boxes of nails. It was marvellous.

'I know you, don't I?' Colette said at last, her cheeks slightly rosy. 'We were at school together.'

Claud did some rapid blinking and swallowing.

'Yes,' he croaked at last, 'you were younger.'

Colette laughed and the dimples were shown off to marvellous effect. How could Claud possibly resist her?

'I still am. You've changed!'

'So have you,' Claud said, his mouth hanging open a bit.

And she had changed in a good way, by the look of his expression.

Behind him, Benoît was watching. He raised his eyebrows, snorted down a laugh and flicked me a glance. And then he tactfully took himself off to the truck where I think he pretended to be doing something.

I left them to it. Wasn't it great when a plan came together?

* * *

Jenny was filled with enthusiasm about what she was doing, and if we looked at the colour charts once, we looked at them a dozen times. She did have a tendency to veer off towards magnolia if she wasn't stopped, but in the end she decided on pale green. It was a lovely feeling to know she was working in the next room. It was the first time we had co-operated like this for many years. We were bonding over the house now, not just there together. I wondered if that had been Sheila's plan?

The trouble was it would soon be time for both of us to go back to England.

Every day the builders took something else away: the digger, the cement mixer, the scaffolding tower. They were finishing things off; the day would come soon when their work was done. And then what?

Sometimes I made myself think it through. We would put Jolies Arbres up for sale and eventually someone would buy it. Maybe it would be someone's holiday home. One day we would drive away and never return.

Every time I contemplated this, I felt a shiver of unease. I couldn't imagine doing that. I couldn't. There was so much here I loved. The clean air, the tranquillity, and, yes, the people I had met too.

I liked how I felt here, grounded and safe, something I didn't think I had ever felt before. I had been clinging to things, to people, to routine, to make me feel in control. Here, I didn't need to try. I fitted here; I belonged here. Was that possible?

Gigi and her kittens didn't seem to mind the upheaval going on in the house, and the cat hopped in and out of her cupboard when she felt like it, occasionally sitting on the windowsill and looking out over the garden.

Colette was a daily visitor, bringing little treats for the new mother, and the kittens were thriving. It wouldn't be long until she could take them back home. I had the funny feeling Jenny would miss them.

There was no doubt too that Colette's calls also included considerably longer visits to chat to Claud. There was definitely something going on there. A lot of giggling and dimpled smiles from Colette, and foot-shuffling and blushing from Claud. He'd taken to using some sort of hair product too and looked rather pleased with himself.

* * *

That day I took myself off down the garden, just to get away from everything. The garden was coming into full bloom now, and every time I turned my back a new patch of weeds appeared.

I think I was suffering with what might be described as gardener's burnout. Like executive burnout but with more mud. And terrible fingernails. And a rubbish wardrobe.

I sat on the little wall and slumped a bit. For the first time since we had arrived here – well, for the first time, really – I was feeling my age. And I was tired. The more I thought about everything, the more complicated it became. Still, I straightened up and flexed my shoulders. I suppose I couldn't expect to be continually positive. Heaven knew Jenny hadn't been. We had both had to cope with things we hadn't expected, but the great thing was now we had each other, just as we used to.

I looked over to the house; I could see her in the window, wearing paint-splattered overalls, hard at work with a roller.

I looked at the pool and, without much hope, went to feel the temperature of the water.

Yes! That was the answer!

It had taken ages for it to reach an acceptable twenty-six degrees. When I finished this bit of weeding, I would go in for a dip. Then I would sit on the side of the pool with a glass of wine and relax, just as I had imagined doing. That was a good plan.

After lunch, Jenny went off, very excited, to buy more paint, and at last I got into my new swimming costume.

Bertrand was painting the shutters outside the front of the house with grey primer; the Bisset men were doing something in the new room. I made sure that they were busy on the other side of the house, out of view.

I didn't really want them seeing me in my swimming costume. It was so unfair that women of all shapes, ages and sizes got cellulite and men – even old and overweight ones who had never seen the inside of a gym – didn't. Sometimes I wondered if Victorian bathing machines might make a comeback.

I slipped off my dressing gown and walked into the shallow end.

It still felt a bit of a shock, but I soon got used to it. It was absolutely blissful. It felt marvellous, christening my own pool.

I did a bit of swimming underwater and I spotted Dom's sunglasses, lying neatly folded on the bottom of the pool. I retrieved them and put them on the edge. Perhaps I would send them to him; perhaps I wouldn't.

I did a few lengths and then lay on my back, floating and watching the clouds drifting past above me. That moment was absolutely worth all the weeks of work and mess and muddle that had preceded it. But would there be someone else enjoying this pool soon? Children shouting and splashing with excitement? Perhaps they would have a blow-up shark, or a flamingo chair with a drinks holder. That funny little chill of unease gripped my stomach again.

Perhaps while I still had the chance I would get up early every morning and do forty lengths. I probably wouldn't. Maybe Jenny and I could do aquarobics. I tried lifting one leg and waving it about above the water. Of course, I was no synchronised swimmer and I sank under and resurfaced, snorting and coughing, my hair in my eyes.

'Please don't drown yourself,' someone said from the side of the pool.

It was Léo, back at last from wherever he had been. And, of course, fate being what it was, he had caught me doing something stupid. And in a swimming costume that was now slightly too big. All that gardening had obviously done me some good.

I hauled inelegantly at the straps and went over to the side of the pool where I could hide a bit.

'Where have you been?' I said, looking up at him.

'I had a job to start, over near Plouvien. An extension. Every-thing was going wrong, one thing after the other.'

No use beating about the bush.

'I thought you were avoiding me,' I said.

'Why would I want to avoid you?'

'You were very cross when I last saw you.'

'I was, wasn't I? The water looks lovely. Would you mind?'

He sat down on the edge of the pool and took his boots and socks off. And then he rolled his trouser legs up and dangled his feet in the water.

'Oh, *mon Dieu*, that's great,' he said, his eyes closed. 'I don't seem to have relaxed for days. There's always something.'

His phone rang and he made a cross little noise. 'See what I mean?'

Well, this was a bit awkward; neither of us could really go anywhere. He had his feet in the water, and I was hiding underneath it, my arms resting on the side of the pool. The afternoon sun was warm on my back. I looked at his feet, which were large. Hmm.

I rested my cheek on my arms, smelling the scent of the *produits chimiques* that were so evocative of every pool I'd ever known. I looked at Dom's designer sunglasses, lying on the ground in front of me. A butterfly landed on them, right in the middle of the bit that had gone over the top of Dom's remodelled nose, flexing its wings. And then I thought about how long I had been here, and how long I might stay and then of course I considered the prospect of going home. And I was unexpectedly rattled. My thoughts were firming up; I had to accept that it was nearly time to leave here. To go back.

Home to me was a flat with some window boxes, a concrete car park, dogs, the smell of fast food, the sound of traffic and people. It was nothing like this, nothing at all.

Here there was peace, or at least there would be when the builders had finished. There was the scent of freshly mown grass. Birdsong, the rustle of leaves, the occasional tractor rumbling along the lane. Hens coming through the hedge, the sea glittering in the distance, proper French bread, cobbled village streets, a cat and kittens in the cupboard, the sound of church bells in the still air. A good feeling. One that suited me, that I wanted to keep.

Léo ended the call, put his phone away in his jacket pocket, and then slung it over the back of one of the chairs nearby.

'Perhaps you need a break from all this, Kitty?'

'No, I'm not unhappy, just tired,' I said.

I looked up at him, still sitting with his feet in the water.

'So are you going to tell me what all that was about? That day when Dominic Delors came here and there was all that chaos?'

There was a long silence, which, uncharacteristically, I didn't fill.

At last, Léo took a deep breath. 'Delors is... he is the man who had an affair with my wife.'

'Oh, *Léo!* Why didn't you tell me?'

'She wanted me to build a pool in our garden. I wasn't keen, but in the end she contacted his firm. He turned up to do a site survey and one thing led to another. We were divorced after many months of her indecision; they went off to live in his holiday home in Spain but I heard the relationship didn't last. She stayed there. I didn't know he was back here again. I was hoping I had seen the last of him.'

'Ah, I see.'

'And then when I saw him here, when Benoît saw him, knowing what he had done, I fear he lost his temper.'

'You should have told me; I might have been able to help.'

Though what I could have done I had no idea.

'Benoît will apologise to you, I'm sure.'

'There's no need,' I said. 'Benoît must have felt it very badly too.'

'He did. He was at an impressionable age, I suppose, when it all happened. It was a long time before he could speak to his mother without tears or argument. She thought it was all my fault. I think they have come to a better place now. But there was still no excuse for his behaviour.'

'It was very exciting, all the same,' I said.

I looked up at him and we smiled at each other.

'There was no excuse for my behaviour either,' he added. 'I have been *distrait*, difficult with you. I needed to sort out my thoughts. I have been very confused. I have enjoyed your company more than I thought possible. And yet I had to keep reminding myself that you were going to leave. Do you see?'

'Yes,' I said quietly, 'I know. I've been thinking about that too.'

I picked up Dom's sunglasses and looked at them.

'These are his. Dom's. Benoît knocked them off. I've just got them from the bottom of the pool. He said they were valuable, some particular brand that I've never heard of. Verruca?'

Léo took them and looked at them, then with a swift motion he chucked them away into the bushes. Perhaps that was what happened to Sheila's sunglasses. Who knew?

'Are you all right?' he said suddenly.

All right in what way?

My mind picked through what he might have meant but I couldn't come up with a satisfactory answer.

'What do you mean?' I said at last.

'I mean you, this house, being away from your life in England for so long. From your job and your friends. Do you miss it all? Is that the problem? Do you want to go home?'

Did I want to go home? But *this* place felt like home. More like home than anywhere I had ever lived. It had begun to fit me like a pleasantly worn slipper. Okay, it wasn't smart or particularly convenient. Everything required a car journey. I had no idea where the nearest doctor was or dentist. I hadn't even found the best supermarket or garden centre. I didn't know how long I was even allowed to stay, although I had researched residence permits one night when I couldn't sleep.

'Here's the thing,' I said, wondering what I was going to say. 'I couldn't understand why Sheila had bought this house when I first came here. It wasn't close to a historic town or the mountains. And the village was nothing special. It didn't even seem the right place for an artist, because it was so dark inside and gloomy. The house felt neglected and rather sad, but underneath that was this sense of something solid. I understand now. It felt as though someone was very happy here. Perhaps it was Sheila; maybe it was someone else.'

I stopped talking, a bit uncomfortable because after all, I was literally up to my neck in warm water and he was still sitting on the side, listening to me ramble on.

'You are right,' he said, 'she was very happy here. In the time I knew her she was well liked. My father…'

'What?' I said.

'Did you ever find that portrait? I think it was the only one she ever did. It was of my father. I really would like to see it if you find it.'

I swished my feet about in the water for a bit. 'We could go and look? I have to decide what to do about all those paintings we put into the storage place. I still have the business card for Capitaine Picard somewhere.'

Léo looked puzzled, so I explained. 'An art dealer we met in Quimper. He said he would be interested if we wanted to sell them.'

'You still haven't answered my question,' Léo said. 'Do you want to finish this house, sell it and go home?'

My wet hair was beginning to dry in the sunshine, and I could almost feel it frizzing. I needed to get some conditioner on it. I dunked my hair back in the pool, enjoying the feeling as the cool water ran across my scalp. Did I want to go home?

But what would I do if I didn't?

I'd never imagined I would seriously consider this. I mean, I had always thought myself quite adventurous, I had the childhood scars to prove it. By the way, never jump off a stepping stone in the middle of a stream in the hope that the next stone is secure.

I looked up at the blue sky. Selling the house to strangers was absolutely unthinkable. It would be like giving a child away, something I had cared for and nurtured and come to love.

The moment was suddenly a quiet one, the possibilities opening up in front of me, unformed and seductive. But now I could think properly. There was no noise from the builders, from the house, almost as if it too was listening. Even the breeze across the garden was quiet, the leaves waiting for my answer.

'No,' I said at last, 'I don't want to. I like it here.'

I felt a bit odd, actually. As though I was having an out-of-body experience. That someone else had taken over and was making my decision for me.

'That is excellent news,' Léo said, laughter in his voice.

He rolled over onto his side and then he leant down towards the water and kissed me, just very lightly.

'Have you forgiven me? Are we friends again?' he said.

I smiled up at him and nodded, feeling even odder, almost sick with excitement. What was happening here?

'Then it is decided,' he said.

'It is?'

'Oh, *bien sûr*, certainly.' He nodded. He kissed me again and sat up, dangling his feet back into the water.

'Would you like to share what has been decided with me?' I asked.

I was grinning so much I must have looked rather crazy.

'But you were here; you were the one who decided,' he said, shrugging. He leant over again, touching my face with one hand.

I grabbed hold of his arm and tugged as hard as I could, pulling him into the water.

He came up spluttering.

'You are a crazy woman,' he said, 'completely crazy.'

He grabbed me and kissed me properly. And then he leant back and looked at me and all I could do was laugh. And he chuckled and dragged me under the surface and kissed me again. And the whole world was blue and warm and wonderful.

We broke the surface of the pool in a huge sploosh of water, still hugging, still kissing. I didn't think I'd ever felt so happy.

'*Now* what are you doing?' Jenny said from the edge of the pool, but this time she was smiling.

'Nothing,' I said in a stroppy teen voice, pushing my hair out of my eyes and looking up at her.

'I have the feeling you are as daft as each other,' she said. 'Now come and see what I've bought. I have paint and some lovely little hooks shaped like flowers and two new dressing gowns, one each. One blue and one yellow. You can choose.'

'Good heavens!'

28

'I will have to go back,' Jenny said that evening, 'and so will you. Or you'll lose your job, your flat might be broken into, your car battery will certainly be flat. That's if it hasn't been stolen.'

'None of those things bother me,' I said.

We were in our new sitting room. Me on one sofa, Jenny on the other with Gigi next to her.

'I thought you said the cat wasn't allowed on the furniture?' I said.

Jenny reached down and rubbed the cat's ears. 'She isn't.'

'Looks like it.'

'Well, she deserves a break from those kittens once in a while,' Jenny said. 'But I mean it, I have to go back and sort things out. For all I know Paul and the trollop have moved in and are creating a little love nest. And that's not the idea.'

'What are you going to do, then?'

I rested my head back. I wasn't really listening too closely; I was thinking about Léo and wondering what I really was going to do next. It was all very well saying I didn't want to go back to England, but doing it meant a huge shift in my life, not to mention the prospect of the paperwork and officialdom.

'I am planning to sell the house, give Paul whatever he is entitled to, always remembering half the house is yours, then I'll give you whatever is due to you.'

'And then?'

'It's all so complicated. There's this house to consider too. I'd need the money from the sale to be able to afford somewhere half decent. And I have a sneaking feeling your plans are changing.'

'Well, yes. I think they are,' I said.

'Go on?'

'I don't want to go back to Bristol,' I said.

Jenny stopped stroking Gigi's furry head and the cat lifted a disapproving paw.

'You don't want to go back? What, *ever*? But what will you do? Stay here?'

'Yes, I think that's about it.'

'Because of Léo? I mean, I know he's nice and quite attractive, but it seems another of your mad impulses. And they've done you no favours in the past.'

'No, it's absolutely not because of Léo,' I said. 'I like it here. I like this house; I like how it feels and more importantly, I like how I feel in it. If I stayed here, you could visit any time and so could Ace.'

'But what about your flat?'

'I'll sell it. I've never liked it and I've never felt as happy there as I do here.'

Jenny sat thinking for a few minutes and, taking advantage of the distraction, Gigi crept into her lap.

'It sounds as though you're going to have all the fun. As usual. But what am *I* going to do?' Jenny said.

'Well, you could do several things. But if I were you, I'd divorce Paul, sell the house, and move somewhere else.'

'Move where?'

'Anywhere. Move near Nantes. Live nearer to Ace.'

'We can't both move to France,' Jenny said, puzzled. 'That would be weird.'

'Why? It's quite a big country, you know. There's room for lots of people.'

'But I don't speak French.'

'Then learn. Ace would help. I bet he knows some sexy, grizzled professors at the university who would teach you all sorts of things.'

'Trust you to think of that,' she said with a wry smile.

'Or you could stay here for a bit while you find your feet and decide what to do.'

'Hmm, maybe not. I'd rather we stayed friends,' Jenny said, 'and if we were living here together without the house renovations to focus on, I think we might get on each other's nerves.'

'Yes, perhaps that wouldn't be such a good idea. We need to think what to do about the paintings too. They can't stay in storage forever.'

'Anyway, isn't Léo going to feature in your plans? It looked like you were getting pretty friendly.'

'Well, he might,' I said, 'but he might not. I don't know.'

'I don't think I could ever – you know – get *close* to another man. In that way,' Jenny said.

'You mean sex? I've told you before, you worry too much about things that may never happen. But on the other hand, if you go and live near Ace he might introduce you to some French intellectual who will want to discuss René Descartes and all you need to say is *Perfect numbers, like perfect men, are very rare* and then stick your lower lip out and look bored.'

Jenny shook her head in disbelief. 'How do you come up with all this stuff?'

'No idea.'

Gigi, meanwhile, had been edging carefully up until she was purring directly into Jenny's face.

'And you could get a cat,' I added.

Jenny shoved the cat gently away. 'I really will have to go home soon. And you need to go too. You might be all loved up with Léo but there are still things you have to do before you can realise this dream of *la belle vie*.'

'I'm not all loved up with Léo, Jenny, I'm all loved up with France.'

* * *

'I've got to go back to England,' I said a few days later.

It was about ten o'clock, Jenny had gone to sleep and I was sitting up in bed with Léo, drinking champagne. I just thought I'd throw that in there.

'I know,' he said.

He had his arm around me and we were having a lovely cuddle.

I looked up at him. 'I was hoping you would go all French and forbid me to leave.'

He laughed. 'I would never do that. But in case you were wondering, I'd rather you didn't go. I will miss you. You will return?'

'Of course I will; I've told you, I want to live here,' I said, holding out my glass for a refill.

'And Madame Jenny?'

I looked at him, exasperated. 'Madame Jenny. Why do you all call her that? It makes her sound much more important than I am. Everyone just calls me Keetee.'

He kissed me. 'But you are much more important, my Keetee. You are vital for the good of my heart.'

I gave a pleased smile. 'I will come back because I am going to live here, in Sheila's house. Forever.'

It was the first time I had said this out loud so boldly. And all at once the little feeling of unease left me, and I knew it was absolutely the right decision.

'I'm going to sell my flat. Bring some furniture over. Sort out those paintings. I don't know what to do with them. I mean, it's not as though we are planning on opening up a museum.'

'I will build you one,' Léo said, waving his champagne glass expansively, 'at the end of your garden. The finest towers topped with spires and flags flying. Battlements and cannons. The tourists will flock in to see such a palace.'

I laughed at the thought of this. I was filled with excitement for the future; a wonderful warm glow was filling my heart.

'And a shed for the chickens when they return, as I'm sure they will. Mimi must be so annoyed with me. By the way, the Claud and Colette thing. What's happening there?'

Léo shrugged. 'I don't know. I don't ask.'

I was exasperated. 'Why on earth not? You men are hopeless. One minute Claud is moping around like a wet cat and now he is happy again. You must have noticed? Aren't you curious?'

'I am but I am his father; we don't tend to have those conversations.'

'Well, in the absence of his mother, I will jolly well ask him,' I said.

'Good. And then you can tell me,' Léo said, grinning, 'and trust me, if you have found a new romance for Colette, I am sure Mimi will forgive you anything.'

'She brings me jam,' I said. 'The last one was pink. It could have been rhubarb. Or radish. I haven't dared taste it yet.'

'Then you are honoured. You may find she likes you after all.'

* * *

I rang Capitaine Picard the next day. He sounded very pleased to hear from me.

'*Chère madame*, I am filled with delight. I was thinking of you only the other day; the painting I had when you called in was sold the day after your visit. I had many expressions of interest.'

'That's good to hear,' I said. 'I wonder if you could advise me.'

'*Bien sûr*, of course, I would be delighted.'

'We have several of Sheila's paintings here; I wonder if you could sell them on our behalf.'

'Of course, of course, *chère madame*, but maybe we should have an exhibition? There would be advertising costs, of course, and some planning.' He sounded very excited.

'And your commission,' I added.

'Well, yes, but I think this would be acceptable, considering the scale of the project. I will take down your details and discuss this with my business partners. I may need a day or two to get back to you. And I should come and see the paintings, to see which would work well together.'

'Of course,' I said, 'that's an excellent idea.'

We exchanged details and I rang off. But which paintings would he want to see? And where was the portrait of Léo's father?

* * *

We carried on decorating and freshening up the house for the next week. Jenny made an excellent job of the spare bedroom, furnishing it with a wooden bedstead and bedroom cabinets. Then we got Claud and Benoît to take the old wardrobe out into the garden and we painted it pale green. Jenny was keen enough to talk about stencilling it but in the end she just replaced the door knobs. It looked splendid – upcycling, I think it's called.

'I can't think why I didn't do this sort of thing years ago,' she said as we stood admiring her work. 'I would have loved to have done this back home.'

'Perhaps you just needed the opportunity?' I said. 'And the encouragement.'

We both thought about this for a moment and then Jenny looked at me and suddenly, she started to cry.

'Oh, Kitty,' she sobbed, 'I was such an idiot for all those years. Letting Paul dominate my life, missing out on so much, missing out on time with you. I remember the day we came here together on the ferry. I was so excited to see you, but I didn't know what to do, so I just sat and read that awful book. And you were trying so hard to make conversation and be nice to me after all the awful things I'd said. I just sat there frozen with fear that we would never be friends again. That Ace was going to be so near and I wouldn't get to see him. That it was too late.'

I went and put my arms around her and gave her a hug.

'Twit,' I said, 'Sheila knew it's never too late. It's never too late to be happy, to fall in love, to change things. And we both still have a great deal of life left and such a lot to do.'

This made her cry even harder.

29

Ace arrived on Friday evening, driving his smart little red sports car that was cool beyond words. Jenny had been like a cat on hot bricks all day, fussing around with flowers in every vase and opening and then closing windows when she changed her mind. I'd made a vast cottage pie because apparently Ace liked it and hadn't had a decent one for years. Aha, so the French might think they were the culinary best but there was still something they couldn't do.

'I hope that new bed is going to be comfortable,' Jenny said as she fussed about a bit more.

'Well, ours are, so I'm sure this one will be.'

'Oh dear, I'm so nervous,' she said, twitching at the curtains, moving a little clock on the bedside cabinet. 'Oh look! He's here!'

She rushed out to greet him, me close on her heels. Ace leapt out of the car, all long legs and beard. He had a huge grin on his face.

'Mum!'

'Ace!'

I held back while they hugged and Jenny gabbled at him, letting them get on with it. But then he turned and saw me standing in the doorway.

'Auntie Kitty! Still causing trouble?'

'I do my best,' I said cheerfully.

We had a hug and then he darted back to his car and pulled out his overnight bag and a huge bunch of flowers, which he presented to Jenny with a flourish.

'It's looking great,' he said, admiring the garden. 'It's so quiet! I'm not used to that. And you've been busy in the garden, I bet? Well done, Mum!'

'Well, it wasn't actually me,' Jenny admitted. 'I didn't do much.'

'Much? You didn't do any of it,' I said, 'but I'll admit you have been busy indoors. She's made such a nice room for you, Ace. Come and see.'

Jenny gave him a guided tour of the house and – nice boy that he was – he admired everything.

I suppose my clearest memories of him had been as a subdued boy, a monosyllabic teenager, in a house that had been dominated by his father. Now he had blossomed into a very cheerful and pleasant young man. And he was nice-looking too, despite the hipster beard.

'Cottage pie! My absolute favourite!' he said with evident pleasure when we sat down to eat. 'So tell me what your plans are now, Auntie Kitty? Mum says you want to stay here, is that right?'

'That's the idea,' I said, 'and your mum has some plans of her own.'

'Well, as long as they don't include my father,' Ace muttered as he helped himself to vegetables. 'I think we've had enough of him to last us both a lifetime.'

'Oh, we don't want to talk about that now,' Jenny said, a bit flustered.

'Well, I do,' I said. 'I've only just got you back; I don't want to see you disappear again.'

Ace gave her a look as he sloshed some gravy over his dinner. Then he handed the jug to Jenny and she gave me a huge grin before she helped herself too. I knew we were both remembering that awful lunch in the Old Duck and Trumpet all those years ago.

'That goes for me too, Mum. You look happier than I've seen you for years. Got a new man?'

'Ace!' Jenny said, horrified. 'Stop it!'

'Well, it wouldn't bother me, Mum. Whatever makes you happy. I'm all grown up now; I'm not going to blame my slow descent into madness and drug-taking on my parents' divorce, am I? What do you think, Auntie Kitty?' He gave me a cheeky look.

Jenny interrupted. 'Oh, Kitty has already got a new man in her life.'

'I remember,' Ace said. 'You're a long time dead. Make the most of life.'

I gave him a pleased grin and opened the wine. A Château Malescot St-Exupéry, which partnered very well with cottage pie.

'When did you get to be so sensible, Ace?'

'No idea. This wine is excellent, where did you get it?'

'The cupboard under the stairs,' Jenny said, raising her glass to clink against his.

* * *

It was such a lovely weekend. Jenny seemed to have bloomed in the space of a few weeks, and she was cheerful, laughing and joining in just as she had been in the old days.

It was terrible what one person could do to another. I suppose you would have had to be a very strong character to withstand thirty years of gaslighting and scorn. There was something to be said for realising that the end of a bad marriage could also mean the start of something new. And that thing could be quite wonderful.

Ace was a revelation. He was cheerful, said all the right things about everything and he could cook too. We took him out to the local market and he charmed all the stallholders in fluent French and bought all the ingredients for a Moroccan tagine, which was fantastic. *And* he did the washing-up afterwards. Perhaps this was the way of this generation, not leaving everything to their mothers and partners to do? There was hope yet.

Be still, my beating heart. No wonder Marie-Odile was phoning him every morning and every afternoon.

He even emptied the dishwasher, a thing I hadn't thought men could do without threats or encouragement. I felt quite David Attenborough-ish watching him do it.

Not often seen in the wild and never before filmed, the behaviour of this young, adult male in Brittany astounded our cameramen.

* * *

We were sitting in the garden late on Saturday afternoon, sharing a bottle of Coteaux d'Aix-en-Provence rosé, which was summery and quite delightful. I wondered how I would go back to less exalted wines in future. The sun was dipping down towards the sea in the distance, birds were tweeting in the trees above us, and Blanche and her crew were pecking about in their usual carefree manner. I had started to think they considered our garden to be merely an extension of theirs.

'This is a lovely place,' Ace said. 'I can see why you want to stay here, Auntie Kitty. But what about you, Mum? What are you going to do when all this is finished?'

'I know what I've got to do.'

'Go on.'

'I have to go back to Budleigh Salterton, and sell the house.'

'I'll come with you. I'll help,' Ace said cheerfully. 'I can clear things with the university for a week, I know I can.'

Jenny took a deep breath and slapped her hands down on the arms of her garden chair.

'Right. Let's do this,' she said.

'Let's finish this excellent wine first,' Ace said, picking up the bottle and looking at the label. 'Do you realise it's quite expensive?'

'Is it?' I said. 'We've had a couple of these. It's quite nice, isn't it?'

He laughed, rather incredulous. 'Yes, Auntie Kitty. It is. Where did Sheila get all this wine, anyway?'

'We don't know; it was just here when we arrived. Someone said perhaps she swapped paintings for wine. It's possible.' I held out my glass. 'I'd like to say a toast: to Sheila. For bringing us all together again.'

We chinked glasses and grinned at each other.

'By the way, did Jenny tell you about all those paintings? They are in a storage place not far from here. I have a chap from an art gallery in Quimper interested in them. He says they might have an exhibition of Sheila's work.'

'Pity you can't do that in the village,' Ace said, 'as she loved it here so much. There's a museum, isn't there? I bet they could do with visitors.'

'It's an idea,' I said. 'Perhaps I'll ask Colette. She works there, doesn't she?'

'If she can ever drag herself away from Claud,' Jenny added.

'And then, Mum? When you've sorted all that out?'

Jenny pulled a face. 'Ah, the innocence of youth. You think it's all going to happen in five minutes, don't you? I'd like to spend some time near here. I wouldn't want to cramp your style or get in the way. But Kitty will be here and so will you.'

Ace reached over and hugged her. 'Top idea, Mum. A real fresh start.'

'Like on *EastEnders*?' I laughed. 'They are always having a real fresh start.'

'Not *quite* like that,' Jenny said.

* * *

They left early on Monday morning. On Sunday, Ace had impressed both of us, making some phone calls, talking at high speed in French and sorting out the following week's workload. Jenny packed a bag and fussed about, wondering if she was doing the right thing, but the fact that Ace was there, back in her life, had given her confidence and a new enthusiasm for life. Five minutes after they left, Léo arrived.

'Good morning, *ma chère*.' He gave me a double kiss, the thing I had wanted all those weeks ago. 'Jenny is not here?'

'She's gone back to England with her son to sort out her house. But then she plans on returning.'

'So you are staying here, finishing all the work? That seems very unfair.'

'Oh, I don't mind. This trip has been about more important things for Jenny than just painting and decorating. She's got her only son back in her life; she's gaining her independence.'

'And you? What are you gaining?'

I thought about it. 'A new home, a new outlook on life. I'm happy.'

Léo put an arm around my shoulder and we walked into the kitchen.

'And you have friends here, new friends,' he said. 'Me.'

'Ah yes, you,' I said. I kissed him. 'I have something for you.'

'Ah yes? What is it?'

'I went to the storage place with Ace yesterday morning, and I've found it.'

'Found what?'

I pointed to the kitchen table where there was a small painting, covered with a tea towel to keep the surprise for a few more seconds. I whipped it off with a flourish.

'What do you think?' I said.

Léo stared for a minute. I think there were tears in his eyes.

'I never thought to see this again. *Mon père*. It is my father,' he whispered. 'I am so happy you found it.'

He propped it up on the draining board and we stood and looked at the portrait. A handsome man, very like Léo, his face turned towards the artist. The look in his dark eyes so clear.

'He looks just as I remember him,' Léo said quietly, 'and yet different. His expression...'

I put my arm around his waist. 'I've looked at this picture for a long time. I think he's looking at Sheila as she was painting him, and I believe he was looking at her with love. I don't think they were just friends; I think he loved her. And she loved him. And that's why when he died, she never painted again.'

Léo nodded and bit his lip. 'I think you're right. How wonderful and yet, how sad. And I never realised it at all.'

We stood together in silence, looking at the portrait, and the more we looked, the more it was obvious. The light in his dark eyes, the slight twist of his mouth into a smile, the care with which the brush strokes had been done. It looked very much as though Léo's father and my aunt had been lovers after all.

'I've told the boys,' he said a little while later.

We had been sitting at the kitchen table eating *pain au chocolat* and drinking coffee before Benoît and Claud arrived to start painting the window shutters.

'Told them what?'

'That you and I...' He wagged his head from side to side, his eyes twinkling.

'Ah, I see. And what did they think?'

He chuckled. 'Who knows with boys? They just said, *Oh yes*, and then asked when the fasteners for the shutters would be arriving.'

'So?'

'So I thought we might actually take our trip to Saint-Malo this weekend. If you still want to go? There is a very good street market I know of, where you might find some interesting things, to make this place feel like home?'

'Home,' I said, 'you've reminded me. I need to go back. And clear out all my things, sell my apartment. The very thought of it is terrible. Shall I just leave it all there? And never go back? The authorities will break in twenty years from now and find the whole place fossilised and covered in dust.'

He laughed and stood up to help me clear the table. 'I'll help you if you want me to.'

'I would love some help,' I said, 'but I'll understand if you suddenly find you are busy that day.'

'We are very polite, aren't we?' he said, and he kissed me.

'And what about us?' I said.

He tightened his arms around me and rested his chin on the top of my head. Well, he was very tall.

'*Je suis soudainement timide*. I'm suddenly shy, Kitty.'

I looked up at him and grinned. 'It's a bit late for that.'

30

A YEAR LATER

In all honesty, I can't say the rest was plain sailing. Far from it. But it's surprising what two sisters can do when they set their minds to it, particularly when they both suddenly see the possibilities and work together to achieve it. We just needed a plan and the determination and confidence to see it through.

I've never been shy of taking a leap of faith. Some might say I've never really made a plan to stick to before. But this time I did, and it feels very different. I'm doing this for me; it is what I want. I'm not going to rocket from one mistake to another any more, from one dead end job to the next. For the first time I am going to take control of my life, to appreciate what I have and accept myself. Flaws, faults, my optimistic ability to hope for the best, my belief in human nature even when rubbish things happen.

Jenny says she can't believe how much I have changed, how sensible I am, but she is the one who astonishes me. She's shed her old life and her old attitude with absolute determination. I'm sure she must have some doubts, but if she does she never voices them to me.

I suppose it's true what they say; when you're over the hill, you pick up speed. And sometimes the bad things in life can lead to the best things that will ever happen to us. I like the thought of that.

The house where we had spent our childhoods and where she had been so miserable was sold to a couple who were thrilled by the 'neutral décor' – in other words, that everything was painted magnolia – so perhaps Paul did one useful thing, after all.

The divorce is underway; Jenny's hoping that the decree nisi will be through by the end of this week, but I've told her not to hold her breath. The finances have been sorted out, heavily in his favour it seems to me, but then, as Jenny said, cheap at the price. She was buying her freedom, after all, and you can't put a value on that.

We did some negotiating over money because we both owned part of each other's houses. But it's all worked out okay in the end. It's a lot easier dealing with a sister who is actually speaking to me. Rather than the Jenny who didn't.

That all seems a long time ago now. And yet today, when I am looking out at the sea and I see a ferry on the horizon, I can clearly remember that spring day, last year, when we met up to come here for the first time. How nervous we both were. Her cold face, our supressed resentment of each other. The misunderstandings and misperceptions, the memories of sad times that are now behind us.

Recently Jenny has bought a little house overlooking the sea just twenty minutes away from Jolies Arbres, and she is making friends with a group of slightly crazy ex-pat Brits who live in the same village. She's learning French at evening classes and she's actually cooking again. She's also taken two of Gigi's tabby kittens and called them Sacha (Distel) and Alain (Delon).

Capitaine Picard, puffed up like a peacock with importance and wearing a red brocade waistcoat for the occasion, came to look at Sheila's paintings and took eight of the largest and best ones for an exhibition in his gallery next month. He phoned me up days later to tell me he had sold one of them as soon as they went onto his website. He sounded as excited as though he had painted them himself. When the exhibition is over, it will be shipped to America and the house of an oil tycoon in Texas with family roots in France. I bet Sheila would have been so surprised.

The rest we have given on loan to the little museum in the village, which has seen the visitor numbers quadruple over the past few months. I had no idea that Sheila was so well-known. They've had to put in new security and re-opened the museum café, which had been closed for over a year because no one ever went there. Colette manages it and it's a thriving little business. She has even been known to sell pots of Mimi's jam there. All the flavours and all the colours. Who knows what they are? Mimi makes labels for them in her spidery handwriting, things like *Confiture Surprise* and *Cœur du Jardin*. Apparently, they are very popular. People like the idea of *Surprise Jam* and *Heart of the Garden*.

And the other day I heard that Colette and Claud are moving in together, something that will delight and appal Bertrand in equal measure, I suspect, partly because they are not married and, more specifically, when she moves out, he is going to be left with only Mimi for company. Well, and Hector, too, I suppose.

Mimi actually speaks to me these days, realising that I am here for good. And also that I am improving my French so she can't mutter things under her breath, believing I don't understand her.

She has given up trying to stop Blanche and her flock from coming over to my garden, and the same goes for Gigi. Her two remaining kittens have grown into sleek little catlings. They are asleep in the garden on the warm stones next to the pool, one eye occasionally opening to keep an eye on the sparrows.

Jolies Arbres is now finished. It is bright and welcoming, and I have a big television so I can watch *Tintin* in colour. Sometimes when I remember how neglected my house was last year it hardly seems possible that it's the same place, but it still has that welcoming, friendly feel to it that I loved when I first arrived. I've moved into the upstairs bedroom that used to be Jenny's, and Léo built me some fitted wardrobes at one end, where I store my new clothes, which are far more attractive and – dare I say it – chic than I was used to.

I've made friends in the village, too. Francine, who runs the *boulangerie*; Yasmin, who has a craft shop in the town square; and Isabel, who has just opened a bookshop. I work there two days a week, and I'm meeting a lot of people and improving my French at the same time. I think the success of the museum shop and café has brought new energy to the village.

And Léo? I love him and I know he loves me, but we still don't live together. We alternate from my house to his and it works very well for both of us. We are happy, we are lovers and also – more importantly – friends, which is something I never was with my other husbands, partners, whatever they were.

Sometimes, out of the blue, someone comes into your life who makes you sit up and take notice. A person who makes your heart flutter and your thoughts race. More often than not it's a policeman behind you on the motorway, but sometimes it's someone like Léo.

I spent my first Christmas here, with Léo, Jenny, Ace, Marie-Odile, Léo's sons and Benoît's fiancée, Louise, and their baby, Gabriel. So perhaps there is a new Bisset boy to carry on the family business.

It is wonderful to be part of them. They are my new people, a proper family who bicker and crowd around the Christmas turkey, arguing about when to baste it and what herbs should be added to the stuffing. Okay, they didn't really understand the jokes in the crackers, but it didn't really matter. And best of all, we sat at the table for hours, passing Gabriel around like pass the parcel. He really is a lovely baby, very accommodating and cheerful, with the promise of the Bisset nose.

The meal took a long time, everyone helped and afterwards absolutely *no one* suggested getting out for a nice walk, so at last I got my wish: a new bottle of Baileys, a book and a snooze on the sofa.

ACKNOWLEDGMENTS

Thank you to the whole team at Boldwood Books, who have been wonderful to work with. Particular thanks must go to my editor, Emily Ruston, ever patient, always helpful.

My agent, Broo Doherty, who is a joy. Unfailingly approachable, responsive to every email and full of good ideas and humour.

Life would have been a lot more difficult without the help of friends and colleagues. The Literary Lovelies (Jane Ayres, Catherine Boardman, Vanessa Thornton-Rigg, Susanna Bavin, Christina Banach), Savvies, many people I have only met over social media but who are always so supportive and encouraging to a fellow writer.

A special mention to Judy Leigh, who pointed me in the direction of Boldwood in the first place – thank you for that!

Finally, as always, to my husband, Brian, my rock. He made everything possible. ILYWAMH&AW.

MORE FROM MADDIE PLEASE

We hope you enjoyed reading *Sisters Behaving Badly*. If you did, please leave a review.

If you'd like to gift a copy, this book is also available as an ebook, digital audio download and audiobook CD.

Sign up to Maddie Please's mailing list for news, competitions and updates on future books.

http://bit.ly/MaddiePleaseNewsletter

The Old Ducks' Club, another feel-good read from Maddie Please, is available to order now.

ABOUT THE AUTHOR

Maddie Please is the author of bestselling joyous tales of older women. She had a career as a dentist and now lives in Herefordshire where she enjoys box sets, red wine and Christmas.

Follow Maddie on social media:

- facebook.com/maddieplease
- twitter.com/maddieplease1
- instagram.com/maddieplease1
- bookbub.com/authors/maddie-please

ABOUT BOLDWOOD BOOKS

Boldwood Books is a fiction publishing company seeking out the best stories from around the world.

Find out more at www.boldwoodbooks.com

Sign up to the Book and Tonic newsletter for news, offers and competitions from Boldwood Books!

http://www.bit.ly/bookandtonic

We'd love to hear from you, follow us on social media:

facebook.com/BookandTonic

twitter.com/BoldwoodBooks

instagram.com/BookandTonic

Made in the USA
Las Vegas, NV
03 September 2023

76989046R00174